romancing the workplace series

Mind The App

alia smith

BAL
KON
media

ALSO BY ALIA SMITH

ROMANCING THE WORKPLACE SERIES

The Plus-One Clause (Novella)

Bookish with Benefits

The Maine Event

The Midnight Meet-Up

Hot Off the Press

Mind the App

MIND THE APP
Published by Balkon Media

Paperback edition ISBN: 978-1-916970-17-5
Also available as an E-book

A CIP catalogue record for this title is available from the British Library.

Edited by Hanna Elizabeth

Cover Design: graphichouse123

www.balkon.media

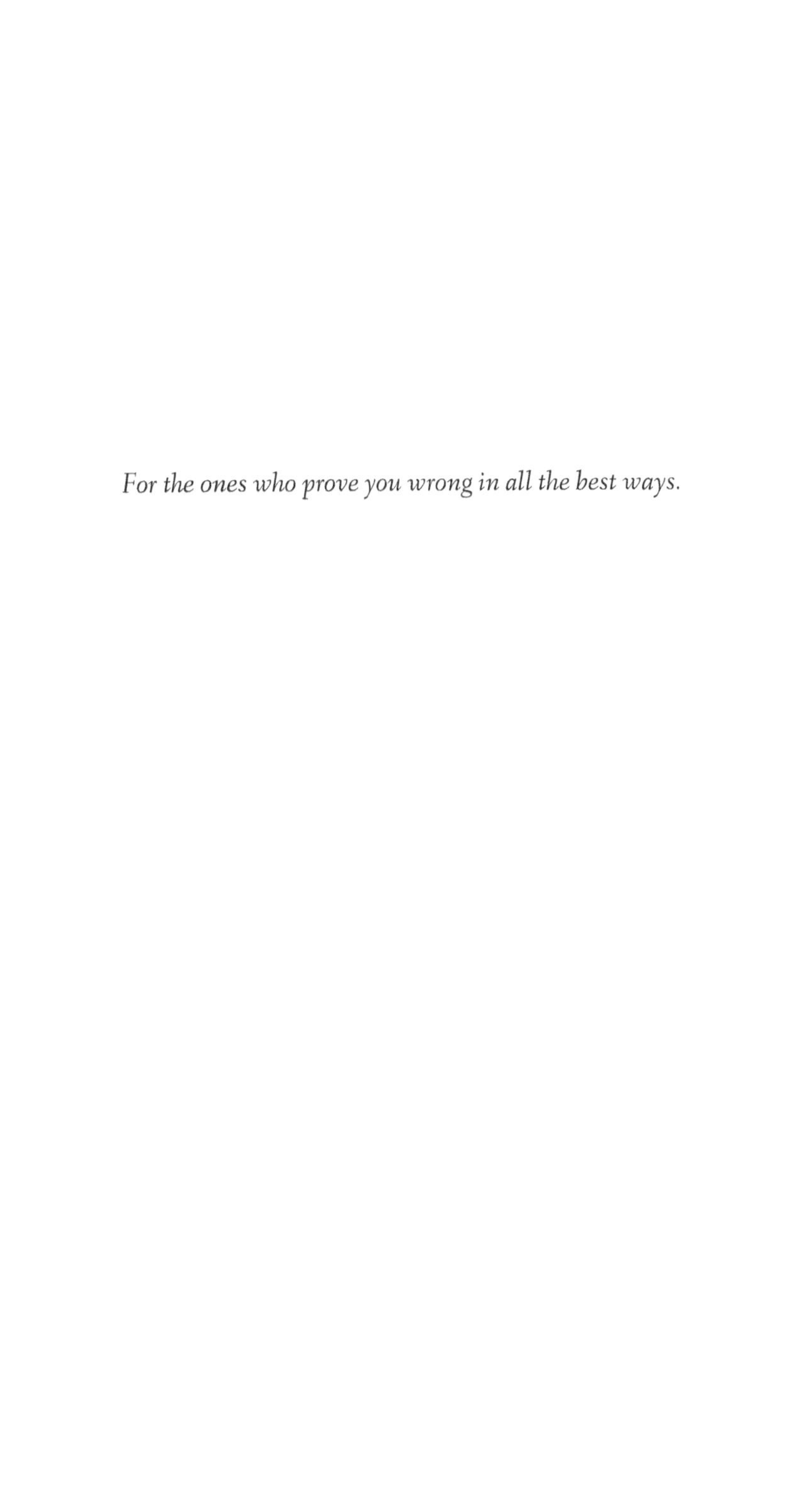

For the ones who prove you wrong in all the best ways.

ONE

DANNY

The gear shifter is mocking me.

"Why," I mutter through gritted teeth, "is it *here?*" My hand flails against the sleek steering column, grappling with the absurdly located lever that refuses to cooperate. It's like trying to solve a Rubik's Cube while blindfolded and mildly concussed. Who decided this was better than a proper gearstick? Americans, apparently.

"Alright, Danny. Breathe. This isn't rocket science. Just twist it into—" A surge of power jolts me forward as the car lurches violently toward the curb. *Brilliant.*

From behind me, a horn blares—a deep, aggressive honk that can only belong to an oversized pickup compensating for something. I glance in the rearview mirror and see the driver gesturing wildly, his face contorted in what I can only assume is either rage or constipation.

"Yes, mate, I hear you. Loud and clear," I murmur under my breath, throwing him a tight-lipped smile through the mirror. Another honk. Brilliant. Now it's a duet of shame because someone else has joined the symphony from further back. Perfect. Nothing like a public audience to really highlight your incompetence.

"Alright. Focus." I square my shoulders and grip the wheel, which feels suspiciously sticky. The rental agency did promise 'thorough cleaning,' but I'm starting to suspect their definition of clean is... flexible.

"Okay, approach slowly. Tiny adjustments. You've got this." My tank-like SUV inches forward, the nose barely nudging into the tight space between a minivan that looks like it's been parked there since 1987 and a shiny red convertible. Of course, the only available spot in this entire town is so narrow it might as well come with a sign that says, "*Good luck, sucker!*"

Another honk erupts, longer this time, accompanied by what sounds like muffled shouting. My anxiety spikes, but outwardly, I plaster on the kind of calm expression one might wear while delivering a quarterly earnings report. Cool. Collected. Not at all about to combust internally.

"One more try," I say aloud, as if the SUV needs reassurance. Glaring at the dashboard, I twist the futuristic gearshift again, gentle this time, hoping it miraculously shifts itself into reverse. Instead, I end up in neutral, the engine completely giving up, mirroring precisely how I feel inside.

"Sure, just take your time, buddy!" comes a sarcastic shout from the pickup driver. His window's down now, and I catch sight of his cowboy hat bobbing as he shakes his head. Cowboy hat. Of course. Why not?

"Thank you for your patience," I mutter under my breath, though every syllable drips with venom. My pulse thrums in my ears as I finally manage to align the vehicle properly. Or as close to properly as one can get when the steering wheel seems to have its own parking-assist agenda and the pavement markings are faded relics of a bygone era.

"Last time I rent a car in a country where they think super-sizing is a personality trait," I grumble as I throw the vehicle into park—or at least I hope it's in park. The flashy lights don't exactly inspire confidence.

With a final, triumphant lurch that feels more like the SUV giving up on me than the other way around, I manage to wedge the tank—sorry, rental—into what might generously be called a parking space. It's crooked. Not just "slightly off" crooked, but "did-a-drunken-raccoon-park-this?" crooked. One tire kisses the curb like it's trying to apologize for my existence, while the rear end juts out into the street with all the subtlety of a toddler's tantrum.

Taking a deep breath, I smooth down the front of my suit jacket and push open the door with as much poise as a man can muster while exiting what is essentially a vehicular crime scene. My shoes hit the pavement, polished leather against small-town asphalt, and I step away from the SUV with an air of calculated indifference. Chin high, shoulders back, as if I haven't just spent ten minutes wrestling with a steering column like it insulted my mother.

And then I hear it—a slow, deliberate clap.

"Well done, sir!" A grizzled voice floats over, tinged with amusement, followed by another clap. And another. I glance up to find an elderly couple perched on a nearby bench, their weathered faces lit with matching grins. The man is clapping slowly, theatrically, while his wife sips from a thermos adorned with stickers that read things like "Live, Laugh, Lobster" and "Willow Cove Forever."

"Bravo!" she adds, raising her thermos in mock salute.

"Thank you, thank you," I say with a dazzling smile, sketching a sarcastic little bow in their direction. "Always happy to provide top-tier entertainment."

"Parking's an art form around here," the old man says,

tipping his flat cap at me. "You'll get the hang of it—eventually."

"Can't wait," I reply dryly, resisting the urge to adjust my tie. Instead, I turn on my heel and stride away, leaving behind the awkwardly parked SUV and my shredded dignity like yesterday's emails.

The air shifts as I move further into Willow Cove, trading the chaos of the main street for something quieter, softer. The faint scent of salt lingers, mingling unexpectedly with cinnamon, and I can't tell whether it's coming from a bakery or some kind of candle shop.

Overhead, strings of bunting crisscross between buildings, their pastel triangles fluttering lazily in the breeze. It's aggressively quaint, like someone took a postcard and made it three-dimensional. The post office sits on the corner, its red-brick façade adorned with cheerful flower boxes. A bell above the door jingles every time someone enters or exits. It's absurdly charming, the kind of detail that would make city planners roll their eyes. But I guess that's the point, isn't it? To scream *small-town America* loud enough that even people in orbit could hear it.

I pass a shop with a hand-painted sign that reads *Scones & Stones: Crystals and Pastries*. Of course. Because why wouldn't you combine baked goods with New Age mysticism? Inside, I catch a glimpse of shelves lined with glittering geodes and a counter piled high with what look like blueberry scones. A woman in a flowing cardigan gestures animatedly at a customer, holding what appears to be a chunk of quartz the size of a small cat.

Despite myself, I take in the details—the tidy cobblestone sidewalks, the clusters of locals chatting outside the hardware store, the way laughter spills out from an ice cream parlor. It's... nice. Annoyingly so. Like someone designed it specifically to make big-city outsiders feel both charmed and out of place. Well, congratulations, Willow Cove. Mission accomplished.

Walking past the ice cream parlor, I catch sight of a sun-bleached newspaper stand tucked between a bench and one of those oversized planters overflowing with petunias. The *Willow Cove Gazette* sits front and center, the bold headline practically shouting to be noticed: *"The App No One Asked For: How Tech is Turning Small-Town Charm into Corporate Blah."*

Charming. Subtle. Definitely not aimed at me.

I stop, tilting my head as if I've misread it. Nope, still there. Still passive-aggressive in font size seventy-two. Beneath the headline, there's a grainy photo of what I assume is the town council office, though the angle makes it look more like a rustic barn. A caption reads, *"Progress or Plunder? Locals Weigh In."*

"Well, this should be riveting," I mutter, paying for a copy. The paper crinkles against my fingers as I flip it open. A faint whiff of ink and newsprint hits me—nostalgic, in a way that feels almost antiquated. Like vinyl records or rotary phones, it's something you wouldn't bother with unless you were determined to make a point about authenticity. I scan the byline: *Riley Hayes, Feature Writer.*

"Right then, Riley," I say under my breath. "Let's see what you've got."

The editorial takes up half the page, framed by an aggressively earnest stock photo of a laptop next to a coffee cup. I skim the opening paragraph, my smirk fading as I read. It's sharp. Too sharp. Words like *"soulless," "exploitation,"* and *"algorithmic mediocrity"* jump out like arrows aimed straight at my ego. There's even a not-so-veiled jab about "tech executives who wouldn't know community values if they tripped over them in their bespoke loafers."

"Ah, good," I mutter dryly. "She's subtle too."

Still, I can't stop reading. Her writing has a rhythm. She

skewers the whole tech-for-the-sake-of-tech mentality, dismantling every talking point my company has ever used to promote our platform. And damn it, she's... kind of brilliant at it. Articulate, passionate, unrelenting. The kind of voice that doesn't just poke holes in your argument but rips the whole thing apart and serves it back to you on a platter, garnished with sass and righteous indignation.

For a moment, I forget to breathe. My chest tightens—not in a *you-may-be-having-a-heart-attack* way, but in a *your-confidence-is-being-flattened-like-roadkill* kind of way.

"Who *is* this woman?" I murmur, scanning for a photo or bio. Nothing. Just her name in neat little italics. *Riley Hayes.* Sounds like someone who's probably wearing practical shoes and glaring at me from some corner of the universe right now.

I fold the paper with more force than necessary, shoving it under my arm. There's a flicker of something unsettling in the back of my mind—half irritation, half admiration. It's maddening. On one hand, how dare she take aim at my project like that? On the other hand... damn, if she doesn't make some valid points. Infuriatingly valid.

"Great," I mutter as I start walking again. "Just what I need. A small-town crusader with a flair for theatrics and a thesaurus."

I stride down Willow Cove's postcard-perfect main street, dodging a gaggle of teenagers on skateboards and a woman walking what appears to be a mop with legs. The folded copy of the *Willow Cove Gazette* burns under my arm like a branding iron, its headline—*"The App No One Asked For"*— seared into my frontal lobe.

"Fix the app rollout," I mutter to myself, as if saying it out loud will somehow summon competence. Get the US launch back on track, earn a hearty pat on the back from the London office, and maybe—just maybe—the product director promotion will be mine. Easy, right? Except, now there's this... *Riley Hayes.* This faceless, word-slinging assassin who's decided my app is the devil incarnate and Willow Cove is her hill to die on.

"Practical shoes," I say under my breath, picturing her as some humorless crusader in orthopedic loafers. Probably wears cardigans with elbow patches. Drinks herbal tea. Owns a cat named Socrates. And yet, even as these snide thoughts churn in my head, I can't shake the sharp-edged brilliance of her writing. It's unsettling. Like discovering a rival chess player who's ten moves ahead before you've even figured out where the horsey piece goes.

Lost in my spiraling thoughts, I almost walk straight past the town hall—a squat, brick structure with peeling paint and a flagpole leaning at an alarming angle. As I veer toward the entrance, something—or rather someone—catches my eye.

She's standing just outside, pinning a brightly colored flyer to the community noticeboard. Her auburn hair is swept up in a messy bun, strands escaping to frame her face in a way that looks effortless, but probably isn't. A battered leather messenger bag hangs off one shoulder, and she's biting her lip in concentration as she smooths out the paper against the board.

For a split second, I forget how to move. She's... striking, in an unpolished sort of way. The kind of person who doesn't try to catch your attention but somehow commands it anyway. But then she glances up—and our eyes lock.

Hazel. Her eyes are hazel. Sharp and discerning, like she's already cataloging every flaw in my existence. My crooked parking job flashes through my mind, along with the slow clap from that elderly couple. Brilliant.

"Hi," I blurt, because apparently, my brain has decided to throw dignity out the window.

"Hi," she replies, her tone flat and vaguely suspicious. There's a flicker of *something* in her gaze—probably my English accent, throwing her slightly. Or maybe I'm imagining things. Either way, her eyes narrow slightly, and my palms start to sweat.

"Nice day, isn't it?" I hear myself say, the words tumbling out before I can stop them. Smooth, Danny. Truly the pinnacle of eloquence and wit.

Her lips twitch, not quite a smile. "If you like salt air and tourists blocking traffic."

"Ah. Yes, well," I stammer, feeling the weight of her judgment—or what I assume is judgment—pinning me to the spot. "Tourists. What a nuisance."

"Mm-hmm." She adjusts her bag, looking me up and down. Not in a flirty way, mind you. More like a mechanic inspecting a car for faults. "You new in town?"

"Just visiting," I say, attempting my most charming smile. It feels painfully forced, like I'm auditioning for a toothpaste commercial.

"Figured," she says, and there's something almost playful in her voice now, though her expression remains unreadable. "Well, welcome to Willow Cove. Try not to run anyone over while you're here. We drive on the left side on this side of the pond."

She turns and pins another flyer to the board—something about a town potluck—and steps back to inspect her work. I can feel her judgment radiating off her in waves, even as she pretends not to be bothered by my existence. It's almost impressive, really. A masterclass in passive-aggressive small-town hostility.

"Right, well," I mutter, adjusting the strap of my laptop bag and trying to summon what's left of my dignity. "I'll just...

get out of your hair, then. Wouldn't want to block any more traffic."

"Good idea," she replies, not even bothering to look at me this time.

Ouch. Okay then. Message received, loud and clear.

I turn on my heel and walk briskly down the street, ignoring the heat creeping up the back of my neck. Honestly, it's fine. Totally fine. If she wants to think I'm some hapless tourist who shouldn't be trusted behind the wheel, so be it. Let her think that. I'm not here to make friends. I'm here to fix an app, prove myself to my bosses, and then get the hell out of Dodge—or Willow Cove, rather.

TWO

RILEY

My boots are propped up on the desk, a lukewarm coffee cup balanced on my knee, and my morning is already circling the drain. The door to the office creaks open, and Elaine strides in like she owns the place, which, technically, she does. She's waving a piece of paper like it's the golden ticket to journalistic doom. Her heels click against the hardwood floor, each step radiating purpose and a subtle warning: brace yourself.

"Good morning, Riley," she says in that clipped tone that tries to sound warm but mostly just sounds like she's about to assign me something awful. My eyes flick to the press release in her hand, and my stomach sinks.

"Let me guess," I say, not bothering to move my feet off the desk. "Another groundbreaking initiative to revolutionize our lives by selling us things we don't need?"

"Close," Elaine replies, dropping the paper onto my desk with a flourish. The words "Artisan App" and "local engage-ment" leap out at me like an unwelcome pop-up ad. "You know that piece you did last week on the *Makers' Mart* app? Well, you got their attention. There's a senior product manager flying in from their UK office. He'll be here for two weeks, leading some community outreach project. They want us to cover it."

I let out a groan loud enough to make Elaine raise an eyebrow. "I think I bumped into him this morning. I can't believe they actively want to engage with me after I tore them a new one. Wow. It's brave, I'll give them that."

"Look, just meet the guy, see what's going on."

"A tech firm thinks they can waltz into Willow Cove with their sleek apps and overpriced lattes and call it 'engagement'? This town doesn't even have decent cell reception half the time."

"Well, apparently, they think we're worth the effort," Elaine counters, crossing her arms. "And since you're our resident cynic with a penchant for colorful commentary, I thought you'd be perfect for the follow-up story."

"Perfect?" I repeat, sitting up straight and giving her my best incredulous look. "Elaine, I'm allergic to PR fluff. You know this. It's in my medical records."

"Riley," she says, leaning over the desk, voice dropping into her no-nonsense editor mode. "You're doing it. Like it or not. The Chronicle needs this coverage, and you need a byline this week."

"Fine," I say, grabbing the press release and scanning it with a mix of irritation and dread. "But if this ends with me having to write about how some British guy redefines the meaning of artisanal bread, I'm quitting."

"Noted," Elaine says with a smirk. She turns on her heel and heads toward her office, leaving me to stew in my misery.

I stare at the press release again, the name "Daniel Winter" glaring back at me like a neon sign. Senior Product

Manager. UK Office. Local Engagement Initiative. I shake my head, tossing the paper onto the desk.

"Welcome to Willow Cove, Daniel Winter," I mutter under my breath. "Prepare to be unimpressed."

I stop just inside the door of the town hall, boots scuffing against the freshly buffed wood, and take in the spectacle before me. There it is—the pop-up tech booth in all its misplaced glory, smack dab in the middle of the room where we usually hold bake sales and PTA meetings. A sleek black banner hangs above a glossy table, its minimalist white font declaring: *"Create. Connect. Share."* The words practically beg for an eye roll, so I oblige them. Twice.

There are iPads. Of course, there are iPads. They're propped up on little stands, their screens glowing with what I assume is some kind of app demo, complete with pastel graphics and soft-focus stock images of suspiciously happy people holding pottery. My gaze drifts to the far corner, where a stack of branded tote bags sits. Each one is stamped with the company's logo—a stylized swirl that looks vaguely like a cinnamon roll trying too hard to be modern art.

"Because nothing says 'support local artisans' like mass-produced corporate swag," I mutter under my breath.

The setup couldn't be more out of step with Willow Cove if it tried. This is a town where the farmers' market still uses handwritten signs, where Mrs. Callahan's honey jars come with crooked labels she prints on her ancient inkjet. The last time someone tried to introduce anything "cutting-edge" here, it was Mayor Thompson's ill-fated attempt at a digital suggestion box. The thing crashed within a week, mostly because half the town still refuses to use anything newer than AOL.

I scan the room again, noting the perfectly symmetrical arrangement of chairs around the booth, the carefully placed flyers fanned out across the table like some kind of corporate peacock display. Everything about it screams calculated precision, and I hate it. It's too slick, too polished, too... fake. Like they think they can slap a shiny veneer over their intentions and no one will notice what's underneath.

"Not on my watch," I mutter, digging into my bag for my notebook. The leather cover is battered from years of abuse, but it feels solid in my hands as I flip it open and click my pen.

"Pop-up booth at town hall," I scrawl at the top of the page, then underline it twice for good measure. My handwriting slants unevenly, the way it always does when I'm annoyed. Below it, I start jotting down notes: "iPads everywhere—overkill" ... "banner looks like something from a dystopian startup" ... "tote bags = insult to actual artisans."

My pen hovers midair as another phrase bubbles up in the back of my mind, sharp-edged and insistent. I hesitate for a moment, then write it down in bold capital letters: "*DIGITAL COLONIALISM.*"

It's a loaded term, sure, but it fits. This isn't just about an app; it's about outsiders coming in and pretending to understand our community, acting like they're saving us while they quietly dismantle everything that makes this place unique. The thought fuels a fresh wave of irritation, and I press my pen harder against the page, underlining the words until the paper tears slightly.

"Perfect," I mutter, flipping the notebook closed. My gaze shifts back to the booth, where a couple of stand builders are fussing over the placement of yet another flatscreen display. One of them steps back, tilts his head, and gestures toward the banner like he's Michelangelo critiquing the Sistine Chapel.

"Yeah, that'll really win over the guy who whittles spoons

for a living," I say under my breath, shoving the notebook back into my bag.

The fork in my hand hovers over the half-eaten pile of sweet potato fries on my plate as Ava raises an eyebrow at me, her grin downright wicked.

"Okay, so tell me again," she says, leaning forward with her elbows on the table, "why you're not *at all* interested in the cute British guy who's apparently taken over town hall with his floppy hair and boyish good looks?"

"First of all, 'cute' is subjective. Second, if by 'taken over town hall,' you mean he's set up a soulless tech shrine to late-stage capitalism, then fine. And third"—I stab a fry into the ketchup for emphasis—"I'm just doing my job, Ava. This isn't about him."

"Uh-huh." She drags out the word, her tone dripping with disbelief. Her coffee cup hovers near her lips as she takes a slow sip, watching me over the rim like she's waiting for me to crack. "So it has nothing to do with how you've said the word 'tech bro' approximately seventy-three times since we sat down?"

"Tech bro is a *genre*," I shoot back, waving the fry dramatically. "He's not special. He's... he's just another corporate pawn here to sell us snake oil and call it innovation."

"Right," Ava drawls, smirking. "And that's why you were glaring at his pop-up booth like it personally insulted your mom."

"Because it did," I snap, pointing the fry at her now. "Metaphorically speaking. My mother is this town, Ava. And he"—I gesture vaguely toward the direction of the square, even though we can't see it from here—"is here to exploit her."

"Wow." Ava sets her coffee down and clasps her hands

together like she's praying. "You're officially projecting onto Willow Cove. I'm impressed, really."

"That's not—" I start, but she cuts me off with a raised hand.

"Don't get me wrong, I love this for you," she says, grinning wider now. "The passion, the outrage. It's all very... Jane Austen's heroine meets Erin Brockovich. But you know what they say about the lines between hate and other feelings being razor-thin, right?"

"Stop it."

"Riley Hayes," she crows, clapping her hands together. "You're flustered! Oh my God, you have a crush on the tech bro!"

"Absolutely not," I say, stabbing another fry. "What I have is a healthy disdain for everything he represents. The accent and cheekbones don't change the fact that he's bad news wrapped in a well-tailored suit."

"Again, *very* specific observations for someone who's not been paying attention," Ava teases, popping a fry into her mouth.

"Ugh." I drop my fork and press the heels of my hands against my forehead. "This is why I hate having lunch with you. Everything turns into some kind of rom-com subplot."

"Hey, I'm just saying—" Ava starts, but I cut her off with a pointed look.

"Enough. I don't care about him. What I care about"—I sit up straighter, jabbing a finger at the table for emphasis—"is making sure this town doesn't get steamrolled by some slick app that thinks it can replace actual human creativity with algorithms and buzzwords. That's it. End of story."

"Uh-huh," Ava says again, clearly unconvinced but mercifully letting it go. For now. She sips her coffee like she knows something I don't, and it takes every ounce of self-control I have not to throw a fry at her face.

"Anyway," I say, grabbing my notebook from where it's wedged under my elbow. "I've got work to do."

"Of course you do," Ava says. "Just try not to swoon too hard while you're, you know, dismantling the patriarchy or whatever."

"Goodbye, Ava," I mutter, standing up and slinging my bag over my shoulder.

"Good luck, Riley!" she calls after me.

Outside, I take a deep breath and square my shoulders. Whatever Ava thinks, this isn't personal. It's about Willow Cove—about preserving what makes this place special. I'll dig deeper, ask the tough questions, and expose this whole initiative for what it is. No distractions. No nonsense.

"Game on," I mutter under my breath, heading back toward the square.

The sound of a heavy-duty stapler misfiring is what first catches my attention.

"Come on, you bloody—" The voice, clipped and British, slices through the late afternoon air like it doesn't belong here. Like it's wandered in from a BBC period drama and gotten lost in small-town Willow Cove.

I glance up from my notebook—just a quick look, I tell myself—and there he is. Mr. Big Tech himself, the guy I bumped into this morning, standing next to that pretentious pop-up booth, wrestling with a piece of poster board that's come loose.

He's tall, annoyingly so, his dark hair styled so perfectly it probably has its own HR department. His shirt looks like it costs more than my monthly rent, and he's wearing some kind of tailored navy blazer that screams *Look at me, I'm important!* It's all very polished. Very corporate. Very... not Willow Cove.

And yet, despite his whole *Bond, Jame Bond* vibe, he's currently losing a very public battle with a staple gun.

"Really?" I mutter under my breath, leaning against the wall to watch the show. "This is the guy they sent to save us?"

Danny—or whatever his name is—yanks the stapler back and examines it like it holds the secrets of the universe. He frowns. Adjusts his grip. Tries again. The sound of another misfire ricochets around the room, followed by an exasperated sigh loud enough to rattle the bunting hanging above the stand.

"Brilliant," he mutters to himself, his accent thickening with frustration. "Just brilliant."

I can't help it. A laugh slips out before I can stop it, quiet but sharp. He freezes, his head snapping up in my direction like he's just realized he's being watched. For a second, his eyes meet mine—blue and piercing, the kind that probably makes boardrooms go silent when he walks in.

"Problem?" he calls out, his tone all crisp politeness layered over obvious irritation.

"Not for me," I say, raising my eyebrows. "But you might want to switch to tape before you staple your fingers together. Just a suggestion."

His jaw tightens, and I feel an almost smug sense of satisfaction at the way his carefully curated mask cracks, just a little. He glances down at the stapler, then back at me, like he's debating whether to engage further.

"Thank you for the... advice," he says finally. "But I think I'll manage."

"Sure you will." I push off the wall, slipping my notebook into my bag. "If you survive the stapler, that is."

"Very funny," he mutters, turning back to his poster board.

"Welcome to Willow Cove," I call over my shoulder as I walk away, my voice laced with sarcasm. "Try not to break anything while you're here."

As I cross the square, I can't resist one last glance over my shoulder. He's still there, still struggling, but now there's something... almost endearing about the way he's muttering to himself, trying to wrestle the board into submission. Almost.

"Digital colonialism," I mutter to myself, pulling out my pen and underlining the phrase in my notebook. "Yeah, this is going to be fun."

THREE

— ♥ —————————

DANNY

The Willow Cove Saturday Market is... quaint. No, that's underselling it. It's aggressively quaint. Like someone took an Instagram filter labeled *Rustic Charm* and cranked it up to eleven.

Wooden stalls painted in soft pastels line the gravel path, draped with cheerful bunting that flutters in the breeze. The air is thick with the mingling scents of cinnamon, fresh bread, and something floral. A fiddler plays in the distance, because of course there's live folk music. Why wouldn't there be?

Vendors are already setting up shop, chatting with customers, laughing, and exchanging pleasantries. Everyone knows everyone. It's like stepping into a Hallmark movie, except I'm the antagonist who's here to ruin Christmas—or in this case, introduce e-commerce capabilities *'for doers and makers.'*

"Morning!" chirps a woman passing by with a basket of apples. She smiles so brightly, I nearly squint. What is it with these people and their relentless friendliness? Do they train for this?

"Morning," I reply, forcing a smile that feels more like a grimace. She doesn't seem to notice, thank God, and continues on her way. Meanwhile, I adjust my satchel strap and scan the market, trying to locate my first target—I mean, potential vendor.

"Soap. Perfect," I mutter to myself, zeroing in on a stall that looks like it was curated by Pinterest itself. *Nora's Soaps* has hessian sacks draped over wooden crates, roughly cut slabs of soap, and pastel labels with calligraphy so elegant they could probably make me cry if I stared long enough. And behind it all stands Nora, the artisan soap vendor herself—mid-thirties, denim-blue Dungarees, hair swept into a messy bun that somehow looks intentional.

"Hi there!" I start with what I hope is an approachable grin. *Too much teeth? Not enough? God, why do I feel like I'm about to audition for a toothpaste commercial?*

"Good morning," she replies, her tone suspiciously neutral as she arranges bars of soap shaped like seashells. She glances at my satchel, then at my pressed shirt, and I can practically hear her brain filling in the blanks: Outsider. Tech guy. Corporate shill.

"Lovely setup you've got here," I say, gesturing broadly at the display. "Really... uh... cohesive branding." *Cohesive branding?* Cringe.

"Thanks," she says, not looking up. Her hands move efficiently, rearranging soaps for no apparent reason other than avoiding eye contact with me.

"Right, well, I'm Danny Winter," I continue, extending a hand over the table. She gives it a brief, polite shake, her grip firm but quick. "I'm here on behalf of—"

"That app thing," she interrupts, finally meeting my eyes. Hers are sharp, calculating. Not unkind, exactly, but definitely skeptical. "Mayor Thompson mentioned you'd be coming around."

"Ah, yes! The app thing," I say, laughing lightly, like that's its official name. "It's actually called *Makers' Mart*. It's designed to help artisans like yourself reach global audiences while maintaining—"

"Global audiences?" she cuts in, arching a brow. "I can barely keep up with local orders as it is. Why would I want to add shipping internationally to the mix?"

"Well, it's not just about shipping," I explain, shifting my weight awkwardly. "It's about visibility. Expanding your brand's reach. Think of it as—"

"How much are the transaction fees?" she asks bluntly, folding her arms over her apron. Her expression is as smooth and impenetrable as one of her soap bars.

"Uh..." My brain scrambles for the exact percentage. "Well, it's competitive. And scalable. Very scalable." I immediately regret the corporate buzzwords—the way her mouth tightens tells me she does too.

"Right," she says, her tone as dry as the air before a thunderstorm. "So I pay you to let someone else pay me? Sounds efficient."

"Okay, fair point," I say quickly, trying to save face. "But the exposure, Nora. Can I call you Nora? Your branding is incredible—" I gesture wildly at a label featuring hand-drawn peonies and a tagline that reads: "*Small-town charm, hand-crafted calm.*" "This? This deserves to be seen on every bathroom counter across America. Maybe even Europe."

"Flattering," she replies, tilting her head slightly. "But exposure doesn't pay bills. And frankly, I prefer selling face-to-face. Builds trust. Relationships. You don't get that from an app."

"Well, sure," I say, nodding so hard I might dislodge something. "But imagine combining the two. Face-to-face sales *and* digital—"

"Look," she says gently but firmly, holding up a hand. "I've received all the emails, seen your adverts and appreciate what you're trying to do here, but this"—she gestures between us—"isn't really my thing. Good luck, though. You'll need it."

"Right," I say, stepping back and nearly tripping over a rogue crate. "Thanks for your time."

"Mm-hmm." She turns back to her soaps, humming softly, as if I've already faded from memory.

"Brilliant start, Danny," I mutter under my breath, retreating to regroup. "One stall down. Only the rest of the market to go."

I pivot away from Nora's stall, her humming trailing behind me like the theme music to my public humiliation tour. I make a beeline for the next vendor's stall—*Baldwin Woodworks*. Surely, a guy who spends his days carving things by hand will appreciate innovation, right? Right?

"Wow," I say, stopping in front of a table laden with cutting boards, birdhouses, and intricately carved wooden bowls. "Hi, I'm Danny. How are you?"

"Ed Baldwin, and I'm here to sell, not buy."

Okay then. Time to turn on the charm. "This is... seriously impressive craftsmanship. Did you make all of these yourself?"

Ed looks up from where he's sanding a block of walnut, his expression suggesting he's already regretting this interaction. He's older, maybe mid-fifties, with forearms that could double as tree trunks, and an aura of "don't waste my time."

"Yup," he says curtly, not bothering to pause the rhythmic scrape of sandpaper against wood.

"Fantastic," I continue, undeterred. "The detail on these" —I pick up a small jewelry box with delicate floral carvings— "is just incredible. Must take hours."

"Days," Ed replies, still sanding. His focus doesn't shift an inch.

"Right. Days. Amazing." I put the box down carefully, as if it might shatter under my touch. "Listen, I wanted to talk to you about this app I'm working with. It's designed to help artisans like you reach a wider audience. Global, even. Imagine your work being appreciated in homes across the world."

"Imagine that," Ed mutters, dry as sawdust. He finally pauses standing to give me a once-over, his eyes narrowing. "You the guy behind that app?"

"Uh, well, kind of. Yes." I straighten my posture, hoping to channel some authority. "Why do you ask?"

"Because I used it. Your app kept freezing every time I tried to upload pictures of my stuff," he says flatly. "And don't get me started on the time I lost my entire inventory because of one of your 'updates.'"

"Ah," I say, swallowing hard. "That's... unfortunate. I assure you, we're constantly working on improvements—"

"Maybe you should improve it *before* pitching it to people," he cuts in, picking up his sandpaper again. "Just a thought."

"Thanks for the feedback."

"Mm-hmm," Ed grunts, returning to his sanding as if I've ceased to exist.

Two stalls down, and I'm getting nowhere. At this rate, I'll be lucky if I leave here with my dignity intact, let alone new users.

"Excuse me! Hi there. Are you Jake?" My voice comes out a little too excited, and I immediately want to kick myself. *Tone it down, Danny. This isn't Old Spitalfields Market.*

Jake looks up from behind his pottery wheel with wide-eyed surprise, clay smeared generously across his forearms and the bridge of his nose. He's younger than I expected, maybe early twenties, with shaggy brown hair that sticks out in every direction like he's been wrestling with his kiln. "Uh, yeah? That's me."

"Jake, great," I say, trying to channel something between approachable tech guru and non-threatening neighbor who offers to watch his house while he's on vacation. Spoiler: I'm neither. "I'm Danny Winter. I'm here with Makers' Mart—you signed up for our beta program a few months ago, but didn't list your products. I wanted to see if I could help you with that?"

"*Makers* what?" His head tilts, genuinely puzzled, and I falter for half a second before recovering with a tight grin.

"Makers' *Mart*." I gesture vaguely, like the words alone should spark recognition. "The app connecting crafters and artisans to local—and global—customers?"

"Oh, right." He wipes his hands on an already ruined apron, leaving streaks of terracotta everywhere. "The one everyone's been grumbling about today."

"Grumbling?" I repeat, pretending my ego isn't currently cringing into a fetal position. "That's... feedback. We love feedback."

"Yeah, uh, cool." Jake doesn't seem convinced, but at least he's still standing here, which is more than I can say for Ed or Nora. "So, how does it work?"

"Glad you asked!" Relief floods through me as I dive into the pitch, pulling out my phone like some kind of digital Excalibur. "You create a maker's profile—it's super intuitive—and upload photos of your work. Like these mugs here—" I point to a neatly arranged row of ceramic cups painted in soft earth tones. "And customers can browse, purchase, and even leave reviews. Plus, we've got analytics tools so you can track sales trends and customer behavior."

"Whoa." Jake leans closer, his interest visibly piquing. "You mean I could see, like, who's buying my stuff and when?"

"Exactly!" Finally—*finally*—a win. "And if you complete your sign-up today, I can get you a free trial for the first three months. No transaction fees at all."

"Seriously?" A grin splits across Jake's face, genuine and warm, and it hits me like sunlight after days of rain. "Okay, yeah, that sounds awesome. Sign me up!"

"Brilliant." For once, the word doesn't feel sarcastic coming out of my mouth. I watch as Jake eagerly types his email into my phone, my earlier doubts melting away like wax under a blowtorch.

"Done. Thanks, man," Jake says, handing my phone back. "This could be a game-changer for me."

"Happy to help," I reply, and for once, I actually mean it.

FOUR

RILEY

The cursor blinks at me like it's taunting me. Blank document, zero ideas, and my pen taps out an erratic rhythm against the desk like a tiny SOS. I resist the urge to throw it across the newsroom. Instead, I mutter to myself, "Riley Hayes: local journalist, former software developer, and now, apparently, professional roaster of tech bros. What a career trajectory."

I lean back in my chair, dragging a hand through my hair—messy, as usual. Elaine wants a follow-up on *that app*. Makers' Mart, aka Danny Winter's mishmash of coding hubris and startup clichés. My first article on it wasn't exactly kind, but no one asked me to be kind. They wanted clicks, and boy, did they get them. But a sequel? A second round of public skewering? That feels... cheap.

"Just what every writer dreams of," I groan under my breath, "becoming the Perez Hilton of small-town tech drama."

"Talking to yourself again, Riley?" Elaine's voice cuts through the newsroom chatter. She appears beside my cubicle like a caffeinated specter, her black blazer sharp enough to cut glass. Her grin is the kind that makes you brace for incoming bad news.

"Only because no one else listens," I say, spinning my chair to face her. "Let me guess. You're here to ask about progress on the article?"

"Yep," Elaine says, crossing her arms. "Your Makers' Mart piece last week? Highest traffic article we've had all year. Got quoted by TechCrunch and Wired."

"Fantastic." My voice drips with sarcasm. "I'll alert the Pulitzer Committee immediately."

"Don't sell yourself short," she quips, ignoring my tone. "People loved it. Well, most people. Look, Riley, this is an opportunity. We can't let it fizzle out. The town's still buzzing about Makers' Mart, and you've got two options here." She ticks them off on her fingers. "One: finish him off. Go full scorched earth, take the whole app apart piece by piece. Or two: dig deeper. Explore whether this Danny guy actually has a scrap of redemption in him."

"Redemption," I repeat flatly, raising an eyebrow. "This isn't a Hallmark movie, Elaine. It's a glorified Etsy knockoff."

"Maybe," she counters, her smile unyielding, "but it's your job to find out. And let's not pretend you don't enjoy shredding nonsense when you see it."

"Sure. When it deserves it," I shoot back. "But do we really want to become 'that paper'? Writing mean-spirited fluff just because it gets a reaction?"

"Mean-spirited or not, it works," Elaine replies, her tone all business now. "And the way I see it, Riley, you're not just writing about the app. You're writing about what it means for this town, and towns just like ours across the country. The good, the bad, the... whatever Danny Winter is trying to do over there. People care. You made them care. So do it again."

I open my mouth to argue, to point out that turning Danny

into a caricature might be easier than digging for actual nuance, but Elaine's already pivoting on her heel.

"Follow him around while he's here. Get under the hood of the app. Interview some of the artisans who sign up," she tosses over her shoulder. "Make it count."

"Great. No pressure," I mutter, yanking my bag off the back of my chair and slinging it over my shoulder. The strap digs into my collarbone, but I'm too irritated to care.

The newsroom hums around me—phones ringing, keyboards clacking, someone laughing way too hard at a joke that probably wasn't funny. It's the soundtrack of deadlines, exhaustion, and caffeine-fueled chaos. My kind of place, usually. Today? Not so much.

"Finish him off or give him a redemption arc," I grumble under my breath as I push through the glass doors and step out onto the sidewalk. "Like I'm writing fanfiction now."

The air outside is crisp, sharp with the tang of autumn leaves and the faint smell of coffee drifting from the café down the street. I shove my free hand into my jacket pocket and start walking, my boots crunching against the sidewalk. The town hall isn't far, but it feels like miles when you're dragging behind you the weight of journalistic integrity *and* Elaine's peppy expectations.

"People care," she'd said. Sure, they care. Because everyone loves a good train wreck. And Makers' Mart? It's teetering on the edge of the tracks, daring me to give it one last shove.

But that's not who I am. Or... it's not who I want to be.

Pushing open the heavy wooden door, I'm hit with a wave of chaotic small-town earnestness. The slick pop-up has... expanded. Folding tables are crammed into every available inch of space, their surfaces littered with laptops, tangled charging cables, and those flimsy plastic signs that buckle if you breathe on them wrong. A whiteboard leans precariously in the corner, half-erased sketches of flowcharts and arrows smudged across its surface like someone gave up halfway through explaining their master plan.

The coffee machine in the back wheezes like it's moments away from a breakdown, churning out what looks more like sludge than actual coffee. Someone's taped a handwritten sign to it: *"Out of order, but still trying its best."* Fitting.

At least thirty people mill around the room—some seated, some standing, all talking at once. There's a frazzled woman in a Willow Cove High sweatshirt juggling three Styrofoam cups, a teenage girl typing furiously on a battered Chromebook, and a balding guy in a plaid shirt squinting at his phone. The whole scene has this scrappy, DIY energy that's almost charming. Almost.

"Okay," I mutter under my breath, scanning the room. "Let's see what disaster looks like up close."

"Now, see, Mrs. Williams, you just tap here—" Danny's voice, smooth as polished oak, floats over the noise of the room, pulling my attention like a thread caught on a nail. I spot him near the far side of the chaos, crouched beside an elderly woman in a sweater that looks like it might've been knitted during the Nixon administration.

"Here?" Mrs. Williams' gnarled finger hovers over the screen, shaking slightly.

"Exactly. And then watch this—" He leans closer, his dark hair catching in the fluorescent light as he taps a button for her. The tablet screen flickers, loading what looks like a photo of a necklace that could double as medieval chain mail. "Voilà. Your product is uploaded and ready to dazzle the masses."

"Well, isn't that clever?" Her voice creaks like an old rocking chair, but there's a smile tugging at the corners of her mouth. Danny beams back at her like he's just handed her a winning lottery ticket.

I fold my arms and lean against the doorframe, watching as he patiently explains how to add a price tag to the listing. He wipes a bead of sweat from his temple with the cuff of his immaculately tailored shirt, his tie slightly loosened but still annoyingly perfect. Even when he's sweating, he looks like he's stepped out of a tech industry recruitment poster: *"Join Us— We Sweat Elegantly!"*

"Of course he's charming," I mutter under my breath. "They always are."

The problem is, he doesn't look like some smug corporate suit phoning it in. No, he's crouched there, eye-level with Mrs. Williams, nodding encouragingly as though uploading photos of discount gemstone brooches is the most important task in the world. His voice is low, soothing, his enthusiasm tempered just enough to avoid coming off as patronizing. It's almost... disarming. Almost.

"Great work," he says, stepping back to let her try navigating the app herself. His hand hovers nearby, ready to assist, but he doesn't interfere. She taps the screen hesitantly, her brow furrowed in concentration, before the next image appears. Her face lights up, and Danny grins like he's just won first prize at the county fair.

But even as I glare at him from across the room, that irritating little part of my brain—the part I usually ignore—whispers something traitorous: *Maybe he's not completely full of it.*

"Ugh." I bite down on the thought, hard, and focus on the beads of sweat forming along his hairline instead. Surely someone who's trying this hard has to be compensating for something. Right?

I force myself to stay put, arms crossed tightly as I watch him move on to another table, this time helping a woman in her forties figure out why her phone camera keeps snapping blurry photos of her pottery. Every movement is deliberate, every word chosen to encourage without overwhelming. He's working the room like a politician at a pancake breakfast—but with less smarm and more... What? Earnestness?

"Seriously?" I whisper to no one in particular. "He's actually trying?"

It's infuriating. People like Danny Winter aren't supposed to *try*. They're supposed to waltz in, toss around buzzwords like "global opportunity" and "scalability," and leave a trail of broken promises and bad PowerPoints in their wake. But here he is, sleeves rolled up, kneeling on the scuffed linoleum floor while explaining pixels and resolution to someone who thinks Facebook is a brand of cereal.

"Don't start feeling sorry for him," I warn myself, pulling my messenger bag tighter against my shoulder. "Just because he's sweating doesn't mean he's sincere."

Still, I don't move. I continue to linger, watching him navigate the makeshift demo station with the kind of patience that should be bottled and sold to parents of toddlers. It's frustrating. Annoying. Possibly commendable—but I'm not going to admit that out loud.

I clear my throat, a sharp sound that slices through the hum of chatter and the low whir of the coffee machine on its last leg. It's enough to make Danny freeze mid-sentence, his hand hovering over the elderly jeweler's phone screen like I've just caught him committing some kind of tech crime.

He turns slowly, blinking at me as if I've materialized out of thin air. For a split second, there's something almost vulnerable in his expression—dread mixed with resigned amusement. Then his face rearranges itself into that polished, confident mask he probably practices in the mirror every morning.

"Ah, Riley Hayes," he says, straightening up from his crouch by the table. His tone is dry, but there's a glint in his eye that screams trouble. "To what do I owe the pleasure? Here to live-blog my public shaming? Or perhaps you're working on a hard-hitting exposé about my tragic overuse of PowerPoint animations?"

"Tempting, but no," I shoot back, taking a step closer. The linoleum floor squeaks under my boot, punctuating my words. "I'm here to see if your app has evolved past being a glorified Etsy knockoff or if it's still a UX nightmare. You know, for journalism."

"Naturally," he replies, brushing invisible lint off his sleeve. "Because nothing says 'objective reporting' like storming into a community pop-up unannounced." He gestures grandly toward the folding tables around us. "By all means, take notes. Maybe include my good side—assuming I have one."

"Your marketing department invited me actually, requested a follow-up to my article last week," I say, though I can't help noticing how effortlessly he commands attention, even when he's being insufferable. "Let's start with the onboarding process. Why does it feel like trying to assemble IKEA furniture without instructions? Is confusion part of the brand aesthetic?"

Danny's smirk falters, just slightly. He exhales through his nose, tilting his head like he's deciding whether or not to fight back. "Fair point," he concedes, leaning casually against the edge of the table. "That was... an oversight. In our defense, the original design team thought *minimalism* meant leaving users to fend for themselves. Very avant-garde."

"Avant-garde?" I arch a brow, crossing my arms. "It's like you designed it for people who think sourdough starters are personality traits."

"Touché." He chuckles, rubbing the back of his neck.

There's a bead of sweat there, catching the fluorescent light, and for a moment, he looks more human than tech overlord. "We've been reworking that. Turns out, actual humans appreciate guidance. Who knew?"

"Shocking revelation," I say. "And the payment flow for vendors? Still as clunky as it was in the beta, or have you managed to figure out how to let people, I don't know, *actually* receive the money they've earned?"

"Work in progress," he admits, holding up his hands in mock surrender. "Look, I'll be the first to say it wasn't perfect. Okay, maybe it was objectively terrible. But we're fixing it. Slowly. Painfully. Like teaching a cat to swim."

"More like teaching a cat to code," I mutter, shaking my head. But my lips twitch, almost forming a smile, before I catch myself. Damn it. He's too quick with the self-deprecation—it makes it harder to hate him outright.

"Any other grievances you'd like to air, Ms. Hayes?" Danny asks, folding his arms now, mirroring my stance. He quirks a brow, smug but somehow inviting the challenge. "Or should I just assume you're filing this under 'lost causes' and call it a day?"

"Don't tempt me," I reply, narrowing my eyes. But there's a spark in the way he holds my gaze, like he's daring me to keep going. And, annoyingly, I want to.

"You know what?" Danny says, dragging out the word as if it costs him something. He gestures toward a nearby folding table, where his laptop sits surrounded by a battlefield of tangled cables and empty coffee cups. "You want to tear it apart properly? Be my guest. Here's the latest release. I'm all ears."

"All ears, huh? That's new for you."

"Consider this your golden opportunity to single-handedly save the artisan economy from my evil corporate clutches."

"Wow. What an honor." My words are flat, but my feet

betray me, carrying me toward the table anyway. The skeptic in me is screaming *trap*, but curiosity has already taken the wheel.

The laptop is open, displaying the Makers' Mart homepage—sleek, polished, and obnoxiously cheerful with its pastel color scheme. It looks... better. Not great, but better. I pull out the rickety chair across from his and sit down, leveling him with a look. "If this crashes your server, that's on you."

"Agreed," Danny says, leaning casually against the table. His sleeves are rolled up now, revealing forearms that should probably come with a warning label. Great. As if his hair wasn't smug enough.

Focusing, I click into the app and start navigating. The interface is smoother than last time, but it still takes three clicks too many to find the "Artisan Portal"—a button that sounds more like a Renaissance Fair attraction than a functional tool. I jab at it. "Okay, first off, this name? No. Just no."

Danny winces but nods, pulling out his phone to take notes. "Got it. Too whimsical?"

"Too ridiculous," I say. "This isn't Etsy on acid. Call it something that actually tells people what it does. Like 'Manage Your Shop.' Short, simple, doesn't make anyone cringe."

"Fair point," he concedes, typing away. "What else?"

"Your onboarding process still assumes everyone using this app has a degree in computer science," I say, clicking through a series of tutorial pop-ups that feel less like guidance and more like a punishment. "This right here? A wall of text explaining how to upload product photos? Nobody's reading this. Add visuals. Arrows. A short video. Literally anything less painful."

"Working on a visual guide," Danny replies, his tone almost apologetic. Almost. "It's harder than it looks."

"Try harder," I shoot back, narrowing my eyes at him before turning back to the screen. "Oh, and the payment setup? Still a mess. Why do I have to input my bank details twice? Once is annoying enough."

"Twice?" He frowns, stepping closer to peer over my shoulder. His cologne drifts into my personal space, warm and woodsy, and I force myself to ignore it. "That's not supposed to happen. Must be a glitch."

"Must be," I echo dryly. "Good luck explaining that to someone who needs to sell a dozen hand-knit scarves to pay for groceries."

"Point taken." He straightens, rubbing the back of his neck, and I catch a flicker of something in his expression—a flash of genuine concern beneath the polished exterior. "I'll flag it with the dev team tonight."

"Tonight?" I glance up at him, surprised despite myself. "You're actually going to fix this stuff?"

"That's kind of the idea," he says, meeting my gaze evenly. For once, there's no trace of sarcasm in his voice. "Contrary to popular belief, I don't enjoy failing."

"Could've fooled me," I say. I turn back to the screen, scrolling further into the app. Flaws aside, there's something… earnest about the updates. Like maybe he's actually been listening. Maybe.

"Anything else, or are you just going to keep glaring at the screen?" Danny asks, leaning against the table again, his posture casual but his eyes sharp.

"Give me another five minutes," I say, clicking into another page. "I'm sure I'll find something else to hate."

"Can't wait," he replies, the corner of his mouth lifting again. Only this time, I don't bother hiding my almost-smile. God help me, this might actually get interesting.

The door of the town hall creaks shut behind me, and I'm immediately hit by a wall of sunlight that makes me squint like I've been living underground for a decade. Typical small-town fall—bright enough to blind you, but still cold enough to make you wish you'd brought a winter jacket. I shove my hands into my jean pockets and start down the sidewalk, the heels of my boots scuffing against the cracked concrete.

He's a terrifyingly competent menace. I should be furious. Or at least annoyed. That would be the normal reaction to someone who has turned my carefully written takedown into some kind of personal challenge. But instead, all I can think about is the way he looked when I handed him back his laptop —grin fading slightly to let something real slip through. It wasn't much, just a flicker, but it was there. Determination. Maybe hope. God help me if it was sincerity.

I shake my head, trying to dislodge the memory, but it clings stubbornly, like gum on the bottom of my boot. "Focus, Riley," I mutter. "This isn't complicated. He's the guy with the app. You're the journalist. He pitches, you critique. End of story."

Except it doesn't feel like the end. Not with the way he toasted me with that stupid coffee cup, like we were in on some kind of private joke. Not with the way he actually listened to what I said, even when I was ripping his app apart piece by piece. And definitely not with the way my stomach did a weird little flip when he said, "Challenge accepted," like I was the one being dared to prove something.

I stop at the corner, waiting for the light to change, and glance up at the sky. The sun's already dipping low, casting long shadows over Willow Cove's quiet streets. There's a faint buzz of activity from the diner across the road—plates clinking, muffled laughter, the hum of a life so familiar it almost fades into white noise.

And yet, here I am, standing in the middle of it all,

thinking about a man who doesn't belong here any more than I belong in his world of polished pitches and market research presentations. A man who, for all his flaws and frustrating charm, might actually be trying to do something decent.

"Get a grip, Riley," I tell myself as the light turns green. "It's just an article. Just a follow-up."

FIVE

━━ ♥ ━━━━━━━━

DANNY

I pace the kitchen like a man trying to wear out the linoleum. My earbuds are in, one hand tugging at my hair. The other hand clutches a mug of coffee so strong it might double as paint thinner. I'd kill for a flat white right now, but Willow Cove doesn't know what that is. Instead, I've got this bitter sludge from an ancient drip machine that rattles ominously every time it brews.

The clock above the stove ticks louder than it should, counting down the minutes until I have to face HQ. London. The board. VC-funded execs who probably had their cappuccinos served on silver trays this morning, while I was busy explaining the difference between an email address and a username.

With a sharp inhale, I tap my laptop trackpad, bringing the Zoom window to life. And there they are. A grid of polished faces staring back at me from the London office, all immaculate lighting and muted backgrounds. I offer them my best I-totally-have-it-together smile.

"Afternoon—or, well, morning for you lot." My voice comes out breezy, even as I feel the weight of their collective judgment through the screen. "Apologies for the... rustic backdrop. Small-town charm, am I right?"

"Afternoon, Danny," comes the clipped reply from Fiona, the director of product development. She looks like she hasn't smiled in a decade, which I suppose is fitting for someone who once described Excel spreadsheets as her "happy place."

"How's our American adventure treating you?" asks Mark, the marketing director, his tone just shy of patronizing.

"Ah, the land of the free and the home of the deep-fried Twinkie," I quip. "It's going... well. If by 'well,' you mean navigating cultural minefields with all the grace of a toddler on roller skates."

There's a smattering of polite chuckles, though Fiona remains stone-faced. Tough crowd.

"Care to elaborate?" she prompts, folding her hands neatly in front of her like a school principal about to assign detention.

"Gladly," I say, flashing a grin that feels more confident than I actually am. "First, let me introduce you to the concept of 'local color.' Apparently, here in Willow Cove, that means everyone knows your name, your business, and whether or not you've paid for your subscription to *The Willow Gazette*. Privacy? Optional. Gossip? Mandatory."

"Sounds quaint," Mark says, smirking.

"Quaint. Sure, let's go with that. It's also meant rethinking some of our features. Turns out, people here don't love the idea of anonymous reviews. They prefer confrontation—but, you know, politely. Passive-aggression wrapped in a smile."

"And the metrics?"

"Early days," I reply smoothly, pivoting like a pro. "But initial feedback has been... colorful. Jake the ceramist called it 'a nifty little thingamabob,' which I believe translates to 'positive user engagement' in small-town vernacular."

Mark nods. "That sounds positive. How about new merchant sign-ups? It seems flat on our end. What's your feeling on the ground?"

"Here's the thing," I start, fingers drumming on the table just outside the webcam's view. "The app, as it stands—" I pause for effect, glancing at the screen where their faces hover in varying levels of disinterest, "—isn't working here and it won't work."

"That's... bold," Fiona says, her voice icy enough to cool the mug of tea in her hand. "Go on."

"Bold? Maybe." I lean forward, meeting her stare dead-on. "But let's be honest: trying to parachute a one-size-fits-all model into a place like Willow Cove is about as effective as teaching a fish how to climb trees. They don't want slick value-add features or vendor league tables. What they want is connection—something real. Something that feels like *them*."

"Connection?" Mark interjects, leaning closer to his mic. "What does that even mean in this context? We're not building a dating app, Danny."

"Thanks for clarifying," I reply dryly. "The point is, this town, and all the thousands like it here, run on relationships. People care who they're buying from—they care about the story behind the product. So instead of pushing an impersonal marketplace, we lean in. We need to redesign with the community in mind: expanded profiles that highlight the artisan, local-focused filters, and a feature that lets buyers see the craft process—videos, photos, Q&A, you name it. Craft-first commerce."

The silence that follows is deafening. It stretches so long that I can hear the hum of my fridge in the background.

"Craft-first commerce," Fiona repeats slowly, like I've just proposed setting fire to her stock options.

"Yes," I say firmly. "It's not a pivot—it's an optimization. A way to meet the market where it actually is, rather than where we wish it were."

"Sounds expensive," Mark mutters, rubbing his temple like I've personally given him a migraine.

"Not necessarily," I counter, keeping my tone even. "We're not overhauling the entire system; we're adapting its presentation. Think of it like... redecorating a house. The foundations and walls stay the same, but we're swapping the IKEA furniture for something handmade. Bespoke. Local craftsmanship is the future, folks."

"How nice for the future," Fiona cuts in, her sarcasm razor-sharp. "But we live in the present, where budgets are real, and shareholders don't care about bespoke coffee tables or 'local filters.'"

"Which is why," I say, holding her gaze through the screen, "we start small. A pilot within the pilot. Limited rollout, measurable metrics. Low risk, high potential reward."

"Potential being the operative word," Mark says, crossing his arms tighter.

"Look," I say, exhaling hard but refusing to lose my footing. "We're trying to plant roots in a place where people still barter eggs for lawn-mowing services. Do you really think fancy dashboards alone are going to win them over? This isn't Silicon Valley. It's Willow bloody Cove. If we want them to buy in, we have to make it *theirs*. If we crack Willow Cove, we crack America, and that's what's going to excite the shareholders."

"Still sounds like a gamble," Fiona says, though her tone has thawed slightly, curiosity flickering behind her skepticism.

"Sure," I admit, shrugging. "But isn't everything we do? At least this way, we're gambling with insight instead of igno-rance. Right now, we don't have a US business. Maybe this will unlock it."

Another stretch of silence. To flinch is to lose, so I keep my expression calm, professional—even as my fingers dig into the edge of my desk.

"One month," Fiona says finally, her words clipped. "You'll get one month to prove this 'craft-first commerce' concept has legs. But if it doesn't deliver, Danny—" She lets the threat hang, her meaning crystal clear.

"Understood. Right, let's talk about Jake," I say, leaning forward and clasping my hands like a motivational speaker on their third espresso of the day. The screen flickers slightly, Fiona raising one skeptical eyebrow while Mark rubs his temples like he's bracing for me to sell them magic beans. Classic.

"Jake the ceramist?" Mark asks flatly, like I've just suggested we brand the app with dancing llamas.

"Yes, Jake the ceramist," I reply, unfazed. "Jake, who, until recently, was selling his pottery at farmers' markets for what-ever spare change people had left after buying artisanal honey. Jake, who, thanks to our trial run, is now fully booked through next month for custom orders. His latest piece? A mug so beautiful it practically made me reconsider my relationship with caffeine."

"Wonderful," Fiona says, clearly unimpressed. "A single potter in a town of— What? A few thousand?"

"Ah, but Jake isn't just any potter," I counter, holding up a finger like I'm revealing the twist ending of a murder mystery. "He's proof that if the platform feels personal—rooted in the community—the locals *will* engage. They'll trust it. And once they trust it, they'll use it. It's not just commerce; it's connection."

"Connection doesn't pay bills," Fiona says, folding her arms. "We're here to scale, Danny, not play matchmaker between small-town artisans and their grandmothers."

"Which is why," I say smoothly, ignoring the jab, "Jake's success story is just the beginning. Imagine this happening across every category: bakers, seamstresses, woodworkers—hell, even pet groomers. If we make Willow Cove the template, we can replicate this in other towns. But first, we have to prove we can do it here."

"Fine," Fiona says, though she doesn't sound convinced. "And Riley Hayes? Her editorial last week didn't exactly paint us as the heroes of small-town America."

"Riley..." I trail off, feeling the heat rise to my face. Of course, someone had to bring her up. My nemesis in flannel and combat boots. I clear my throat, shifting slightly in my chair. "Riley... Well, she's—" I pause, searching for the right words.

"She's what?" Mark prompts, looking far too amused for my liking.

"She's... like a cat near a radiator," I blurt out, then immediately regret it. Three pairs of eyes blink back at me through the screen, waiting for clarification. I press on, because what other choice do I have? "You know, standoffish at first, all claws and suspicion. But give her time, and she starts to warm up. Slowly. Grudgingly. Like it's against her better judgment."

"That's your strategy?" Fiona asks, incredulous. "Hoping she warms up?"

"Let's call it... fostering mutual understanding," I say, managing to keep a straight face. Mostly. "Look, her concerns aren't baseless. She's protective of the community, and frankly, that's an asset. If we can win *her* over, we're golden. She's got the ear of half the town."

"Or she could tank this whole thing with another scathing article," Gareth points out. Ever the optimist, that one.

"True," I admit, leaning back in my chair. "But I'd argue she's more interested in solutions than sabotage. I'm convinced she doesn't want us to fail; she just wants us to get it right. And I—" I stop myself before saying something vulnerable, like how much I maybe, possibly, kind of respect her. Instead, I flash a tight smile. "I'll handle Riley."

"Good luck with that," Fiona says, a hint of amusement creeping into her voice.

"Thanks," I reply dryly. "I'll need it. Cats are notoriously difficult to herd."

"Alright," Fiona says, clicking her pen into the mic like she's trying to puncture my eardrum all the way from London. "We'll let you get on with it. One month, Danny, under these conditions: limited scope, minimal budget impact, and measurable metrics by the end of thirty days. Can you deliver that?"

"Sure. Why not? But I'll need to tech team to drop everything if I need to push through a new feature or update."

"They'll fit you in when they can," Fiona interjects, her tone clipped. "You wanted the chance to test your little... 'craft-first commerce' idea. Now you've got it. But mark my words"—she leans in closer to her webcam for emphasis, her face suddenly uncomfortably large on my screen—"if this tanks, you're taking full responsibility. End of discussion."

"Got it," I say dryly, though my palms dampen against the tabletop. "Anything else? Should I vow to sacrifice my firstborn while we're at it?"

"Just the metrics, Danny." Mark again, ever the dull hammer to Fiona's sharper blade. "We need hard numbers. Engagement rates, transaction volume, retention. If they don't match the growth rates we've seen across Europe, we pull the plug."

"Understood." I force a smile, even as the weight of their expectations settles squarely on my shoulders.

"Good luck," Fiona says before she disconnects. One by one, the others vanish from the call until it's just me staring at the blank screen.

I exhale sharply, slumping back onto the couch like a marionette whose strings have been cut. My head tips against the cushion, eyes fixed on the water-stained ceiling of my rental's kitchen.

For a moment, the silence feels deafening, the enormity of the task pressing down on me. But then, almost involuntarily, my lips curve into a wry smirk. Game on.

I shove my laptop aside and pull the roadmap up on my tablet. It's a mess. Like trying to untangle Christmas lights that someone decided to braid into a Gordian knot. My fingers swipe across the screen, dragging boxes and arrows into some semblance of order. The one-month deadline looms over me like a doomsday clock set to chime on my career's funeral.

"Pilot users," I mutter under my breath, tapping a box labeled *community collaborators*. A laughable term for what is essentially "people who don't hate me yet."

Jake the ceramist comes to mind—his clay-stained thumbs-up during our last chat practically screamed local buy-in. But then there's Julie Marsh, the baker, who looked at me like I'd stomped on her sourdough starter. And let's not forget Riley Hayes: Queen of Skepticism, Empress of Judgmental Eyebrows.

The mere thought of her has my stomach twisting in a way that's... uncomfortable. Not bad exactly, but definitely not good. Riley is an enigma wrapped in flannel and tied with a bow of dry wit. Half of her comments are scathing; the other half, she's actually helpful. Infuriatingly so. Like when she pointed out the app's search function wasn't optimized for rural Wi-Fi speeds—something my entire team missed.

"Friend or foe?" I ask the air, circling her name on my mental list of potential allies-slash-problems. If I could just figure out where she stands, maybe I'd stop second-guessing every interaction we have.

"Focus, Danny," I say, shaking off the distraction.

Riley's role in this pilot is pivotal, whether I like it or not. She knows this community better than anyone. But trusting her feels like handing a matchbook to someone standing next to a pile of dynamite.

Still, the numbers don't lie. Her editorial piece brought more engagement than any of our paid ads. People listen to her. For this to work, I need her on board—and not just begrudgingly. She needs to believe in the vision. Which means I need to convince her without, you know, accidentally insulting her hometown traditions or stepping on her fiercely independent toes.

My phone's already in my hand before I even realize what I'm doing, thumb hovering over friend, confidante, and sarcasm-queen Lara's contact like it's some kind of panic button. It's late in London, but she's a night owl—no doubt writing a follow-up to her best-selling debut novel— and I'm banking on her being awake and at least mildly caffeinated enough to absorb the chaos I'm about to unload.

"Right," I mutter under my breath, pressing record on the voice note.

"Hey, Lara," I start, pacing again because apparently sitting still is too much to ask of myself right now. "So, quick update from your favorite expat marooned in Small-Town, USA. Spoiler alert: I've officially lost the plot."

I pause, glancing at the roadmap sprawled across my laptop screen on the counter. Lines and arrows crisscrossing like a conspiracy board, complete with digital sticky notes in varying shades of neon chaos.

"The good news? I have a plan. The bad news? That plan involves convincing Riley—yes, *that* Riley—to help me sell this community-driven redesign idea to people who think 'user interface' is what happens when you smile at a stranger in the supermarket."

I let out a dry laugh, leaning against the counter. "You'd love her, by the way. She's got this whole... unshakable small-town wisdom thing going for her. Like if sarcasm and stubbornness had a baby and raised it on a locally sourced kombucha. Naturally, she also thinks I'm a walking plummy British stereotype, which isn't entirely unfair, but still stings. A little."

I sigh, dropping my head back to stare at the cracked ceiling. "Honestly, though, she's brilliant. Annoyingly brilliant. Her scathing editorial piece brought more engagement than any of our marketing campaigns combined, which is equal parts impressive and infuriating."

I rub the back of my neck, a wry smile tugging at my lips despite myself. "The worst part is, I think she might actually enjoy watching me squirm. Like, there's this glint in her eye every time I fumble over another town tradition or accidentally insult someone's great-grandmother's prized pie recipe. It's... God, it's driving me mad."

I stop pacing, leaning forward onto the counter as my voice softens. "But then there are these moments—rare, fleeting moments—where she lets her guard down. Just for a second. And I see this... this determination in her. This fire. And suddenly, I'm not thinking about metrics or deadlines or how much coffee I've consumed in the last twelve hours. I'm just... watching her. And wondering why the hell she doesn't hate me as much as I probably deserve."

I blink, realizing I've gone completely off-script. "Anyway," I say quickly, clearing my throat. "That's the update. Hope you're enjoying your tea and biscuits or whatever it is you do at two in the morning. Say hi to Rory from me. Talk soon. Probably. Unless I spontaneously combust first."

I hit send before I can overthink it, collapsing onto the couch with a groan.

SIX

— ♥ —

RILEY

The scent of cinnamon and caramelized sugar lingers in my nose as I type the final sentence of my piece on Willow Cove's annual pie bake-off. It's fluff, sure, but the kind of fluff that makes readers smile over their morning coffee. I sit back, crack my knuckles, and take a sip from my mug—lukewarm, naturally. My fingers hover over the keyboard, debating whether "decadent" or "indulgent" better captures Mrs. Harper's Best-In-Show pecan pie, when my screen pings with the first email. Then another. And another.

"RILEY," the subject line screams in all caps, "HELP!"

"Great," I mutter under my breath.

Setting down my mug, I click into the inbox, where emails are piling up like it's Black Friday promotion week. Mrs. Callahan from Willow Cove Honey is panicking about her vendor profile not loading. Shannon, from one of the artisanal soap stalls, says her orders have vanished into the ether. Even George, who usually communicates exclusively through grunts and head nods, has managed to type out an alarming, "WHAT IS WRONG WITH THE APP????"

"Why are they emailing *me*?" I groan, shoving my chair back with a screech.

I glance around the newsroom for someone—anyone else—to pass this off to. Peggy's door is closed, her blinds drawn, which means she's either on a call or pretending to be, so she doesn't have to deal with crises. Lucky her. Elaine will throw it back at me and tell me it's related to the app, so I need to deal with it. The intern is nowhere to be found, probably hiding behind the copier again. Figures.

"Okay, Riley," I tell myself, tapping my fingers against the desk—a nervous tic I thought I'd left behind when I traded coding for column-writing. "It's just an app issue. Danny needs to fix it. Not your circus, not your monkeys."

But the circus feels uncomfortably close when I picture the weekend market vendors pacing their kitchens, wringing their hands over unsold jars of jam and unscented candles. Willow Cove's Saturday market isn't just some quaint community event. Not anymore, anyway. It's become an important revenue stream for most of these folks and is something of a tourist attraction, welcoming visitors from across the entire state and beyond. No sales money tied up in stock and materials, which means no rent, no groceries, no peace of mind. And despite my better judgment—or years of corporate burnout screaming *don't get involved*—I feel that tug. That stupid, inconvenient sense of duty that always seems to land me in situations I'd rather avoid.

"Ugh." I rub my temples. Maybe if I ignore it, the problem will magically solve itself.

"Is this your idea of a slow news day?"

I look up from my desk to find Danny Winter standing in the doorway of the *Gazette* office, looking like he's just stepped out of a wind tunnel and directly into a fight he knows he's losing. His dark hair is doing its best impression of a distressed bird's nest, and his usually crisp suit has taken on the crumpled charm of someone who's either been wrestling with existential crises or office furniture.

"Let me guess," I say, folding my arms and leaning back in my chair. "You heard I was enjoying my morning and decided to ruin it personally."

"Not quite," he replies, stepping further inside, hands raised in mock surrender. "More like I saw the car crash that is our app situation currently and thought, 'Who better to blame —uh, consult—than Riley Hayes?'" He flashes a sheepish grin, one that would probably charm a weaker person. Unfortunately for him, I'm not feeling particularly weak today.

"Consult? Really?" I arch an eyebrow. "Because it sounds like you're here to dump your mess in my lap and hope I don't throw it back at you."

"Harsh, but fair," he says, shoving his hands into his pockets. "Look, I know tech issues aren't exactly your wheelhouse anymore, and believe me, I wouldn't be here if I had even a shred of a clue how to fix this. But it's the middle of the night in the UK. Our tech support team is offline, and the vendors are panicking. If I don't get this working, our entire US business is at risk, and I... well, I've already tried turning it off and on again. Twice."

"Twice, huh?" I scoff. "Wow, you're really pulling out all the stops. Why can't it wait until morning? In the UK, I mean."

"I've just won over these people," he says, sincerely. "They're beginning to trust the app. To trust me. If there's friction with their experience, they'll abandon the whole idea and I'll never get them on board again."

I roll my eyes, muttering something under my breath about corporate types and their inability to handle anything that doesn't come with a preloaded tutorial. But as much as I'd love to shove him out the door and let him figure this out on his own, the image of Nora's trembling hands clutching unsold jars of peach preserves keeps flashing in my mind like a guilt-ridden screensaver.

"What makes you think I can help?"

"I read your LinkedIn. You used to code, didn't you? I just—"

"Fine," I interrupt, pushing back my chair with a sigh. "Show me the damage."

"Thank you, you're a lifesaver," he says, placing his laptop on my desk and logging in.

"Don't thank me yet. I've no idea if I'm going to be able to help."

"Just take a look. That's all I ask," he says, opening a program. "So, this is our back-end, it's... messy. Features built on top of features, very little forward planning, lots of technical debt, and sometimes... it just falls over.

"Like right now," I say.

"Yep."

"But what is it you want me to do?"

"See if anything stands out. See if you can see what's causing the app to crash."

I look at his laptop screen, watching the log files scroll in a steady, relentless stream of data, populating faster than my eyes can follow. "Sorry. I'm not the right kind of developer."

"Oh. What do you mean?"

"This app is written in PHP. I'm a C-Sharp programmer."

"Tomato, *tomahto,* aren't they the same but different?"

"Yeah, pretty much, so let's see how well you get on reading the teachings of Confucius in their original Chinese."

"Okay, fair point," he concedes. "Sorry, I just thought—"

"Fine, I'll take a look, but no promises." I pull the laptop in front of me, my fingers hovering over the keyboard that looks like it's seen more spilled coffee than actual typing. For a moment, I hesitate, my reflection staring back at me from the glossy black screen. It's been years since I've touched code—really touched it—and the thought of diving back in, feels like reopening a chapter I'd slammed shut for good reason.

"Everything okay?" Danny asks, his voice light but edged with concern.

"Peachy," I lie, squaring my shoulders. With a deep breath, I crack my knuckles and start typing commands, the keys clicking beneath my fingers like a familiar rhythm I didn't realize I still remembered.

"Wow," Danny murmurs behind me. "You actually know what you're doing."

"Don't sound so surprised," I retort, without looking up. "But just so we're clear, if this works, you're buying me coffee for a month."

"Done," he says, watching the screen over my shoulder. "Assuming you don't burn the whole system down first."

"Keep talking, London," I warn him, my lips twitching despite myself. "See how fast I make you regret it."

The unfamiliar code blurs across the screen, and for a moment, I feel like I've been dropped into someone else's life—someone who actually enjoys this sort of thing. But then, somewhere between the syntax errors and the nested loops, something clicks.

It's muscle memory. Like riding a bike. Or reciting your ex's Netflix password after two margaritas.

"Okay, so you're... What? Hacking into the Matrix?" Danny's voice drifts from behind me, thick with amusement. He's leaning over, arms crossed, like he's waiting for me to pull a rabbit out of my laptop. "Should I be worried you're about to summon Skynet?"

"Only if you keep talking," I mutter, squinting at the lines of code. Somewhere in here is the problem, buried like a splinter, and I'm going to find it if it kills me. Which, judging by the state of this system, it might. "Seriously, don't you have anything better to do than hover?"

"Not really," he says, unbothered. "I'm enjoying the show. You look..." He pauses, as if searching for the right word. "Intense."

"That's because I *am* intense, Danny," I say. My focus locks on a suspicious string of commands, and I dive deeper, my hands moving faster now. It's almost instinctive, the way my brain picks apart each segment of code like unraveling an old sweater.

"Impressive," he murmurs, and there's something different in his tone—less teasing, more... sincere?

"Are you just going to stand there and narrate, or are you planning to contribute?" I say without looking up.

"Contribute? To whatever dark sorcery you're performing? Hard pass." He gets to his feet. "But I'll tell you what—I'll start on those coffees that I owe you. You take yours black, right? Matches your soul?"

"Har har. Yes, black. Now, go away."

"Going," he says, retreating. "Try not to erase anything while I'm gone."

"Only if you hurry."

He disappears, and for a blissful stretch of minutes, it's just me and the keyboard. The rhythm of typing feels oddly soothing, each keystroke unlocking some long-dormant part of my brain. I didn't realize how much I'd missed this—solving problems, fixing things. It's like hearing an old song on the radio and remembering all the words without trying. Familiar, but bittersweet.

I'm so absorbed that when he returns, sliding a steaming cup of coffee onto the desk beside me, I barely notice. "Any progress, or should I start drafting my apology email to the vendors?"

"Shh," I say, waving him off. "I'm thinking."

"Right. Thinking." He falls silent, but I can feel his gaze on me—warm, curious, and very distracting. Ignoring him, I lean closer to the screen, my mind already racing ahead to the next step.

"Got it," I mutter, the lines of code finally snapping into place like puzzle pieces that were hiding under the couch all along. My fingers hover over the keyboard for a second longer, as if waiting for some cosmic green light to confirm I'm not about to accidentally nuke half the app's functionality.

"'Got it' as in you've fixed it, or 'got it' as in we're still doomed and should start selling artisanal apology cards on the app instead?" Danny's voice is as dry as ever, and I can feel him leaning closer behind me without having to look.

"'Got it' as in I've found your problem." I glance over my shoulder at him, raising an eyebrow. "Your precious app has been choking on its own caching system."

"Ah, yes. Caching bugs. Naturally." He says it like he has any clue what that means, folding his arms and nodding sagely. "And... what do we do about that?"

"First, you stop breathing down my neck," I suggest, turning back to the screen. "Second, you let me patch in a temp fix so your vendors don't riot."

"Riot seems strong," he counters, but I don't miss how his voice tightens just a fraction. For all his polished bravado, the guy is wound tighter than a dollar-store rubber band.

"Look, this isn't brain surgery," I say, pulling up the offending lines of code. "Your app's backend is trying to cache way too much data. It's like a squirrel hoarding nuts for the apocalypse. All I have to do is tweak this function here"—I tap a few keys with precise intent—"and redirect the overflow. A

Band-Aid, but it'll hold until someone smarter than you gets a proper fix in place."

"Lovely," he says, but I catch the faintest tug of a smile. "And how do I help?"

"By not touching anything," I reply immediately.

He moves closer anyway, peering over my shoulder as if sheer proximity will give him tech wisdom by osmosis. I sigh and gesture for him to sit beside me, mostly because his looming presence over my shoulder unnerves me.

"Fine. Just—watch this, okay? You're going to deploy the fix once I'm done."

"Deploy. Right. Sounds official."

He drops into the chair next to mine, far too close for my liking, and leans toward the keyboard. Our shoulders almost brush, and I swear I catch a faint whiff of something expensive —cologne, probably, though it could just be his ego.

"Don't touch anything yet," I warn, typing rapidly. My focus locks on the code, each line falling into place with satisfying clarity. It's almost too easy, and I hate how much I missed this—the rush of solving a problem no one else could.

"Okay," I say after a minute, sitting back and exhaling. "That should do it. Now, when I tell you, hit Enter."

"Hit Enter. Got it. Very technical," he quips, moving his hand toward the keyboard.

"Not yet!" I bark, slapping his wrist away without thinking. His skin is warm under my palm, and there's a brief pause where neither of us moves. My hand lingers for a beat too long before I snatch it back like I've touched a live wire.

"Sorry," I mutter, keeping my eyes glued to the screen.

"Don't mention it," he says lightly, but his voice is softer now, almost unreadable.

Out of the corner of my eye, I see him flex his fingers as if testing whether they still work.

"Alright," I say briskly, breaking the moment. "Now you can hit Enter."

"With great power comes great responsibility," he murmurs, reaching for the key.

This time, our fingers brush over the edge of the keyboard —barely a whisper of contact, but it sparks like static electricity. I freeze, my breath hitching, and for half a second, the air between us feels charged, heavy, like we're standing on opposite sides of a fault line.

"Enter," I repeat, sharper than necessary, shoving the tension aside.

"Right. Enter." He presses the key, and the screen floods with refreshed data, the error logs clearing out like magic.

"See?" I say, pushing back from the desk with forced nonchalance. "Not brain surgery. Even you could handle it."

Danny's screen changes dramatically. The red and amber warning icons vanish, replaced by the smooth, refreshingly green dashboard that signals everything is back in working order. I exhale sharply, leaning back in the creaky desk chair, while Danny lets out a noise that's somewhere between a laugh and a relieved groan.

"Yes!" he practically shouts, pumping a fist in the air like we've just won the World Series. "Riley, you're a genius. A literal genius. Like, Einstein-level brilliance wrapped in flannel."

"Calm down, London," I say, swiveling my chair away from him and grabbing my coffee. It's lukewarm, but I sip it anyway because I refuse to let him see me smile. "Don't get any ideas about putting my name on a plaque or whatever corporate nonsense you people do. No one needs to know about this."

"Wait, what?" He turns to me, his face lighting up with what I can only describe as mischievous disbelief. "You solve a crisis of *epic proportions*, save the entire North American launch, and you don't want credit? That's... criminal."

"Not criminal." I set the mug down hard enough to make the ceramic clink against the desk. "Practical. Last thing I need is every vendor in town asking me to fix their toaster ovens or how to edit PDF documents. My plate's full enough, thanks."

"I should at least write a poem. Maybe commission a statue."

"Do that, and I'll sabotage the app myself," I say flatly, and hand Danny back his laptop. "Come on, fresh air."

The *Gazette*'s back steps are rickety at best, downright dangerous at worst, but they're my favorite spot to sit when I need a moment. The view isn't much—just the town square with its mismatched benches and stubborn patches of grass—but this morning, it feels... peaceful. Quiet, even.

"Not bad," Danny admits, lowering himself onto the step beside me. He sets his coffee cup down, fingers drumming absentmindedly against the lip. "Could use some landscaping, though. Maybe a fountain."

"Right, because nothing says 'small-town charm' like a miniature version of the Trevi Fountain. I glance at him sideways, catching the faint smirk tugging at the corner of his mouth.

"Hey, don't knock it till you try it. Could be revolutionary."

"Or tacky. But sure, dream big, Danny."

For a while, we just sit there, sipping our lukewarm coffees and watching the world go by. The hum of conversation fades into the chirp of crickets, and for once, neither of us says anything. It's... nice. Unsettling, but nice.

"Okay, real talk." Danny breaks the silence, tilting his head toward me. "Why didn't you stick with it?"

"Stick with what?" I ask, even though I already know where this is going.

"Tech. Coding. Whatever magic you just worked in there." He gestures vaguely toward the *Gazette* building behind us. "You're clearly good at it—like, stupidly good. So why bail?"

"Because not everything's about being good at something," I say sharply, more defensive than I mean to. "Sometimes it's about... other things."

"Like what?" His tone is softer now, less pushy, but still curious. Too curious.

"None of your business," I reply, standing up before the conversation goes any deeper. "And seriously—don't make a habit of needing me to bail you out. Next time, you're on your own."

"Next time?" He grins, rising to his feet with frustrating ease. "So you're saying there *will* be a next time?"

"From what I saw of your code base, you can count on it." I empty the last of the coffee from my cup into the drain and start walking back inside, leaving him sitting there.

SEVEN

DANNY

I wake up to the distinct sensation of my spine protesting its very existence. The bed—if it can even be called that—is a lumpy relic from some bygone era, likely constructed during a time when comfort was considered an indulgence. My neck cracks audibly as I move, and I groan, rolling onto my side only to encounter a spring digging into my ribs with unrelenting determination.

"Brilliant," I mutter, swinging my legs over the edge and rubbing my face. "Nothing like starting the day feeling like I've been hit by a truck."

The apartment's heater wheezes in the corner, valiantly trying to warm the drafty space but failing spectacularly. I glance around at the peeling wallpaper, the mismatched furniture, and the faint smell of mildew that seems permanently embedded in the air. It's charming in that quaint, small-town way that might appeal to someone else—someone *not* accustomed to Egyptian cotton sheets and Nespresso machines within arm's reach.

I shuffle to the kitchen counter where my laptop sits, glaring at me like an accusatory ex. The Wi-Fi router blinks erratically, as though it, too, is in on the conspiracy to ruin my life. I refresh the page I've been trying to load for the past fifteen minutes—still nothing.

"Of course not," I say aloud to the empty room. "Why would functional internet exist in Willow Cove? That would just be too convenient."

Resigned, I grab my phone instead and flop back onto the couch with all the grace of a collapsing deck chair. Scrolling through my messages, I land on Lara's name. Best friend, professional meddler, and the only person who could make me laugh at this ridiculous situation without wanting to throttle her. I open the chat window, thumb hovering over the keyboard, then decide against typing. Too much effort. Instead, I hit the voice note icon.

"Morning, Lara. Or should I say afternoon? Evening? Whatever ungodly hour it is in London right now. Just a quick update from your favorite expat tech genius-slash-glorified babysitter." My voice is thick with sarcasm, but it's the kind that keeps me sane. "App crash? Still a disaster. Wi-Fi? About as reliable as a chocolate teapot. Oh, and the bed I'm sleeping on? I think it's cursed. Pretty sure it's actively trying to murder me in my sleep."

I pause for dramatic effect, staring at the blinking cursor on my screen as if it'll somehow fix itself. It doesn't.

"Anyway, I hope you're enjoying your flat with its functioning plumbing and walls that don't look like they've survived a hurricane. Meanwhile, I'm here trying to figure out whether the locals are being nice because they're genuinely friendly or just because they want to sell me overpriced artisanal jam."

I hit record again, leaning back against the couch that is even less comfortable than the bed. The app crash deserves a proper recap—mainly because I need to vent, but also because Lara thrives on my misery.

"Right, so picture this," I start. "The app goes down. Completely. Like Titanic-level sinking. Users are freaking out, my phone's blowing up, and I'm stuck in this charming little town where 'tech support' means unplugging it and praying, or waiting for someone's grandson called Nathan to come home for Spring Break."

I let the memory of yesterday's disaster wash over me. "Enter Riley Hayes. Local journalist-slash-technical savant-slash... Well, I don't actually know what else she does, but she swoops in like some sort of flannel-clad superhero. She figures out the glitch in about five minutes flat, while I'm still waiting for our supposed IT team to log on for the day. It was... fine." I wave a dismissive hand, as if downplaying her skills will somehow lessen the blow to my ego.

"She didn't even gloat," I add, almost begrudgingly. "Not really. Just gave me this look, you know? That 'I'm smarter than you, but too polite to say it' look. Infuriating. Anyway, she patched things up, saved the day, and went back to whatever small-town superheroes do when they're not making product managers like me feel entirely useless."

I hover over the send button, debating whether I should mention how Riley's hands moved so quickly across the keyboard that it was almost hypnotic. Or how she bit her lip in concentration, completely unaware of the chaos around her. Nope. Not going there. Instead, I click send and brace myself for Lara's inevitable commentary.

Her response pings almost immediately—a string of laughing emojis followed by:

> 😂 😂 😂 😂 Flannel-clad superhero? Danny, you've got to stop watching Hallmark movies before bed.

"Very funny," I mutter under my breath, rolling my eyes as her next message pops up.

> So let me get this straight. You, the self-proclaimed tech genius, were rescued by a local journalist who probably fixes laptops on the side for fun? And she didn't rub it in your face? Are you sure she's human?

"She's very human," I grumble, though I refuse to elaborate. My phone buzzes again.

> What's next? Is she going to teach you how to churn butter or knit a sweater from scratch? Honestly, Danny, I think I love her already. Riley sounds iconic.

"Yeah, well, you're not stuck in the same town with her," I shoot back in a voice note. Because the truth is, Riley isn't just 'iconic.' She's sharp, capable, and annoyingly difficult to dislike —even when she's proving me wrong.

> Oh, poor Danny. Stuck in a small town with someone who doesn't fall for your usual charm routine. How exhausting for you.

"She's not immune to me," I mutter, though it sounds weak even to my own ears. My fingers hover over the screen, debating whether I should leave her on read out of spite.

But Lara follows up:

> Face it, Danny. She's got your number. You can't smirk your way out of this one.

> That is objectively false.

> I've been perfectly professional. And charming, by the way. She just… doesn't appreciate it.

Uh-huh. Translation: she's making you work
for it. This is new territory for you, isn't it? No
instant swooning? No breathy laughter at your
jokes? Tragic.

Okay, first of all, my jokes are objectively
hilarious, thank you very much. And second

I pause, struggling to find a point that doesn't sound like I'm trying too hard.

She's not making me do anything. Riley Hayes
is… complicated. That's all.

Complicated

Sure, Danny. Keep telling yourself that while
you stare longingly at her like a lovesick
teenager.

I start to type, "*I do not—*" I stop mid-protest because, well, I kind of did. But it wasn't longing. It was… curiosity. Professional curiosity. Completely normal when dealing with someone who defies every logical pattern you've ever encountered in human behavior.

"Fine," I say aloud to the empty apartment, scrubbing a hand over my face. "Maybe she's a little different. Big deal."

My phone buzzes with the incoming call. It's Lara calling to gloat.

"Alright, enough," I say, dropping back against the couch with a groan loud enough to startle the neighbor's cat outside the window. "If you've got something helpful to say, now's the time."

"Helpful?" Lara's voice crackles through my phone's speaker, the tinny quality doing nothing to soften her tone. "When have I ever been *unhelpful?*"

"Do you want the list alphabetically or chronologically?" I

mutter, swiping at the keyboard to give my hands something to do. The spreadsheet on my screen still refuses to load, and I resist the urge to punt my laptop into the nearby wall. It wouldn't be the first casualty of this godforsaken town.

"Stop deflecting." Her voice shifts, the teasing edge smoothing into something quieter, sharper. "What's really going on, Danny?"

"Define 'really,'" I hedge, but even I can hear the strain in my voice. There's no point fighting it when Lara gets like this— she's practically made a career out of cutting through my nonsense. It's annoying how good she is at it.

"Really, as in why you sound like you just lost a fistfight with self-doubt and let it pin you to the mat." There's a pause, heavy with expectation. "Talk to me."

I press my thumb and forefinger to the bridge of my nose, squeezing until stars dance behind my eyelids.

"I don't know if I can pull this off."

"Pull what off? A functioning Wi-Fi connection? Because I hate to break it to you, but small-town America isn't exactly known for its broadband speeds."

"Ha ha." I force a laugh, though it comes out choked. "No, I mean... this whole thing. Willow Cove. The app relaunch. Fixing a system I didn't even build in the first place while trying not to offend literally everyone in a twenty-mile radius. All while sharing oxygen with Riley Hayes, who might just be actively plotting my demise."

Lara hums thoughtfully, which is worse than outright mockery. Mockery, I can handle. Thoughtful Lara means she's about to get serious, and serious makes me squirm.

"Let me ask you something," she says finally. "When was the last time you felt like this?"

"Like what?"

"Like you were out of your depth. Unsure. Vulnerable."

She lets the word hang there, daring me to flinch. "Because if I remember correctly, that's not exactly your default setting."

"Gee, thanks for the reminder," I grumble, shifting uncomfortably on the couch. One of the springs digs into my lower back, a physical manifestation of everything wrong with my current situation. "And no, it's not. Which is why this feels so bloody awful."

"Maybe it's supposed to," she counters, her voice softening but staying firm. "You're used to being the guy with all the answers, Danny. But maybe this time, you're not supposed to fix things. Maybe you're supposed to listen instead."

"Listen to what? Angry New Englanders shouting about bugs in their software?" I snort, but the words ring hollow even to me.

"Listen to them," she says simply. "To what they actually need, not just what the algorithm says they should want. You're brilliant with data, sure—but you're better with people. When you stop trying to impress them and just... connect."

"Connect," I echo, rolling the word around like a piece of hard candy that won't dissolve. "Right. Because I'm such a natural at *that*."

"More than you give yourself credit for," she says firmly. "It's why you're good at what you do, Danny. People trust you. They just need to see that you trust them, too."

"Trust *them*?" I repeat, staring at the ceiling where a single cobweb waves smugly in the draft. The idea feels foreign, uncomfortable in the way new shoes pinch until they're broken in. But somewhere beneath the skepticism, there's a flicker of something else. Something warmer, softer. Hope, maybe.

"Look," Lara continues, "I know you love a good control freak moment, but maybe it's time to let go of the data for a second and actually talk to these people. Really get to know them. Figure out what makes them tick. And yeah, maybe that includes Riley."

"Riley doesn't tick," I mutter. "She detonates."

"Then find out why," Lara shoots back without missing a beat. "You might surprise yourself."

"Or end up as collateral damage," I grumble, but the fight's gone out of me. Instead, I let her words settle, their weight pressing down like the lumpy cushions beneath me.

"Just think about it," she says gently. "That's all I'm asking."

"Fine," I sigh. "But if this goes horribly wrong, I'm blaming you."

"Blame away," she chirps. "But don't forget—you're still the guy who knows how to make people feel seen, Danny. Even if you're too stubborn to admit it right now."

"Great pep talk," I say, but a reluctant smile tugs at the corner of my mouth despite myself.

"Anytime, Daniel Anthony Winter. Now go figure out how not to screw this up."

"Noted," I reply dryly, but as I hang up, her words linger. Trust them. Listen. Connect. Easier said than done—but maybe, just maybe, worth a shot.

From my perch by the window, Willow Cove's main street stretches out below in all its postcard-worthy glory. The cobblestones gleam faintly, kissed by dew and sunlight, while the mismatched storefronts—the bakery with its striped awning, the antique shop with its peeling sign—look like something straight out of a film set. A couple of locals wander past, coffees in hand, chatting like life isn't just one long series of impending deadlines. It's infuriatingly quaint.

"Talk to these people," Lara's voice echoes in my head. "Figure out what makes them tick."

I snort under my breath, leaning back against the lumpy couch arm. What makes them tick? Croissants and small-town gossip, from the looks of it. Not exactly untapped reservoirs of groundbreaking insight.

Still, the light catches on the bakery's windows, turning the glass into molten gold, and I can't help but stare. There's something about the way the whole street feels awake—not in the caffeine-fueled, rush-hour sense I'm used to, but in a slow, deliberate way, like the town takes its time stretching and unfolding itself. Like it knows exactly what it is and doesn't feel the need to prove anything.

My phone buzzes with another message from Lara. I swipe it open, already bracing myself.

> Prediction: Riley will be your meet-cute breakdown. Calling it now.

> Professional interest only.

> Denial looks good on you, babe 😄

> Goodbye, Lara

I text back firmly, tossing the phone onto the coffee table like it's physically capable of transmitting her smugness if I hold it any longer.

But even as I stare out at the glowing storefronts again, the laughter emojis still dancing annoyingly behind my eyes, I can't quite stop the thought from creeping in. What makes Riley tick? And why do I suddenly care so much about figuring it out?

I get up off the couch, groaning as my lower back protests like I've just aged forty years. My hand automatically rubs at the spot where a particularly aggressive spring has been stabbing me, no matter how much I try to avoid it. This rental's furniture is actively trying to kill me, I'm convinced of it.

"Definitely living the dream," I mutter, shuffling toward the coat rack by the door. My coat, still hanging there from yesterday, looks like it's mocking me with its lopsided slouch. I grab it anyway, shaking off some imaginary dust that isn't there, because apparently I need to assert dominance over inanimate objects now.

As I slide my arms into the sleeves, I catch a glimpse of myself in the mirror by the door. Hair sticking up in places it shouldn't, a shadow of stubble making me look more hungover than sleep-deprived, and an expression that screams "man spiraling." Excellent. Just the image of professionalism and charm.

"Riley would definitely find this hilarious," I grumble under my breath, tugging the lapels of the coat sharply to straighten them. The thought of her smirking at my disheveled state makes my jaw tighten—and not in the way I'd prefer. She already thinks I'm hopelessly out of my depth here; no need to give her more ammunition.

And yet, as I grab my keys and turn toward the door, I feel something unfamiliar tugging at the corner of my mouth. A flicker of... amusement? Curiosity? God forbid, optimism? Whatever it is, it feels suspiciously like the first crack in the armor I've spent years perfecting.

"Don't get used to it," I tell my reflection before pulling open the door and stepping out into the crisp autumnal air. The morning sunlight hits my face, warm and annoyingly cheerful, and for a second, I pause on the porch, letting it sink in.

Willow Cove awaits, bustling with small-town charm and,

probably, Riley lurking somewhere with her sharp tongue and infuriating ability to make me question why I care so much about what she thinks. I shake my head, stuffing my hands deep into my pockets as I head down the steps.

"Let's see what fresh hell today brings," I mutter, but the faint, reluctant smile clinging to my lips betrays me entirely.

EIGHT

RILEY

I push open the door to Ava's printing studio, and the scent hits me first—ink, paper, and just a faint undercurrent of frustration. It smells like creativity on a deadline. Amidst the chaos, Ava stands like some weary goddess of stationery, surrounded by what looks like a crime scene of misprinted postcards. She holds one up for inspection, her mouth set in a grim line.

"Vintage vibes," she mutters, her voice dripping with disdain, "and they chose *Comic Sans*." She flicks the card onto the pile with dramatic flair.

"Clearly, they have an eye for design," I say, setting my bag down on the counter. "Tragic they weren't born fifty years earlier; they could've been pioneers of bad taste."

Ava snorts, grabbing another postcard and shoving it into my hands. "Behold," she says, gesturing like she's unveiling a masterpiece at the Louvre. "The pinnacle of modern typography."

I glance down at the offending card, where the words

"*Love is Timeless*" are sprawled across a faux-parchment background in bold, unapologetic italics. I can't help it—I laugh, sharp and sudden, breaking through the usual weight that seems to follow me wherever I go.

"Timeless," I say, holding it up to the light like it might reveal some hidden message. "Timelessly hideous, maybe. Did they also request Papyrus for their wedding invitations?"

"Don't tempt fate," Ava replies, smirking as she takes the card back and tosses it onto the growing reject heap. "So, what brings you here? Just come to mock my suffering?"

"Always," I say, leaning against the counter. "But actually, I was curious about the designs you want to sell through the app. Thought maybe I'd help you upload them—if you're ready to risk another round of tech roulette."

Ava freezes mid-reach for another postcard, turning to narrow her eyes at me. "You mean *that* app? The one that crashed so hard last time I nearly lost a week's worth of work?"

"That would be the one," I say, trying not to sound defensive. "Supposedly, it's been fixed. New updates, fewer glitches, less soul-crushing despair. You know, all the things you look for in a functioning platform."

"Mm-hmm." Her skepticism is palpable, thick as the ink smeared on her fingertips. She crosses her arms, tilting her head at me. "And this sudden interest wouldn't have anything to do with a certain disheveled Brit who thinks he's Silicon Valley's answer to James Bond?"

"Absolutely not," I say too quickly. "Believe it or not, I'm capable of caring about something without ulterior motives. Shocking, I know."

"Uh-huh," Ava says, but there's a glint of amusement in her eyes now. She reaches under the counter and pulls out a neat stack of new postcards, handing them over with a flourish. "Fine. Knock yourself out, Riley. But if this thing wipes out my portfolio again, I'm billing you for the therapy."

"Deal," I say, taking the stack and flipping through the designs. They're gorgeous, of course—clean, clever, and unmistakably Ava. If anyone deserves a wider audience, it's her. And if this stupid app actually works, maybe she'll finally get one.

"Okay, let's get this over with," I mutter, sliding my laptop across Ava's cluttered worktable. A stray pencil rolls off the edge and clatters to the floor, but neither of us bothers to pick it up.

Ava leans against a stack of cardstock, arms crossed, watching me like I'm about to summon a demon instead of open a browser.

"Don't look so excited," she says dryly, sipping her iced coffee. "You might pull a muscle."

"Trust me, I've got my expectations set appropriately low." My fingers fly over the keyboard as I navigate to the app's login page. The familiar logo pops up—sleek, modern, and just pretentious enough to remind me who designed it. Great. Even the loading screen has Danny's smug fingerprints all over it.

The homepage loads, and... huh. That's not what I remember.

"Well?" Ava nudges me with her elbow. "What's the verdict, O Wise One?"

"Hold on." I squint at the screen, clicking through a couple of tabs. The dashboard is clean, almost annoyingly so. Filters that used to be buried under ten layers of nonsense are now front and center. Pricing options? Clear as day. Upload tools? Actually functional. It's like someone took everything that used to make me want to throw my computer out a window and... fixed it.

"Ugh," I groan, leaning back in my chair. "It's... not terrible."

"Wow. Stop the presses," Ava says, raising an eyebrow. "Did Riley Hayes just say something wasn't terrible?"

"Don't get used to it," I say. My gaze drifts back to the screen, and despite myself, I can't help but admit that this is—dare I even think it?—impressive. Clean design, intuitive features, logical flow. It's like someone actually listened to feedback for once.

"Look at you," Ava says, her voice dripping with mock sympathy. "You're practically glowing. Is this what betrayal looks like?"

"Please," I scoff, clicking into another tab. "I'm just surprised it works at all. Given its track record, I was fully prepared for it to crash the second I touched it."

"Uh-huh," she says. "And this sudden burst of magnanimity wouldn't have anything to do with... Oh, I don't know... A certain tech bro we know?"

"Absolutely not," I say too quickly. The words are out before I can stop them, and Ava's grin widens like she's just won a bet I didn't know we were having.

"Sure, sure," she says, waving me off. "Whatever helps you sleep at night, Riley." She gestures toward the screen. "But admit it—you're kind of impressed."

"Impressed" is a strong word, but I keep that thought to myself. Instead, I grumble something noncommittal and turn my attention back to the app. The truth is, as much as I hate to admit it, the improvements are undeniable. And if I weren't so stubborn—or, you know, morally opposed to giving Danny any credit—I might even call it good.

"Fine," I say finally, dragging the word out like it physically pains me. "It's functional. Happy?"

"Ecstatic," Ava says, smirking over the rim of her coffee cup. "This is going in the scrapbook."

"Okay, here goes nothing," Ava says, cracking her knuckles like we're about to hack into the Pentagon instead of uploading some postcard designs. She leans over my laptop, her elbow perilously close to my iced coffee, and I push it out of her splash zone. "You're sure this thing isn't going to implode halfway through?"

"Not making any promises," I mutter, even as I begrudgingly navigate the app's sleek dashboard. The clean layout mocks me with its functionality. "But hey, at least it hasn't caught fire yet. That's new."

I plug in Ava's USB drive and click through the steps: upload, categorize, price, shipping options. It's all unnervingly smooth, the app practically begging for compliments with its idiot-proof features. A couple of clicks later, Ava's entire portfolio is sitting pretty in a virtual gallery, complete with zoomable previews that shouldn't annoy anyone with functioning eyes.

"Well, damn," Ava says, leaning closer to inspect the screen. "That was... painless."

"Don't say that like it's a good thing," I grumble, because it *was* painless, and now I've got this weird sinking feeling in my stomach. Like the universe just slipped a love letter under Danny's door, signed by me against my will. "It's suspicious. Too perfect. Probably cursed."

"Or maybe it's just... good?" Ava says, smirking like she knows exactly how much that word hurts to hear me say out loud.

"Unlikely," I shoot back, but the argument feels weak even to me. My fingers hover over the touchpad, hesitating for reasons I refuse to unpack right now.

"Mm-hmm," she hums, clearly enjoying herself. "So, this sudden burst of tech enthusiasm... should I be thanking you, the app, or Mr. Smug McSmugface?"

"Are you serious?" I ask, spinning my chair to face her.

Her grin only widens, which is both impressive and infuriating. "This has nothing to do with him."

"Right, because you always get this flustered while using an app." She folds her arms, her eyes sparkling with mischief. "Come on, Riley. You can admit it. He's tall, he's kind of charming in that 'I-own-too-many-shoes' way—"

"Charming? He's an algorithm in chinos!" I cut in, my voice rising despite myself.

"Sure, sure." Ava waves me off, her expression downright gleeful now. "An algorithm who somehow managed to build this app you're trying very hard not to call brilliant."

"Functional," I correct sharply, glaring at her. "It's functional, not brilliant. There's a difference."

"Uh-huh," she says, drawing the syllables out like she's savoring them. "So, no feelings whatsoever about the man behind the code?"

"Zero," I insist, crossing my arms. "If anything, I pity him. Can you imagine being that British all the time? Exhausting."

"Right," Ava says slowly, dragging out the word until it's practically its own sentence. "But he's not *completely hopeless*, right?"

The words slip out before I can stop them. "Not completely hopeless, no."

Silence. Deafening, soul-crushing silence. Ava doesn't even move. She just stares at me, wide-eyed, like I've just confessed to secretly loving Nickelback or something equally heinous.

"Forget I said that," I say, heat rushing to my face as I march past her toward the porch. "Erase it from your memory. Pretend it never happened."

"Too late," she calls after me, her tone downright gleeful. "It's already burned into my brain forever. Riley Hayes, offering a compliment? This is historic!"

"Enjoy your iced coffee while you still have teeth," I grumble, stepping outside to escape her self-satisfaction. The sun hits me full force, warm and relentless, and I drop into one of the porch chairs with a huff. Ava follows, unbothered, handing me a sweating glass of iced coffee like she hasn't just ruined my day.

"Okay, but seriously," she says, settling into the chair next to mine. "That's the most invested I've seen you in anything work-related since... I don't know, Seattle? Remember Seattle? You used to talk about tech like it was your soulmate."

"Seattle was different," I say quickly, too quickly. The words land flat, even to my own ears.

"Was it?" Ava presses, sipping her drink. "Because from where I'm sitting, it looks like a certain tall, scruffy Brit has managed to yank you out of your tech-induced retirement, whether you want to admit it or not."

"Let me make one thing clear," I say, pointing my straw at her for emphasis. "This has nothing to do with him. Or the app. Or anything remotely related to either of those things. I'm just making sure the people here don't get taken for a ride. That's it."

"Sure," Ava says, smiling over the rim of her glass. "Whatever helps you sleep at night."

"You're reading too much into this," I say, my voice as breezy as the faint autumnal wind stirring the curls that have escaped my bun. "I helped you upload some postcards to an app, Ava. It's not exactly a career renaissance."

Ava snorts softly, tipping her drink to her lips. "If you say so. But your face lit up like the Fourth of July when you figured out that AI background feature. Don't think I didn't notice."

"I was *curious*," I counter, crossing one leg over the other with forced casualness. My boot scuffs against the peeling paint of the railing, and I focus on it like it holds the meaning of life. "Curiosity doesn't mean anything. People get curious about serial killers; it doesn't mean they want to be one."

"Right," Ava says slowly, dragging out the word in a way that makes me want to shove her iced coffee off the porch. "So, you're saying tech is now the Ted Bundy of career paths? Got it."

"Exactly," I reply, before realizing how ridiculous that sounds. "Wait—no, that's not what I meant."

"Just keep digging. It's fun to watch," she says, clearly enjoying herself.

I glare at her, but the words sink in anyway, insidious and persistent, like water seeping through cracks in plaster. Because here's the thing: she's not entirely wrong. And I hate that.

While Ava scrolls through her phone, I find myself staring out at the street, where a dandelion has sprouted defiantly through a crack in the sidewalk. Something about it sticks with me. Resilient, stubborn, completely unnecessary—and yet, there it is. Thriving.

Kind of like what I used to feel when I'd solve something no one else could, back in my coding days. That electric surge of satisfaction when everything finally clicked into place. The thrill of untangling messy problems and turning them into clean, elegant solutions. I haven't felt that in... Well, since Seattle, if I'm honest. And maybe Ava's right—maybe helping her today scratched an itch I didn't even know I still had.

But then there's the matter of *why* I even cared enough to scratch it. My brain, traitorous as ever, conjures up an image of Danny Winter, all windswept hair and infuriating smirks, leaning over my shoulder to explain some algorithm while pretending not to look pleased with himself. I grit my teeth. No. This isn't about *him*. And it's not really about helping my neighbors, although that is certainly a nice byproduct. If anything, it's about proving I can still do this stuff better than he ever could.

Still, I can't shake the memory of his latest work—the stupidly intuitive interface, the streamlined navigation, the way everything just... worked. It's annoying how satisfying it was. And, begrudgingly, I have to admit it: Danny played a role in that. Not willingly, of course. He probably stumbled into it by accident, like a toddler building a sandcastle that doesn't collapse immediately.

"Ugh," I mutter under my breath, scrubbing a hand over my face.

Ava glances up from her phone.

"Something you want to share with the class?" she asks, raising one eyebrow.

"Not really," I reply, finishing the last of my drink in one long gulp. The ice rattles in the empty cup, loud and jarring.

"Now, if you'll excuse me, I need to go remind myself why I left this nonsense behind in the first place."

"Sure, sure," she says, waving me off. "But don't be surprised if you start dreaming in code again. Old habits die hard, Riley."

"Not a chance," I call over my shoulder.

NINE

DANNY

My phone pings just as I'm about to dig into a perfectly mediocre ham sandwich at my desk. An app logo—a smug little leaf, because of course it is—glares at me from the screen. Ah, the Willow Cove Community app, my daily reminder that I'm the outsider playing SimCity with real people's lives.

"Potluck in the Square!" the event listing chirps, complete with a cheery banner image of mismatched dishes and sunlit picnic tables. My eyes skim past the details (because honestly, who cares about the suggested dress code for a potluck?) until I reach the note tagged at the bottom: *"Bring something home-made... or don't. Up to you."*

It's signed "R.H.," which I immediately decode as Riley Hayes, local journalist, professional thorn in my side, and unofficial president of the Danny Is Ruining Our Town club. The woman has made an art form out of skepticism and smirking.

"Trap or truce?" I mutter to myself, leaning back in my chair. It's probably neither. More likely, it's her way of luring me into some quaint culinary Thunderdome, where everyone judges my worth based on the flakiness of my pastry crust and how soggy my bottom is. She knows full well I don't cook. I've declared this publicly, proudly even. Still, there's something intriguing about the challenge hidden in her words.

I can hear her voice in my head now, dripping with mock innocence: "Oh, didn't expect you to show up, Mr. Technology."

Smugness bubbles up in response. Oh, I'll show up, all right. And I'll bring a quiche so perfect it practically sings "God Save the King" when you cut into it. I just hope the dilapidated oven in the kitchen is up to it.

By late afternoon, I'm weaving through Willow Cove's town square, quiche box in hand, feeling like ten pounds of over-dressed in a five-pound bag. The air smells of charred hot dogs, sugar-dusted funnel cakes, and the faint tang of baked pumpkin. Bunting crisscrosses above the rows of folding tables, fluttering in the breeze like overenthusiastic cheerleaders. Kids dart between the legs of frazzled parents, clutching balloons and cookies. It's chaos, but the cheerful kind—the sort of scene that would make a Londoner weep quietly into their takeaway coffee.

"Store-bought," I mutter under my breath, glancing at the pristine packaging of my quiche. Riley's going to have a field day with this. But honestly, what was I supposed to do? The oven, it turns out, was just for show. I did splash out at the store, opting for the most expensive quiche on offer—a premium choice for a premium occasion—or so I tell myself as I step further into the fray.

"Afternoon, Danny!" one of the town council members chirps, waving a spatula like a scepter.

I offer my best British grin, the one that's gotten me through countless awkward networking events, and nod. Keep moving, keep smiling. Blend in. Never let them see you sweat.

I spot the dessert table first, a technicolor display of pies, brownies, and cakes so elaborate they'd make Mary Berry blink twice. Nearby, the savory section looms, slightly less glamorous but no less intimidating. Someone's brought a casserole dish the size of a small country, its contents still steaming. I glance down at my quiche, suddenly feeling inadequate.

"Well, well, if it isn't Mr. Marks & Spencer himself," Riley's voice slices through the hum of the potluck like a knife through—well, a store-bought quiche.

I turn, squaring my shoulders. She's standing there, arms crossed, a smirk curling one corner of her mouth. Her auburn hair's doing this wild, half-escaped thing from a bun, but of course, she manages to make "chaotic" look effortlessly cool.

"Riley," I greet, keeping my tone light. "Lovely to see you. And here I was worried I might get through this afternoon unscathed."

Her eyes flick down to the quiche in my hands. "Oh, you're definitely not getting through *unscathed*." She promises. "Let me guess: spinach and goat cheese? Or are you more of a Lorraine kind of guy?"

"Spinach and ricotta, actually." I lift the box slightly, as if presenting evidence. "Only the finest pre-packaged delicacy for Willow Cove's discerning palates."

"Ah, yes. Nothing says 'community spirit' like outsourcing your culinary contribution to a corporate chain." She gestures at the tables, groaning under the weight of homemade casseroles and pies. "You do realize people here show up with recipes passed down from their great-grandmothers, right? Not receipts."

"Well, forgive me for not having a great-grandmother on call," I shoot back, leaning in. "Although I'm sure this will hold its own against... whatever that bubbling monstrosity over there is." I nod toward the casserole dish, still steaming ominously.

"Careful, Danny," she warns, though her grin widens. "That 'monstrosity' happens to be Martha Cleary's tuna bake. You slander that, and they really will have you flogged and burned as a witch."

"Got it." I glance at her messenger bag slung casually across her body, ready to capture all my missteps, no doubt. "Should I expect a write-up in the next edition of *The Willow Gazette*, or are you saving your takedown of my cultural insensitivity for the Christmas issue?"

"Depends," she replies, tilting her head. "How much material are you planning to give me?"

"Well, if you're hoping for a scandal, I'm afraid I'll have to disappoint you," I say smoothly. "Though, judging by that smirk, disappointment isn't exactly new territory for you."

"It's not." She laughs, a quick, genuine sound that catches me off guard. It's brief, though, because the next moment, a third voice cuts in.

"Trouble in paradise?" chirps Helen, one of the committee members, appearing out of nowhere like some sort of apron-clad fairy godmother. She's holding a clipboard and has that glint in her eye that tells me whatever she's about to suggest is going to be... inconvenient.

"Hardly," Riley says, shooting me a look that borders on conspiratorial. "Just a little friendly banter."

"Friendly, was it?" Helen muses, tapping her pen against her chin. "Because it sounded to me like a challenge."

"Challenge?" Riley echoes, her brow furrowing slightly.

"Yes!" Helen claps her hands together, clearly delighted. "A cook-off! What better way to settle your differences than over a stove?"

"Settle our—" I start, but she's already bulldozing ahead.

"Riley, you'll take sweet. Danny, savory. Perfect balance. Everyone loves a good showdown!" Helen's practically vibrating with excitement now, and I swear the surrounding crowd starts to tune in like they can smell drama brewing.

"Wait a minute," I protest, holding up the quiche as if it'll shield me. "I didn't sign up for—"

"Neither did I," Riley cuts in, crossing her arms again. "But I'm not one to back down from a challenge."

"Challenge? This isn't a—" I stop, catching the raised brow she's leveling at me. Ah, there it is. The gauntlet. Well, damn it all. "Fine," I snap. "But don't blame me when your dessert ends up second place to my culinary genius."

"Big talk for someone holding a pre-made quiche," she says, biting back a grin. "Hope you know how to boil water, London."

"Hope you know how to handle miserable public defeat, Ms. Hayes," I fire back, before Helen gleefully announces the rules and we're ushered toward makeshift cooking stations.

This is ridiculous. Utterly ridiculous. But as Riley rolls up her sleeves, her expression sharp and determined, I feel something unfamiliar stir—a mix of dread and adrenaline. God help me, I think I might actually want to win this.

"Right, so this is what rock bottom looks like," I mutter under my breath, staring at the assortment of ingredients dumped unceremoniously onto my makeshift station. A bag of Arborio rice, a handful of mushrooms, some sad-looking parsley, and a block of Parmesan that looks like it's seen better days. This isn't cooking—this is survival training.

"Cheer up, Gordon Ramsay," Riley quips from the next table over, her voice dripping with mock cheerfulness. She's already elbow-deep in flour, strawberries gleaming like little rubies in a bowl beside her. "At least you didn't get stuck making dessert. You'd probably set the Jell-O on fire."

"I'll have you know I make an excellent toast-and-tea combo. Michelin-star-worthy, really."

"Fascinating," she says, not even looking up as she drops spoonfuls of dough on top of her cobbler with the precision of someone who's far too confident for her own good. Then, without missing a beat, she adds, "Oh, by the way, you might want to rinse the rice first. Unless you're going for 'gritty disaster chic.'"

"Thanks, Nigella," I reply, though now I'm second-guessing whether rinsing the rice *is* a thing. Damn it. She's already in my head.

The square around us buzzes with energy—kids darting between tables, the warm hum of chatter, the occasional clatter of pans. Somewhere behind me, Helen is narrating the cook-off like it's the Wimbledon final, her enthusiasm enough to draw in every curious passerby. The bunting flutters over-head, casting dappled shadows across the crowd. It should be charming. It would be, if I weren't currently locked in culinary combat with a woman who's made it her life's mission to torment me.

"Careful there, Danny. That's a lot of oil," Riley calls out again, her tone innocent but her smirk anything but.

"Would you *please* focus on your cobbler and let me ruin my risotto in peace?" I say, sloshing the olive oil into the pan with more confidence than I actually feel. "Unless you're scared, I might actually pull this off."

"Scared? Of you? Oh, please." She laughs, loud enough to draw attention from a cluster of local mums nearby.

They glance over, clearly intrigued, and I swear one of them mouths, *Is he single?* Great, just what I need—an audience.

"Besides," Riley continues, tossing her hair over one

shoulder as she layers strawberries into her dish, "I don't need to sabotage you. You're doing a perfectly good job of that all on your own."

"Funny," I mutter, stirring the rice and trying to ignore the fact that it's sticking to the bottom of the pan. My heart sinks slightly as I realize I've definitely added too much stock. Or not enough. I don't know. This wasn't covered in product management school.

"Need the instructions again?" Riley pipes up, holding the rice packet aloft like a trophy. "It says, and I quote, 'Stir continuously for twenty minutes.' Think you can manage that, or should we call in backup?"

"Would you *stop* reading over my shoulder?" I growl, snatching the packet out of her hand.

She just grins, completely unfazed, and resumes sprinkling sugar over her cobbler like a French pastry chef.

But then—miraculously—the risotto starts to come together. The mushrooms soften, releasing an earthy aroma that mixes with the nutty scent of toasted rice. The Parmesan melts into creamy perfection. By the time I plate it up, garnishing with a flourish of parsley because why not, it actually *looks* edible. Dare I say... impressive?

"Well, well," Riley says, leaning over to inspect my dish as I set it down for judging. There's a note of genuine surprise in her voice, though she quickly masks it with a smirk. "Didn't think you had it in you, London."

"Neither did I," I admit, glancing at the risotto as if it might suddenly betray me. But it holds steady, gleaming under the sunlight like a beacon of hope.

The surrounding mums clap politely, one of them even exclaiming, "That smells divine!"

"Not bad for a beginner," Riley concedes, though her eyes are still dancing with challenge. "Don't get used to it, though. Victory will taste sweeter—literally, in this case."

"Enjoy your moment while it lasts," I reply, unable to suppress a grin. "Because next time, Riley, I'm coming for your cobbler crown."

"Big words for a man with parsley in his hair," she shoots back, and I instinctively reach up, cursing under my breath when I find she's right.

As the crowd gathers closer, the applause swelling, I can't help but feel a flicker of something unexpected—a mix of pride and disbelief. Maybe I'm not as hopeless as I thought. Or maybe, just maybe, I'm starting to enjoy this ridiculous competition more than I should.

"Alright, folks!" Helen shouts with excitement into the microphone. "The moment we've all been waiting for—time to crown the Cook-off Champion! Cheer for your favorite: savory or sweet!"

The crowd shifts, a sea of plaid shirts and knitted sweaters pressing closer around the judging table. My risotto sits there, steaming gently, looking almost smug in its perfectly plated glory. Next to it is Riley's cobbler, its golden crust practically glowing under the sunlight, as if it knows it's about to win prom queen.

"Team Savory!" Helen shouts, gesturing towards my dish with a flourish.

"Let's go, Danny!" someone yells—a mum from earlier, I think, her toddler perched on her hip, waving a sticky fist in solidarity.

A respectable cheer follows, loud enough to make me stand a little taller, though not so loud as to get cocky. Not that I would. Cockiness is for people who don't have rice stuck to their sleeve.

"Not bad," Riley mutters beside me, folding her arms and tilting her head to shoot me a sideways smirk. "You might actually have fans here, Danny."

"Jealous already?" I counter, keeping my voice light even

as my pulse quickens. "Don't worry, you can always try again next year."

"Bold words for a man who needed instructions to boil rice."

"Moving on!" Helen interrupts before I can fire back. Her arm sweeps dramatically toward Riley's cobbler. "And now—Team Sweet!"

The reaction is instantaneous and deafening. Children scream like it's Christmas morning, and half the mums are clapping as if they're auditioning for *Stomp*.

Riley raises her eyebrows at me, lips twitching in mock pity.

"Well, well," she drawls. "Looks like dessert's got a fan club. Surprised you didn't see this coming, London. Everyone loves sugar. Even you."

"Unfair advantage," I say flatly, nodding toward a particularly enthusiastic kid holding what appears to be his third bowl of cobbler and sporting a vanilla ice cream mustache. "I demand an independent investigation."

"Did you just accuse a child of corruption?"

"Only if he votes against me."

Helen holds up her hands for quiet, though the crowd doesn't exactly oblige. She leans into the mic again because, apparently, this is now the Super Bowl. "And the winner—by a single vote—is... Team Sweet!"

The crowd erupts. Riley throws her arms up, basking in her victory like a triumphant gladiator. The cobbler kid lets out another ear-piercing shriek, which feels like overkill, frankly. I clap along, mostly to avoid looking like a sore loser, though I can feel Riley's self-satisfied grin burning a hole in my peripheral vision.

"Don't cry," she says, turning to me as the applause dies down. "Losing builds character."

"Don't gloat," I reply. "It's unbecoming."

"Face it," she says, picking up her empty dish. "You never stood a chance."

"Next time," I say, pointing at her with my wooden spoon, "I'm bringing pudding. And when I do, Riley, you'd better be prepared to lose."

"Looking forward to it," she fires back, and for a moment, the tension between us simmers down into something almost... fun. Almost.

By the time the tables are cleared, the bunting packed away, and the last crumbs of food scraped off serving plates, the square has emptied out except for a handful of volunteers. Riley and I are among them, standing side by side at the sink in the community hall's tiny kitchen. She scrubs, I dry, and the ridiculousness of this domestic tableau isn't lost on me.

"Didn't think you'd stick around," Riley says finally, breaking the silence. Her tone is casual, but there's something sharper underneath—something like curiosity. Or maybe accusation. Hard to tell with her.

"Why wouldn't I?" I ask, keeping my eyes on the tea towel as I wipe down a stubborn casserole dish.

"Because you don't seem like the type," she replies, glancing at me over her shoulder. There's no smirk this time, no teasing lilt. Just a matter-of-factness that lands heavier than expected. "To hang out after losing, I mean. Or to show up at all."

"Ah," I say, stalling while I process that one. "So, you assumed I'd flake. Good to know where I stand."

"Can you blame me?" she says, shrugging as she rinses a plate. "You've got 'too busy' written all over you. The suit, the phone, the fancy quiche." She pauses, then adds, "People like you... You don't usually want to mingle with people like us."

"People like us?" I repeat. "Careful, Riley, you're starting to sound territorial."

"Maybe I am," she admits, setting the plate aside and meeting my gaze. "This town means a lot to me. And honestly? I wasn't sure you'd get that."

"Fair enough," I say after a beat, surprising even myself with the honesty in my tone. "But for the record, I'm not just here for the quiche."

"Good," she says, her lips curving into a small, genuine smile—the first one I've seen all day. It's fleeting, but it lingers long enough to throw me off balance. Long enough to make me wonder what else I've underestimated about her.

"Any feedback on my dish-drying technique?" I ask lightly, trying to steer us back to safer ground.

"Definitely," she says, handing me the last plate. "But hey —next time I'll print out some instructions."

"Truth is, I nearly didn't come, you know," I say, sliding the last stack of chairs into place. The metal legs screech loudly against the pavement, punctuating my words in the most dramatic fashion imaginable. "Would've saved myself a crushing defeat and a mild case of heatstroke."

Riley looks up from where she's folding a tablecloth with extreme precision, her hands moving like clockwork. "Let me guess," she says, arching an eyebrow. "Too many people? Too much sunshine? Or was it the fear of mingling with us small-towners?"

"All of the above," I shoot back, leaning casually on the now-empty table.

"So, why did you?"

"I didn't want to give you the satisfaction of making me look like a coward."

"Ah." She tosses the folded cloth onto a nearby chair and narrows her eyes at me, her smirk inching wider. "So you're saying I *do* intimidate you?"

"Please," I scoff. "I've been stared down by corporate lawyers with sharper tongues than yours."

"Corporate lawyers don't bake cobblers," she says, her voice light but her gaze steady. "Or win cook-offs against men who think risotto is a personality trait."

"That's rich coming from the woman who weaponized strawberries and sugar against me," I counter, crossing my arms. "It wasn't even a fair fight."

"Life isn't fair, Danny," she says breezily, but there's something softer under the sarcasm.

For a moment, neither of us speaks. The din of the potluck cleanup fades into the background—distant laughter, the clatter of dishes being packed away, someone calling for their kids. Riley shifts her weight from one foot to the other, the light catching in her hair as she tucks a loose strand behind her ear. It's such a small, thoughtless motion, but somehow it takes up all the space in my head.

"Well," I finally say, breaking the silence before it swallows me whole, "you were right about one thing."

"Just one?" she teases.

"Yeah," I say, holding her gaze longer than I probably should. "I nearly didn't stick around. But not because of the sun or the crowd or whatever else you think scares me. I just... wasn't sure if I'd fit into all this." I gesture vaguely at the tables, the bunting, the endless sea of cheerful townsfolk. "Your world."

Her smile falters—not in a bad way, but in a way that feels real. Honest. "And now?"

"Now?" I shrug, trying to keep the mood light. "Now I'm reconsidering my stance on small-town charm. It's exhausting, but... tolerable."

"Wow," she says, but there's a faint blush creeping up her neck, barely noticeable unless you're paying attention. And I am. "High praise coming from Mr. Big City himself."

"Don't let it go to your head," I warn.

The pause stretches again, this time deeper, slower. Her eyes flick to my mouth for the briefest second—a blink-and-you'll-miss-it kind of thing—but it's enough to send my pulse into overdrive. I want to say something, crack a joke, do *anything* to break the tension, but my brain refuses to cooperate. Instead, we just stand there, caught in some unspoken middle ground I don't quite understand.

"Well," she says finally, stepping back and breaking whatever spell had settled over us. "Guess I'll see you at the next round of 'Danny vs. Willow Cove.' Try not to embarrass yourself next time, yeah?"

"I'll try," I reply, watching as she picks up her empty casserole dish and starts walking away.

I watch her go, her boots scuff against the cobblestones, her empty dish tucked under one arm like some kind of culinary trophy. There's a little bounce in her step, probably from the sugar rush courtesy of her sickly sweet victory. Or maybe it's just the smug satisfaction of having beaten me by *one vote*. One. Singular. Vote. From a child who probably still thinks ketchup is a food group.

"Enjoy the taste of hollow victory!" I call after her, but she doesn't bother turning around. Just throws up a hand in a lazy wave, her hair catching the last streaks of sunset. The sight stirs something annoyingly unquantifiable, but I shove it aside before it can take root.

"Next time," I mutter under my breath, straightening my tie for no reason other than to feel like I've still got some semblance of control, "I'm coming for her with pudding. Sticky toffee. Treacle sponge. A full-blown dessert arsenal."

Not that I care about proving anything to her. Obviously not. It's more about principle. And pride. And... Okay, fine, maybe I do care a *little* about wiping that self-satisfied smirk off her face. But only because it's insufferable.

She expected me to flake. She said so herself. And honestly, I nearly did. But standing here now, reflecting on the absolute circus that unfolded today—the laughter, the cheering, the sabotage involving rice packets—I don't regret showing up. Not even a little.

Riley Hayes is infuriating, yes. But she's also... Well, intriguing. Sharp. Stubborn. The kind of person who gets under your skin without even trying. And apparently, the kind of person who makes you re-evaluate your entire cooking skill set just so you can beat her at her own game.

Whether it's pudding or potluck politics, Riley Hayes has officially made Willow Cove... interesting. And I'm not sure if I should thank her or blame her for that.

Maybe both.

TEN

RILEY

My phone buzzes on the desk, skittering across the cheap laminate surface like it's got somewhere to be. I glance at the screen, and I'm surprised to see Danny's name.

His message pops up:

> Got a lead you might like. Ed Baldwin.
> Meeting him tomorrow afternoon. Want in?

I blink. Ed Baldwin. As in *the* Ed Baldwin—the woodworking enigma who refuses interviews like they're door-to-door salesmen? The guy whose carved pieces are so sought after that people whisper his name like he's Bigfoot, but with better craftsmanship?

This has to be bait. Some elaborate ploy to distract me while he sneaks another corporate land grab past the *Gazette*'s readership. Still, my gut does a little somersault at the possibility. Baldwin's been on my professional bucket list since before I traded coding for copywriting. But Danny's sudden generosity? How does he even know I want to interview Ed? That smells fishier than the docks after low tide.

"Why me?" I mutter to the empty newsroom, biting the inside of my cheek as I lean back in my chair. My flannel shirt wrinkles against the seat, and I absently pick at the frayed hem of my sleeve. *Did Ava put him up to this? Is this her way of pushing me toward some kind of redemption arc for the smarmy Brit?*

The phone buzzes again. A follow-up text:

> I'll drive. Don't worry, Riley, you can bring your reporter's notebook and glare at me the whole time.

Damn it. If I pass this up, someone else will snag the story. Someone less skeptical, less nosy, someone who won't ask the uncomfortable questions about what Ed thinks of the slick, soulless apps dishing out glossy versions of "authenticity." And God help me, I want to be the one to hear Baldwin's philosophy firsthand. Even if it means enduring a few hours trapped in Danny's smug orbit.

"Strictly professional," I mutter, reaching for my phone. My fingers hover over the keys like they know typing "yes" is tantamount to shaking hands with the devil. This isn't about him. It's about the story. About Ed Baldwin.

Before I can overthink it, I type back:

> Fine. But I'm not here for small talk or charm school, London. Just the story.

His reply comes almost instantly:

> Wouldn't dream of it. Pick you up at 2pm.

"Great," I grumble, tossing the phone onto the desk like it's suddenly radioactive. My reflection in the darkened monitor catches my eye, and I swear I catch a flicker of something resembling excitement. I push it down, shove it under the same mental rug where I keep my grudging admiration for Baldwin's dovetail joints and Danny's irritatingly perfect hair.

"Just the story," I repeat firmly, grabbing my bag and shutting off my computer for the night. It's not like this is a date. It's work. A job. A chance to prove I can follow up on a lead without getting tangled in whatever game Danny thinks he's playing.

And if he tries to make it anything more? Well, I've got a whole arsenal of sardonic comebacks ready to go.

The car smells like leather and Danny's cologne—something expensive and annoyingly pleasant. I'm in the passenger seat of his rental—a brand new black *Santa-Fe*—clutching my coffee like it's a lifeline, while he squints at his phone mounted on the dashboard.

"Turn left in four hundred meters," the GPS on his phone chirps in its polished British accent. Naturally.

"Let me guess," I say, glancing at him sideways. "You've got a personal relationship with your GPS? Name her something cute? Maggie, maybe? Or is she just 'darling' when you're feeling sentimental?"

"Of course not," Danny replies smoothly, without even looking up from the road. "Her name's Eleanor. And she only gets sentimental if I miss a turn."

"Figures." I take a sip of coffee, savoring the warmth. "You'd be lost without her, wouldn't you?"

"Lost?" He finally glances over, smirking. "Literally. But forgive me for embracing technology instead of carting around..." His eyes dart to the floor of the car where my battered messenger bag sits open, revealing a Dictaphone and the corner of a mini-cassette tape case. His smirk deepens. "...artifacts from the Stone Age."

"Artifacts?" I shoot back, raising an eyebrow. "Those artifacts happen to be classics. You know, music recorded by actual humans, not algorithms spitting out Top-40 garbage."

"Ah, yes, because nothing screams modern sophistication like rewinding a mixtape with a pencil." He taps the steering wheel in mock thought. "Do you also press your own cheese, Riley? Knit your own socks?"

"Maybe I do," I say, biting back a grin. "At least I don't have to rely on Eleanor to tell me where my feet are."

He barks out a laugh, and I hate how much I like the sound of it.

"Fifteen love. But let's not pretend you don't have a notebook in that bag with half the pages falling out. What is it this time? Scribbled interview questions or doodles of cats wearing hats?"

"Both," I admit without shame. "And before you ask, no, you can't see them. Some things are sacred."

"Like your cassette tapes, apparently."

"Exactly."

We leave the main road and wind our way through tall pines and narrow gravel paths. The farther we go, the quieter it gets, save for the crunch of tires on dirt and the occasional birdcall. Danny leans forward slightly, scanning for the next turn like he doesn't quite trust Eleanor after all.

"Here," I say, pointing to a weathered wooden sign half-hidden behind a cluster of trees. It reads *Baldwin Woodworks* in faded white paint, with an arrow pointing down an even narrower driveway.

"This has got horror movie written all over it," Danny mutters, turning onto the path. The SUV bumps along, jostling everything inside, including my coffee. I clutch it tighter.

"Don't scratch your fancy car," I tease.

"I think it's impossible to hurt this vehicle. I think it might be bulletproof."

The driveway opens up to a clearing where a modest cedar cabin stands, smoke curling lazily from a chimney. A pile of logs sits neatly stacked beside the porch, and the whole place smells like pine. It's... quaint. Idyllic, even. But there's no time to admire it because the front door swings open, and out steps Ed Baldwin himself.

"Stay here," Danny whispers as he kills the engine.

"Not a chance," I reply, already opening my door.

Ed is taller than I expected, his shoulders broad under a flannel shirt that's seen better days. His face is lined, his beard streaked with gray, and his eyes are as sharp as a chisel as they flick between me and Danny. He doesn't look thrilled to see us.

"Mr. Baldwin," Danny starts, stepping forward with his hand outstretched, all British charm. "Mayor Thompson thought it would be good if—"

"Who're you?" Ed cuts him off, ignoring the offered handshake.

"Daniel Winter," Danny says, recovering quickly. "I reached out about—"

"Don't care," Ed growls, turning his attention to me. His eyes narrow. "Wait a minute. You're that reporter, aren't you? Wrote that piece on old-time craftsmanship last year?"

"That's me," I say, trying not to sound too eager. "Riley Hayes. I've been hoping to meet you."

"Yeah, well, hope's a funny thing," he mutters. "What do you want?"

"Just a conversation," I say carefully. "About your work, your process. I promise it's not an ambush."

"Mm-hm." He crosses his arms and gives Danny a once-over. "And what's his deal?"

"My driver," I say.

Danny shoots me a look, but Ed snorts.

"Fine," Ed says gruffly, jerking his thumb toward the workshop. "You want to talk? We'll talk. But only if *he* keeps his mouth shut about that damn app."

"Deal," I say quickly, before Danny can respond.

"Right," Ed grunts. "Come on, then. Don't waste my time." He turns and strides toward the workshop, leaving us standing there.

"Smooth," Danny murmurs under his breath as we follow. "Really won him over."

"I did slightly better than you managed," I whisper back, earning myself another smirk.

"Watch your step," Ed grunts as he pushes open the door to his workshop, a weathered hand resting on the frame like it's holding up the whole building. "Last thing I need is one of you townsfolk face-planting into my planer."

Danny follows behind me, ducking slightly through the doorway, and whistles low. "This is... something else," he says, voice softer than usual, like he doesn't want to disturb whatever magic lives here.

"Beats your sterile little office app world, huh?" I toss back over my shoulder, smirking when I see him scanning the room like he's trying to memorize every detail. His hands are shoved in his pockets, but his gaze lingers on a half-finished piece—a twisting, organic sculpture that looks more grown than carved.

"Believe it or not, Riley," he murmurs, tilting his head at the piece, "I'm allowed to appreciate things that don't come with a quarterly report attached."

"Sure, sure," I say, drawing the words out, "but do you

even know what you're looking at? Or are you just dazzled by all the... wood?"

"Ha. Ha." He steps closer to the workbench, trailing a finger near—not touching, because even *he* knows better—a set of chisels laid out in ascending order. "I'll have you know I once dabbled in woodworking myself."

"Is that so?" I ask, crossing my arms. "Should I brace myself for some kind of profound revelation about how whittling changed your life?"

"Hardly," he admits, shooting me a sideways grin. "It was compulsory in school. Thought I'd impress a girl by making her a spoon. It ended up looking like a table tennis paddle."

Ed snorts from the corner, where he's adjusting a clamp. "Let me guess—she wasn't impressed."

"She was not," Danny confirms solemnly, though there's a glint of self-deprecation in his eyes. "But good to know I've got a backup career path if this whole tech thing falls apart."

"Backup career?" Ed arches an eyebrow. "Kid, you couldn't carve your way out of a paper bag."

"Fair assessment," Danny agrees easily. It's disarming, seeing him poke fun at himself, like there's a real person under that polished exterior.

"All right," Ed grunts, lowering himself onto a stool that looks like it's seen better days. He gestures for me to take the opposite seat at his workbench, though he doesn't exactly look thrilled about it. The space smells like sawdust and varnish, a quiet hum of activity lingering in the background. Tools hang on the wall in neat rows, each one gleaming with use rather than neglect.

"Let's start simple," I say, sliding into the seat. My notebook is open in front of me, pen clicking once. "How'd you get into woodworking?"

"Simple?" He snorts, leaning back. "Ain't nothing simple

about it. Started young, though. My old man was a carpenter. Learned from him."

"Family tradition," I say, nodding. "And when did you decide to go your own way? You know, focus on these one-of-a-kind pieces?"

"Didn't 'decide' anything," Ed says, his tone clipped but not unkind. "Just happened. Got sick of making the same damn chair over and over. Figured if I'm gonna spend my life carving wood, might as well make something worth looking at."

"Never repeating a design," I murmur, scribbling fast. "That's... bold. Risky, even."

"Yeah, well, safe don't interest me," Ed replies, folding his arms. His gaze darts to Danny, who's standing off to the side, suspiciously quiet for once. "You gonna just stand there like a coat rack or what?"

"Driver," I remind Ed smoothly, not even glancing Danny's way. "Ignore him."

"Gladly." Ed scratches his beard, then continues, "Thing is, people contact me wanting something nobody else has. Something they can't just buy off a shelf. That's why I don't repeat myself. No two pieces are the same—it's personal."

"So, when you're working on something, how do you know it's done? Like, what's the moment where you step back and say, 'This is finished'?"

"Ha," Ed barks out a laugh. "Now that's a question. Thing is, you don't always know. Sometimes you gotta walk away before you ruin it."

"Or," comes Danny's voice, cutting through the moment like a blade, "sometimes you've got to keep going past what feels done. Push it further. See what happens."

Ed's eyebrows lift at that. So do mine.

"Maybe," Ed says slowly, tilting his head. "Sometimes, yeah. But that's a hell of a gamble. And you don't strike me as much of a gambler."

"Depends on the stakes," Danny says evenly, his hands shoved deep in his pockets like he's trying too hard to look casual.

"Fair enough," Ed mutters after a beat. "But you wanna know what makes something *finished*? It's when I can look at it and see it couldn't be anything else. Like it was always meant to be that way."

"Like it's inevitable," Danny says softly, almost to himself.

"Exactly," Ed agrees, nodding once. Then he fixes Danny with a sharp look. "You sure you're just the driver?"

"Positive," Danny says, earning a low chuckle from Ed. Meanwhile, I'm sitting there, blinking at Danny like he's just sprouted a second head. *Where the hell did that come from?*

"Right," I say, clearing my throat and closing my notebook. "Back to the real questions, if we can focus. Ed, let's talk about your philosophy—"

"Thought that's what we were doing," Ed interrupts, smirking.

"Sure," I shoot back, giving Danny a sideways glance, "but without any more unsolicited poetic musings from the peanut gallery."

"Peanut gallery?" Danny echoes, hand to his chest like I've wounded him. "I inspire one moment of awe, and suddenly I'm a circus act?"

"Focus, people," I say, raising an eyebrow at both of them. But my pen hovers over the page longer than I want it to, the words "like it's inevitable" circling in my mind longer than they should.

Outside, the sun has dipped low, casting long shadows across the yard. Ed locks up with a rusty key, his dog—a shaggy mutt with mismatched ears—trotting faithfully at his heels. There's a quiet here that's both heavy and oddly comforting.

"Nice dog," Danny says, crouching down to give the mutt a quick scratch behind the ears. The dog wags his tail once, then ambles off to sniff at something more interesting.

"Guess he likes you," I say, leaning on the porch railing. "Must be the charm. Works on everyone, right?"

"Funny," he replies, straightening up and brushing nonexistent dirt off his trousers. "But no, I think he's just discerning. Probably senses I'm the only one who hasn't insulted him today."

"Didn't realize you were keeping score."

I turn to smirk and drive the point home, but something about the golden light softens his features and makes him look... well, less like the buttoned-up corporate robot I've been pegging him as. More like a guy who's standing here, staring at the same horizon I am, trying to figure out what to do with it.

"Things made to last," he says suddenly, nodding toward the workshop. "That's what Ed said, isn't it? That everything he makes has to mean something. Be inevitable." He looks at me then, and for once, there's no smirk, no deflection. Just curiosity. "Do you think we've lost that? The difference between things built to last and things just... made?"

I blink, thrown by the question—and maybe a little by the fact that he's actually asking *me*. "I think..." I start, then falter, gripping the railing tighter. "I think people rush too much. We're always chasing the next thing, throwing out the old before we even know what it meant. But Ed... he takes his time. Makes sure it matters." I glance at him, searching his face. "Why? You planning to quit your job and join the arts and crafts movement?"

"Not quite," he says, but there's something distant in his tone, like he's thinking about it anyway.

ELEVEN

DANNY

"Seattle, huh?" I lean against the porch railing, arms crossed. The wood creaks faintly under my weight, and Ed's dog plops down near Riley's boots like he's here to listen to the story too. "Funny. You don't strike me as the 'grunge-loving, stock-option-chasing, techie' type."

"That's because I'm not." Riley shoots me a look. "And don't pretend you know anything about Seattle just because you've probably flown first class through it once or twice."

"Twice," I confirm, smirking. "And for the record, it was economy, and I had to connect through Denver both times. Total nightmare."

"Tragic," she says.

"Seriously, though." I tilt my head, studying her. She's got this guarded thing going on, like every word is weighed before it leaves her mouth. It makes me want to press buttons just to see what slips out. "Why leave? I mean, Seattle's practically a Mecca for someone like you. Tech hub, artsy, independent, slightly intimidating in your unwavering opinions."

"Wow," she says, voice dripping with mock appreciation. "What an absolutely condescending summary of my personality. Bravo."

"Thank you. I try." I grin, but it falters when she looks away, her fingers curling tightly around the strap of her bag. Okay, maybe I pushed too hard.

"It wasn't working," she says finally, her voice quieter now, less sharp. "Seattle, I mean. The job was fine, the city was fine, but..." She exhales, and for a second, she looks almost... fragile. Like the wind could knock her over if it tried hard enough. "I felt like I was drowning in 'fine.' Every day, same grind, same people, same everything. I thought... maybe here, I could breathe again."

"Here," I echo, glancing around at the sprawling hills and the fading sunlight painting everything gold. "You came back to Smalltown, USA, to catch your breath?"

"Don't mock it," she says. "Sometimes you need to strip everything back to figure out what matters."

"Fair enough." I nod, surprising even myself by not making a joke out of it. "So, are you figuring it out? What matters?"

"Maybe." She shrugs, but the tension in her shoulders tells me it's not that simple. "And what about you, Mr. Suit-and-Tie? Let me guess—big bad corporate guy wants to find his soul in a pile of sawdust?"

"Something like that." I glance back at Ed's workshop, the smell of pine still lingering in my nose. "I think... I don't know. Lately, it feels like everything I do is just... noise. Apps, metrics, new feature rollouts—it's all so disposable. I want to make something that *lasts*." I pause, realizing how much I've just given away. "Not that I'm planning to whittle spoons anytime soon."

"God forbid," she says. "Though I'd pay good money to watch you butcher another one."

Ed appears from the side of the house, holding something small in his hand.

"London," he grunts, squinting at me. "Catch."

I barely reach out in time to snag the object he tosses—a tiny wooden keyring, smooth and polished, shaped like some kind of leaf. It's impossibly light in my hand, but the craftsmanship's ridiculous. Every detail's perfect, right down to the veins carved into the wood.

"Consider it a souvenir," Ed says, his expression unreadable. "For not being completely useless today."

"Uh, thanks," I manage, turning the keyring over in my fingers. "It's incredible. Really."

He gives me a curt nod before retreating toward his house, the mutt trailing faithfully behind him.

"Well, well." Riley's voice cuts through my awe like a knife, and I glance up to see her smirking at me, arms crossed. "Looks like you've been knighted. Sir Danny of Sawdust."

"Jealous much?"

"Please." She snorts, brushing past me to follow Ed. "But I'll admit, it's nice to see you earn something without the need for a Wi-Fi connection."

"Careful, Riley," I call after her, twirling the keyring in my fingers. "You're starting to sound impressed."

"Don't push your luck," she throws over her shoulder, but I swear I catch the faintest hint of a smile before she disappears into Ed's house.

The keyring dangles from my index finger as I steer one-handed down the winding road back to town, the other hand lazily drumming against the wheel. We ended up spending the whole afternoon chatting with Ed, and it was fascinating.

It's quiet in the car, though—a sharp contrast to Riley's usual quips—but not the comfortable kind of quiet. No, this silence is coiled, like a spring ready to snap. I can practically feel her overthinking in the seat next to me.

"Still basking in your knighthood?" she asks finally, breaking the tension without looking at me. Her tone is light, but there's an edge tucked neatly behind it—like she's daring me to take the bait.

"Just deciding where to mount the plaque," I shoot back, glancing sideways at her. She's staring out the window, her fingers absently tracing the strap of her messenger bag. "Thinking above the fireplace. Right next to 'Employee of the Month.'"

"That'd be fitting," she says. "You really thrive on validation, don't you?"

"Don't we all?" I counter. "Besides, if anyone needs validation, it's the guy who spent forty minutes explaining how he refuses to make the same table twice."

"Some people call that integrity," she says, arching a brow. "But sure, let's reduce it to 'table drama.'"

"Integrity," I repeat, savoring the way the word rolls off my tongue, "is just stubbornness with better PR."

I clear my throat, shifting in my seat. The headlights cut through the dark stretch of road ahead, but I swear I can feel her gaze flicker toward me when she thinks I'm too focused on driving to notice.

"Do you always look at people like they're a puzzle you're trying to solve?" I ask, keeping my eyes firmly on the road.

"Only the ones who insist on being cryptic," she replies smoothly, without hesitation. "Not my fault you've got layers like an overpriced parfait."

"Interesting choice of analogy," I say. "Guess that makes you the spoon."

"More like the critic," she quips, leaning back in her seat. "And so far, this parfait's heavy on the fluff."

"Careful, Riley," I warn, letting my voice drop just slightly. "You might dislike what you find underneath."

"Wouldn't be the first time."

Every now and then, I catch her reflection in the passenger-side window—her profile lit faintly by the dashboard glow, her lips pressed together like she's holding something back. It's distracting as hell. My grip tightens on the wheel, and I tell myself it's just the curves of the road demanding my attention. Not her.

Finally, the town comes into view, its sleepy streets lined with dim porch lights and shuttered businesses. I pull up outside the café where her beat-up sedan's parked, killing the engine but leaving the headlights on. They cast long, slanted shadows across the pavement, making everything feel strangely intimate.

"Well," I say, twisting the keyring once more between my fingers before slipping it into my pocket. "Thanks for tagging along today. Made the whole sawdust experience... bearable."

"Bearable?" she echoes, as she unbuckles her seatbelt. "Wow, don't get too sentimental on me, London."

"Fine," I concede, leaning back in my seat. "I enjoyed it. Satisfied?"

"Marginally." She grabs the door handle, but doesn't open it right away. Instead, she turns toward me, searching my face like she's waiting for something. For once, I'm not sure what to say.

"Night, Riley," I finally muster, leaning in just enough to catch the faint scent of whatever shampoo she uses—something citrusy but not too sweet. My fingers twitch on the steering wheel, like they're debating whether to betray me and do something stupid, like reach out. For half a second, half a breath, the thought crosses my mind, uninvited and entirely inconvenient: *What if I just kissed her?*

But then reality crashes in like an overly enthusiastic intern with bad timing. Riley, sitting there with her hand still on the doorhandle, doesn't look like someone waiting for a grand romantic gesture. She looks... guarded. Like one wrong move from me would send her bolting into her car at Mach speed.

So instead, I chicken out. I straighten up and slap a wall of nonchalance over that split-second lapse in judgment. "Drive safe," I add, my voice easy, casual. Too casual.

For a moment, she just stares at me, as if she's trying to figure out what game I'm playing. Then she smirks, tilting her head in that way she does when she thinks she's one step ahead of me.

"Night, London," she says, her voice low and almost teasing, but there's something softer underneath that makes the back of my neck warm. And then she's gone, shutting the door with a solid *thunk* and walking away without a backward glance.

I watch her in the rearview mirror as she crosses the street, her boots scuffing the pavement with a determined rhythm, her shoulders squared like she's marching into battle. But there's something about the way she hooks her thumbs into her jacket pockets, like she's trying to keep her hands busy, that makes me wonder if maybe—just maybe—she felt it too. Whatever *it* is.

"Idiot," I mutter under my breath, shifting the SUV into drive and accelerating before I sit here all night dissecting her body language like some kind of love-struck teenager.

The door to the apartment swings open, and I half-stumble inside, my keys threatening to fling themselves from my hand like they've had enough of me. The pizza box dangles precariously from my other fingers, grease already seeping through a corner. Classy. I kick the door shut behind me—harder than necessary—and drop the keys on the entry table. They miss, clattering to the floor with a metallic *cha-ching* that echoes louder than it should in the quiet room.

"Brilliant," I mutter under my breath. "Proper Olympic-level coordination there, Danny."

The apartment smells faintly of cedar and something that might be mildew. It's not offensive, exactly, but it's distinctly... temporary. Like everything here. It doesn't help that the place is tiny—more dollhouse than dwelling—but I don't need much. Just a roof, Wi-Fi, and apparently an existential crisis or two. Today? Check, check, and check.

I head straight for the kitchen, dodging the suitcase I still haven't unpacked and the chair that lurks by the dining table like it's waiting to trip me up.

My brain's still running laps around the field trip earlier—the way Riley rolled her eyes when I called her "chief," the precise tilt of her smirk when she said, "What's next, London? A PowerPoint on synergy?" Like I'm some walking TED Talk. Which, to be fair, might not be entirely wrong.

"Synergy," I repeat quietly, tasting the word like it's some kind of punchline.

The pizza sits abandoned beside me, one sad bite taken before I gave up entirely. The grease stains the napkin it's perched on, mocking me. My laptop hums softly, its blank document a glaring spotlight on my procrastination. *Ed Baldwin – artisan case study*, I type in bold at the top of the page. That's as far as I get.

Instead of thinking about Ed Baldwin—local legend, community hero, possibly the most philosophical carpenter alive—I'm replaying this afternoon like it's a Netflix Original I can't stop binge-watching. Riley's laugh keeps sneaking into my head, uninvited and way too loud. It wasn't even the kind of polite chuckle you give someone when they're inept but trying; no, it was full-on, head-thrown-back, eyes-sparkling laughter. Like I'd genuinely surprised her.

"London," she'd said, voice dripping with amused condescension. "You're gonna make me believe you're actually human if you keep this up." And then that smirk. That infuriating, *infuriating* smirk—the one that says she's got my number and isn't afraid to use it.

I lean back in the creaky kitchen chair, rubbing both hands over my face. "Get it together, Danny," I mutter into my palms. "You're here to save the US market launch, not flirt your way into—" I cut myself off because finishing that sentence feels dangerous. Point is: focus. Focus on the task. On the work. On anything but how Riley looked today, like some indie movie heroine.

My fingers hover above the keyboard again. *Ed Baldwin.* What do I even write? "Grew up here, loves fishing, blah blah hometown pride"? Maybe I should just copy-paste his Wikipedia entry and call it a day. But every time I try to form a coherent thought, her voice cuts through. "What's next, Danny? A motivational poster about teamwork?" She'd said it with such disdain I couldn't help but laugh, which only egged her on. "Oh, let me guess—you've got a whole PowerPoint on 'leveraging synergies.'"

God, I wanted to be annoyed, but she made it impossible. It's like she'd built a career out of getting under people's skin. Or maybe just mine.

"Brilliant," I say to the empty room. "Now I can't even think without hearing her critique my entire existence." My pizza stares up at me accusingly, cold and congealed, as useless as I feel right now. I shove it aside, crossing my arms on the table and dropping my head onto them.

This is ridiculous. I'm supposed to be the composed one, the guy who stays cool under pressure. But apparently, all it takes is one sarcastic local with a sharp tongue and a laugh to throw me completely off my game.

It's been two weeks since I proposed a 'craft-first commerce' approach, and it's time to check in with head office. I angle the laptop screen down a touch, catching my own reflection as I do. Hair: fine, bordering on impeccable. Shirt: crisp enough to pass for someone who has their life together, even if the pizza grease stain from earlier is an inconvenient truth lurking just out of frame. Posture: straight as a ruler, though my shoulders feel like they've been holding up the weight of every bad decision I've ever made.

"Showtime," I mutter under my breath, adjusting the camera one more time because, apparently, perfectionism is my coping mechanism now. The little clock in the corner of my screen ticks closer to midnight UK time, and for once, I envy everyone back home who's already asleep, blissfully unaware that I'm about to set this entire project on fire.

With a deep breath, I click into the call, the familiar *ding* heralding my arrival in the lion's den. A grid of faces blinks to life, each one more polished and exhausted-looking than the last. There's Fiona, her perfectly manicured hand poised over some ominous notes. There's Mark, rubbing his temples like he's preemptively bracing for a migraine. Lawrence, the CTO, and, of course, there's the CEO, Victoria Blackwood herself, sitting ramrod straight in a chair that probably costs more than my car, her expression unreadable yet somehow still terrifying.

"Evening, team," I say, trying for casual, but it comes out

clipped, like someone shoved a broomstick where the sun doesn't shine. "Or morning, rather. Thanks for staying up—or waking up—for this."

"Let's cut to the chase, Danny," Victoria says, her tone sharp enough to slice through steel. "How's the pilot performing? Are we ready to scale?"

Ah, there it is. The warm-up act: a question so pointed it could double as a dagger. My hands itch to smooth down my tie—a futile effort, since I'm not wearing one—but I clasp them in front of me instead, fingers interlocked so tightly they might fuse.

"Not quite," I admit, forcing the words out before I can stop myself. "The data... Well, it's not exactly encouraging."

Fiona leans forward, her brow furrowing in that way that screams, *This better be good.* "Define 'not encouraging,'" she says, her voice practically dripping with skepticism.

"Right." I clear my throat, stalling for time, but knowing I can't evade the inevitable. "Engagement metrics are underperforming across the board. Conversion rates—lower than expected. Feedback? Uh... let's just say adjectives like 'clunky' and 'unintuitive' have come up more often than I'd care to admit."

The silence that follows is deafening, broken only by the sound of someone typing furiously—probably Fiona, logging my demise in real-time. I can feel Victoria's gaze boring into me through the screen, like she's mentally drafting my termination letter.

"To put it bluntly," I add, because apparently, I hate myself, "the app in its current form isn't working. But"—I hold up a finger, desperate to regain some semblance of control—"I have a solution."

"Do you?" Victoria's voice is ice wrapped in silk, her arched eyebrow daring me to continue. It's the kind of tone that makes grown men rethink their life choices, but I push forward anyway, because I'm already halfway off the cliff.

"Yes," I say, injecting as much confidence as I can muster. "I think we need to pivot. Reevaluate our approach to the US market. What we're missing—and what the data supports—is a more localized strategy."

"Localized," Fiona echoes, her skepticism cranked up to eleven. "As in, more delays? More money? More potential for failure?"

"More potential for success," I counter, leaning forward. My voice picks up speed, passion edging out the nerves. "We've been treating Willow Cove like it's just another test market, but it's not. It's unique. It's insular. It values community above all else. If we want to win here—and scale across the United States—we need to demonstrate that we understand that. That we *respect* it."

"Respect doesn't pay the bills," Victoria says flatly, her expression unchanging.

"Neither does launching a product that people hate," I shoot back before I can stop myself. My stomach drops the second the words leave my mouth, but there's no taking them back now. Instead, I plow ahead, hoping that momentum will save me. "Look, I know it's a risk. But I'm not suggesting we blow up the whole roadmap. Just... adjust the route. Start small, test big ideas locally, and iterate from there. One step back to take two forward."

For a moment, the only response is silence. Then Victoria tilts her head, her lips curving upward in something that might be a smile—or a grimace. It's hard to tell with her.

"So what are you proposing?" she finally asks.

"Regionally tailored app versions," I say, speaking slower now, letting the weight of those words drop into the virtual room like stones in water. "A micro-team embedded here in Willow

Cove that works directly with the community. Think hyper-local feedback loops, faster iteration cycles, and—" I pause for effect, because timing is everything, "—a product that feels organic, authentic, like it actually belongs to this market, rather than being slapped together in London and parachuted in."

"Organic?" Fiona cuts in, her voice dripping with skepticism. "What are we, a farmers' market now? Danny, do you have *any* idea how expensive it would be to maintain multiple localized versions of the app? The logistics alone—" She shakes her head, mentally calculating what these delays are doing to the company's valuation.

"Yes, Fiona," I say, my tone deliberately calm, like I'm explaining fractions to a particularly obstinate child. "I've run the numbers. And yes, there's an upfront cost. But if we focus on building loyalty in these smaller markets first, we'll create a user base that isn't just large—it's committed. That kind of engagement doesn't just boost growth; it sustains it."

"Sure, until the novelty wears off and they move on to the next shiny thing. Meanwhile, we're stuck managing half a dozen custom app versions and burning through resources."

"Not if we build smart," I counter, the edge in my voice sharpening. "This isn't about gimmicks or throwing money at bells and whistles. It's about trust. People here don't want to feel like they're just another data point in a global analytics report. They want something that reflects their world, their needs. And when they get that, they stay. Long-term loyalty, Fiona. Isn't that what we've been chasing?"

"This 'micro-team' of yours will need oversight. Who exactly is going to manage them? You?"

"Yes," I say without hesitation. "I'm already here. I know the market, I've started building relationships, and—" I hesitate for only a fraction of a second, then press on, "—I believe in this plan. Enough to stake my reputation on it."

There's a beat of silence, the kind that makes you acutely

aware of every tiny sound—the hum of my laptop fan, the distant chirp of crickets outside.

Then Victoria speaks up, her voice measured but curious. "You're very passionate about this, Danny. It's... surprising."

"Passion's part of the package," I reply lightly, though I can feel the tension coiled in my shoulders. "Along with, you know, expertise and a proven track record."

"Don't oversell it," Fiona mutters, but it isn't hostility in her tone, more... wariness. Like she's trying to figure out whether I'm brilliant or completely mad. To be honest, I'm not sure myself.

"Look," I say again, softer this time, leaning back in my chair. "I know this is a risk. But isn't that what we signed up for? Innovation means taking calculated risks, and this one—" I gesture vaguely around me, as if they can see the sleepy streets of Willow Cove through the screen. "This one could redefine how we approach emerging markets. Not just here, but everywhere."

I look directly at each of the execs on the call. I might not have convinced them completely, but they're considering it, and that's encouraging.

"If it doesn't work, you can all say 'I told you so' and happily throw me under the proverbial bus. But if it does work..." I let the sentence hang, the unspoken possibilities shimmering in the air between us.

"Big if," Fiona murmurs, but her voice lacks the conviction it had a few minutes ago. Progress.

"Big payoff," I counter, my smile small but genuine. "Trust me, Fiona. You won't regret this."

"Alright," Victoria says finally, her voice cutting through the tense silence like the crack of a whip. "Let's hear from the top."

I blink, momentarily thrown off. "The... top?"

"The CTO," she clarifies, narrowing her eyes at me

through the pixelated screen as if I've just wasted precious seconds of her life. "The tech team is already spread thin. I need Lawrence's buy-in if we're going to consider localized versions."

"Ah. Right. Of course." My mouth goes dry. This is it. The moment where my meticulously crafted pitch either soars or bursts into flames. No middle ground.

"Well, Danny," the CTO—Lawrence Chase, Head God of All Things Tech and Innovation—leans forward, steepling his fingers like some kind of Silicon Valley Bond villain. His expression? Impossible to read. Classic Lawrence. "It's certainly... unconventional."

"Unconventional" is corporate-speak for "borderline insane," but I choose not to flinch. Instead, I clasp my hands in front of me and sit up straighter, maintaining eye contact with the tiny glowing rectangle that represents him.

"Sometimes unconventional is exactly what we need," I say. My tone is calm, measured, but inside? Inside, I'm already halfway through composing my resignation email. Subject line: *This Was Fun Until It Wasn't.*

"True," Lawrence muses, dragging out the word like he enjoys watching me squirm. Then he tilts his head slightly, contemplative. "And I'll admit, your argument about community involvement has merit. Particularly in new markets. It's... intriguing."

"Intriguing" is better than "unconventional," right? A step up? Or maybe just a slower death?

"Enough to move forward," he continues, and for a split second, I think I misheard him.

"Sorry—" I start, leaning closer to the screen.

"Four weeks," he interrupts, holding up four fingers like this is a game show. "You have four weeks to prove it works. Build your micro-team, implement the pilot, whatever you're calling it. But if there aren't measurable results by then…" He trails off, leaving the threat unspoken but perfectly clear.

"Understood," I say quickly, before anyone can change their mind.

"Good," Lawrence says simply, leaning back again. "Fiona, update me weekly on progress. And Danny"—he pauses, offering me one of those rare, almost-smiles that always feel like a trap—"don't screw it up."

"Wouldn't dream of it," I reply, forcing a grin that probably looks more like a grimace.

"Meeting adjourned," Lawrence declares, and just like that, the call ends.

The screen goes black.

For a moment, I don't move. Don't breathe. Just sit there, staring at my own reflection in the now-empty monitor.

"Bloody hell." The words slip out before I can stop them, barely louder than a whisper.

Four weeks. Four weeks to build something out of nothing in a town where the biggest tech innovation is probably the self-checkout machine at the local grocery store.

But also… four weeks to prove I'm not just another tech bro spouting empty buzzwords. Four weeks to actually, *finally*, make a meaningful impact.

Exhilaration and terror crash over me in equal waves, leaving me dizzy.

I push back from the table, the chair legs scraping against the hardwood floor with an ear-splitting screech. Leaning forward, elbows on knees, I bury my head in my hands.

I flick the laptop shut and lean back in my chair, staring at the ceiling like it holds the answers to life's greatest mysteries. It doesn't. All it does is remind me that the lighting in this apartment is criminally dim. Figures. Perfect setting for a man who just upended his entire career trajectory with one rogue suggestion.

My phone sits on the table, screen dark. My fingers drum against the wood, restless. If there's one person who'd appreciate the absurdity of this situation—and maybe help talk me off the ledge—it's Lara. Of course, she'll also laugh at me, mock me, and probably suggest some wildly inappropriate solution involving tequila, or to ignore it all and read a book. But that's what friends are for, right?

Grabbing the phone, I unlock it and pull up her contact. The cursor blinks at me from the empty message field, taunting me. I start typing:

> So… remember that time you said I should 'shake things up' and stop being such a corporate robot? Congrats, you've officially broken me.

I hit send before I can second-guess myself, then toss the phone onto the table. It buzzes with a response almost instantly. Classic Lara.

> Oh no, what did you do?

> I pitched a hyper-local pilot project in Willow Cove. CTO actually approved it. Four weeks to deliver. No safety net. Send snacks.

Her reply comes in hot:

> Lol, so you're staying on in Willow Cove?? Are you trying to become the tech world's Jane Austen hero? Brooding Londoner goes rustic? Also, snacks won't save you. You'll need divine intervention. Or wine.

She's not wrong, though—the whole scenario *is* ridiculous. Still, hearing (well, reading) her dry humor somehow makes it feel… manageable.

I fire back:

> Wine welcome. Any other pearls of wisdom,
> oh great oracle?

The reply takes a few seconds longer this time, and when it pops up, I can practically hear her voice in the words:

> Yeah—don't screw it up, Danny.

> Joking aside, you've got this. Seriously. Just
> channel whatever madness made you pitch it
> in the first place.

I stare at the screen, rereading her message until the letters blur. *You've got this.* Simple. Direct. Not even remotely mocking. For Lara, that's basically Shakespearean-level sincerity.

TWELVE

— ♥ —————

RILEY

The cursor blinks at me like it's mocking my very existence. A tiny, taunting line on an otherwise empty screen. My fingers hover over the keyboard, poised for brilliance—or maybe just mild competence—but nothing comes. Well, that's not true. I type a sentence:

"Artisan economies thrive in the digital age by leveraging—"

Delete.

"Leveraging" sounds like something Danny Winter would say. All polished and corporate, like he's pitching his next big thing to a room full of start-up investors. No, thank you.

"Artisan economies struggle to maintain authenticity when faced with—"

Delete. Too cynical. Too... me. Elaine will call it "predictable" and suggest I lighten up.

I push back against the booth seat, the faux leather squeaking in protest. The Willow Bean Café smells like burnt espresso and fresh-baked muffins, but even its usual charm isn't working. My notebook sits on the table, filled with scribbles and half-formed ideas that make no sense now that I'm looking at them. Did I actually write "local honey as metaphor" in the margin? What does that even mean?

"Come on, Riley," I mutter under my breath, running a hand through my hair. It's probably sticking out in every direction by now, but who cares? Not me. Definitely not the guy three tables over whose AirPods are in, but who keeps glancing over like he's expecting me to combust at any second.

"*Artisan economies...*" I try again, my fingers tapping out the words slowly, deliberately. But then Danny's voice creeps into my head, uninvited as always.

"Surely there's an opportunity here," he'd said last week, leaning back in his chair during our *discussion*. His British accent made it sound almost reasonable, like I hadn't just spent an hour glaring at him at his town hall pop-up while he spouted nonsense about being both global and local. "We want to be *glocal*, it doesn't have to be a battle between tradition and innovation, you know."

"Maybe not for you, Mr. Disruptor," I'd said, because apparently sarcasm is my default setting around him. "But some of us actually care about things like integrity and community."

And yet, here I am, unable to finish a single coherent thought without his stupid voice echoing in my brain. Is it possible to get writer's block from sheer annoyance? Because if so, this is definitely Danny Winter's fault.

"Artisan economies walk a fine line between preserving their roots and embracing—"

Delete.

God, he's in my head, isn't he? That's what this is. Every time I try to draft a sentence, I hear his infuriatingly logical suggestions or remember the way he tilted his head like he was trying to figure me out. Like I'm some kind of puzzle he could solve if only he had enough data points.

"Ugh!" I slam my laptop shut harder than necessary, earning a startled look from the AirPods guy. Whatever. Let him stare. I grab my pen and jab it at the notebook, circling "local honey" until the paper threatens to rip. If this article ends up being about anything other than how much I hate self-serving tech bros and their endless optimism, it'll be a miracle.

But deep down—like, way, *way* down—I can't shake the nagging thought: *what if he has a point?* What if my cynicism isn't the shield I think it is, but a wall keeping me from writing something real? Something better?

"Artisan economies..." I whisper to myself again, staring at the messy page. My pen hovers, but I don't write. Instead, I sit there, paralyzed, wondering if the problem isn't just the topic or the deadline. Wondering if the real problem is that I don't want to admit that Danny Winter might've actually gotten to me.

"Is this seat taken, or are you saving it for a tall, dark stranger?"

Ava's voice hits me before I even register the floral scent of her chai latte and the bitter notes of an Americano. She slides into the booth across from me, without waiting for an answer, setting the drinks down with a thud that might as well announce *game on.* She's grinning, like she already knows exactly how this conversation is going to go—and she probably does.

"Not now, Ava," I mutter, tapping my pen furiously against the notebook like it's the only thing keeping my sanity intact. The page in front of me is still a graveyard of half-formed ideas and scratched-out sentences, but I'm not about to let her see that.

"'Not now'?" Ava repeats, mock-offended, as she leans back and crosses one leg over the other. "Wow. I bring you caffeine-infused emotional support, and all I get is 'not now'? Someone's touchy."

"Someone's busy," I say, gesturing at my closed laptop and a notepad with more doodles than words.

"Busy writing an exposé on artisan goods? Or..." Her eyes narrow mischievously, and her smile widens. "...busy channeling your feelings about a certain Mr. Darcy into your prose?"

"Excuse me?" My head jerks up so fast I nearly knock over my coffee. "This has nothing to do with Danny Winter."

"Uh-huh." Ava doesn't even try to hide her amusement. She tilts her head toward my laptop—because of course she does—and arches a perfectly sculpted eyebrow. "You know, I read your last draft."

"Congratulations," I say dryly. "I'd offer you a medal, but I might have used all my creative energy writing the imaginary acceptance speech."

"Ha. Ha." Her grin widens, which is never a good sign. "No, seriously. It's... different."

"Different how?" I spin my pen between my fingers, pretending to look busy. Maybe if I just ignore her, she'll get bored and go away.

"Less..." She waves a hand in the air, searching for the word. "Angsty. Like, usually, your stuff reads like a manifesto against capitalism with footnotes made of fire. But this? There's almost—" She pauses dramatically, leaning forward like she's about to share the world's biggest secret. "Hope in it."

"Hope," I repeat flatly, like she's just suggested I tattoo 'Live Laugh Love' across my forehead. "Yeah, sure. That's exactly what I was going for: *hopeful journalism.*"

"Don't be so defensive," she says, tilting her head as she studies me. "It's not bad. It's just... you're usually so cynical, you know? Sharp edges, biting commentary, the whole 'burn-it-all-down' vibe. This feels..." Her lips twitch as she tries not to laugh. "Soft."

"It's not soft. It's nuanced. There's a difference."

"Uh-huh." Ava raises an eyebrow, shooting a pointed glance at my screen. "And would this sudden embrace of nuance have anything to do with a certain British tech guy who, oh, I don't know, might've challenged your worldview?"

"Absolutely not," I reply, the denial automatic. Too automatic.

Ava's grin only grows more insufferable.

"Riiight," she drawls. "So that line about 'bridging the gap between tradition and innovation'—" she makes air quotes so exaggerated they could double as semaphore signals, "—that wasn't inspired by Danny Winter and his big, dreamy ideas about digital transformation?"

"First of all, stop saying his name like that," I say, glaring at her. "Second, my article has nothing to do with him. Or his... ideas."

"You just keep telling yourself that."

I open my mouth to argue, but the words stick in my throat. Because damn it, she's not completely wrong. The shift in tone *is* there, staring back at me from the screen like a neon sign flashing, *liar, liar*.

"Fine," I mutter, slumping back in the booth. "Maybe there's a slight adjustment in tone. But that has nothing to do with him. I'm just... trying something new."

"Uh-huh." Ava's skepticism is practically a third presence at the table. "And this 'something new' just happens to coincide with you spending more time debating artisan economies with Mr. Broody McTech?"

"Coincidence," I insist, but the word feels flimsy even as I say it. Because the truth—the deeply uncomfortable truth—is that Ava's right. My usual edge, my sarcastic bite, it's been dulled lately. Not gone, but softened, like a blade worn smooth from overuse. And I can't help but wonder if that has less to do with burnout and more to do with… him.

"Okay, whatever you say." Ava gives me a knowing smile, the kind that makes me want to strangle her and hug her all at once. "But for the record? I think it's a good thing. Even you deserve a break from being the human embodiment of a scathing op-ed."

"Gee, thanks," I say. Because underneath her teasing, there's a truth I can't ignore: the version of me she's describing sounds suspiciously like the person I used to be. Back when I still believed words could change minds instead of just tear things down.

"Look, I'm just saying"—Ava leans back, cradling her chai like it's a crystal ball—"maybe he's not such a bad influence after all."

"Or maybe I just need better friends," I shoot back.

My gaze drifts back to my notebook, to the words and phrases I wanted to use to frame the article. They don't feel like mine, but they don't feel wrong, either. And that scares me more than I'd like to admit.

"Keep telling yourself that," Ava says with a wink, sliding out of the booth like she's won some unspoken game. "See you later, softie."

"Not soft," I mutter again, but she's already gone, her laughter trailing behind her. Maybe Ava's right. Maybe things are shifting. And maybe—just maybe—that's not entirely a bad thing.

Later that night, I'm on my couch, laptop balanced precariously on my knees, a half-empty mug of tea cooling on the table beside me. The glow of the screen lights up my face as I scroll through the latest draft of my article for what feels like the hundredth time.

It's... different. That much I can't deny. The sentences flow more gently than they usually do, weaving together stories and ideas rather than hammering home an argument like a gavel hitting a courtroom bench. There's something more thoughtful here—maybe even curious.

"Great," I mutter under my breath, slumping back into the cushions. "I've accidentally written a feel-good piece."

I skim back over a section about how small-town artisans are using digital tools to expand their reach without losing their local charm. My usual biting sarcasm has been replaced with... admiration? Optimism? Support? Ugh. This is all Ava's fault. She got in my head earlier, planting seeds of doubt like some smug little gardener. Or maybe it's not Ava. Maybe—

Nope. Not going there.

This isn't burnout. Burnout was thick walls and blank pages and the kind of snark that could cut glass. This... this feels like cracks in those walls. Tiny fissures where light is getting in. And I don't know whether to smash the rest of the wall down or patch it up as fast as I can. Because if I let too much light in—if I let myself hope again, care again—what happens when it all comes crashing down?

I squeeze my eyes shut, trying to block out the intrusive thoughts. But they're persistent, whispering questions I don't want to answer. Is this growth or weakness? A reawakening or a surrender? And why does it feel like every sentence I've written tonight has his voice echoing somewhere underneath it —challenging me, pushing me, softening me?

"Stop it," I hiss, opening my eyes again. The ceiling stares back at me, offering no answers. I grab a throw pillow and shove it over my face, muffling a frustrated groan.

There's no denying it anymore: something's shifted. In my

writing. In my perspective. In me. And I have absolutely no idea what to do about it.

I blame Danny. There's no other explanation for why my brain feels like it's been rewired lately. His voice keeps echoing in my head, replaying snippets of our arguments, his annoyingly reasonable challenges to my assumptions. And somehow, without my permission, those echoes have started bleeding into my writing.

"He's in my articles now," I say aloud, horrified. "He's parasitic."

I lean forward, elbows on knees, scrubbing my hands down my face. Maybe it's just proximity. We've been forced to collaborate so much lately that it's natural some of his overly polished, relentlessly analytical perspective would rub off on me. That's all this is. A side effect. Temporary.

But then I think about the way he watches me when I argue with him—not condescending or dismissive, but curious, intrigued. Like he actually values what I have to say, even when we're standing on opposite sides of the room (both figuratively and literally). It's disarming, that look. Dangerous.

I have to face the fact that he's getting under my skin. Not just professionally, though that's bad enough—what with him making me second-guess every carefully constructed critique I've ever written. No, it's more insidious than that. He's wormed his way into my personal space too, cracking open parts of me I thought were sealed shut. Parts I didn't want opened.

I stare at the ceiling, waiting for it to offer some sort of cosmic clarity. Naturally, it doesn't. My thoughts spiral instead, looping around the same uncomfortable truth: I can't keep pretending his influence isn't affecting me. It is. And that scares me more than anything. Because if Danny Winter can change the way I write, what else might he change?

This is definitely his fault. His polished, insufferable, app-wielding British smugness has infiltrated my headspace. Danny Winter, with his ridiculous hair and maddening ability to argue circles around me without breaking a sweat, has somehow managed to rewire the way I think about everything—my work, my town, myself.

I close my eyes and lean back against the cushions, letting the silence settle around me. But even with my eyes shut, his voice lingers—sharp and teasing, challenging and sincere. And no matter how hard I try, I can't shake the feeling that he's really changed something fundamental in me.

For better or worse? I don't know.

All I know is that I'm not the same writer I was before Danny Winter strolled into Willow Creek with his Power-Point presentations and irritatingly perfect hair.

And worse—so much worse—I don't think I'm the same person, either.

THIRTEEN

♥

DANNY

The bouquet looks like it was assembled by a hyperactive toddler who got lost in a meadow. Wildflowers, they call them —"chaotic" would be more accurate. I shift the stems from one hand to the other, pacing along the sidewalk outside the *Willow Cove Gazette* office like some lovesick fool in a bad rom-com.

"Great idea, Danny," I mutter under my breath, holding up the bouquet like it's Exhibit A in my impending humiliation. "Because nothing screams professionalism, like showing up with flowers for a woman who already thinks you're a walking cliché."

I glance at the glass door of the office, Riley's name etched into my brain like some cruel mantra. Riley Hayes: Destroyer of Egos, Wielder of Sarcasm, Guardian of Small-Town Integrity. She's probably inside right now, rolling her eyes at something—or someone—and looking infuriatingly good while doing it.

"Maybe I should just chuck these in the bin," I muse,

eyeing the trash can next to the door. The flowers are innocent enough: bright yellows, purples, and whites tangled together like they're trying too hard. Kind of like me. "Or better yet, accidentally trip into traffic, so I have an excuse not to go in at all."

But no. I can't do that. Not this time. There's something about Riley—her directness, her ability to see through my polished pitches and charming deflections—that makes me want to try harder. Well, mostly it makes me want to run screaming, but also... try harder.

"Pull it together, mate," I tell myself, standing up straighter and giving the bouquet a little shake. A stray petal flutters to the ground, as if even the flowers are skeptical of my plan. "You're here to ask for feedback, not grovel. Flowers are a peace offering, not a bribe. Totally normal. Totally fine."

With a deep breath, I plant my feet and grip the bouquet like a lifeline. Whatever happens when I walk through that door, I'll handle it. If Riley laughs, so be it. If she throws the flowers back in my face, well, at least I'll have a story to tell.

"Alright, wildflowers," I say, squaring my shoulders. "Let's go charm the dragon."

The bell above the door jingles, and immediately, every head in sight swivels toward me. A bulletin board on one wall is cluttered with flyers, deadlines scribbled in red ink, and what looks suspiciously like a meme about grammar errors.

"Well, well," a voice drawls from behind a desk stacked precariously with newspapers and half-empty mugs. "If it isn't the British charm offensive in the flesh."

I glance up to see Riley's editor, Elaine, with her coiffed hair and fitted pant suit. She's got that look people get when they've seen too much and decided sarcasm is their last line of defense. Her gaze flicks to the wildflowers clutched in my hand, then back to me, one brow lifting like she's just caught me trying to smuggle contraband past customs.

"Good morning to you, too," I reply, plastering on a grin and leaning casually against the counter. "I assume this is your way of rolling out the welcome mat?"

"More like trying to keep the riffraff out," she replies, eyeing my suit and watch like she's sizing up my net worth. "But you've got guts, I'll give you that. She's in her office. Try not to break anything—or anyone."

"I'll try, but no promises." I tip an imaginary hat and step deeper into the chaos, the flowers feeling heavier by the second.

Before I can overthink my next move, Riley appears in the doorway of her office like she was summoned by sheer force of will—or maybe she just has a sixth sense for impending nonsense. Her hair's pulled back, her sleeves rolled up, and there's a pen tucked behind one ear, like she's been preparing to dismantle someone's argument at a moment's notice. Her eyes land on me, then drop to the bouquet, and her expression sharpens into something between confusion and suspicion.

"Are you lost?" she asks, crossing her arms and leaning one shoulder against the doorframe. Her tone is flat, but her lips quirk ever so slightly, like she's already bracing herself for whatever ridiculous explanation I'm about to offer.

"Lost? Not at all," I say, straightening up and letting the grin spread wider. "Though I did get briefly sidetracked by your editor's warm hospitality. Quite the ray of sunshine, that one."

"Yeah, Elaine's a delight," she says dryly, her gaze darting back to the flowers. "So... what's this? Did you get roped into someone's community theater production of *My Fair Lady*?"

"Funny," I reply smoothly, holding out the bouquet. "These," I say with a deliberately dramatic wave of my hand over the wildflowers, "are for my most terrifying beta tester. You know, as a token of my ongoing survival."

Riley's eyebrows lift so high they might hit the ceiling. She doesn't move from her spot in the doorway, arms still crossed like she's preparing to deliver a decisive cross-examination. "Terrifying? That's bold, coming from the guy who just walked in here looking like he's about to pitch me a pyramid scheme."

Her eyes flick back to the bouquet, narrowing slightly. "So, what? You're trying to butter me up now?"

"Butter you up? Never." I hold the flowers closer, shaking them lightly for emphasis. A petal drifts off and lands on the floor between us, which feels like a metaphor I'd rather not unpack. "Think of it more as... gratitude. For your unflinching honesty and very constructive criticism."

"Unflinching honesty," she repeats, finally pushing off the doorframe and stepping closer. Her boots scuff softly against the worn wood floors, her gaze locked on mine like she's daring me to blink first. "That's one way to describe it. The other way is calling me a pain in the ass."

"Well, I wasn't going to say it," I reply smoothly, extending the bouquet her way again. "But since you bring it up..."

She snorts, finally reaching out to take the flowers, though the movement is cautious, like she's half-convinced they'll explode in her hands. The bouquet looks almost comically out of place against her rolled-up flannel sleeves and ink-smudged fingers, but somehow, she makes it work.

"Wildflowers, huh?" she says, turning the stems in her hands like she's inspecting evidence at a crime scene. "What, no roses? No orchids? Did you raid someone's backyard for these?"

"Careful," I warn, mock-serious. "You'll hurt their feelings. And no, I didn't *raid* anything. I went into an actual shop, pulled out actual money, and specifically requested something you wouldn't immediately throw in the bin."

"Bold assumption," she mutters, lifting the bouquet higher. She sniffs once, briefly, then lowers it like she's caught herself mid-softening. Her lips press together, and she fixes me with a look sharp enough to cut glass. "This isn't going to work, you know."

"Still wanted to shoot my shot," I say easily, though the warmth in her voice—or at least the absence of outright hostility—feels like a small victory. "But just to clarify, are we talking about the flowers, or me in general?"

"Both," she replies, tucking the bouquet under one arm like it's a stack of files she's begrudgingly agreed to carry. "Now, are you done playing florist, or is there another act in this little performance?"

"Depends," I say, straightening up and brushing imaginary dust off my sleeve. "If I told you there's interpretive dance involved, would that get me kicked out faster?"

"Try it and find out," she shoots back, already turning toward her office. But the flowers stay tucked securely in her grip, and I can't help the slow, satisfied grin spreading across my face as I follow her inside.

"Right, so," I start, settling into the chair across from Riley's desk with the kind of forced casualness that probably screams *nervous wreck*. "Here's the thing—"

"Careful," she interrupts, dropping the bouquet onto her desk and fixing me with one of those laser-focused stares that makes me feel like I'm being dissected. "If you're about to say 'circle back' or 'leverage,' I might actually throw this stapler at you."

"I won't," I reply, leaning back slightly as if that'll protect me from airborne office supplies. "No corporate catchphrases. Got it. What I was going to say is that we've been working on some new features for the app, and I'd really value your feedback."

"Would you?" Her tone is all razor edges, and she crosses her arms, tilting her head like she's just caught me trying to sell her snake oil. "Because the last time you asked for my feedback, you spent half the conversation defending why my critique was wrong. Or did you forget?"

"Ah, yes, the infamous push notification debacle," I say with a tight smile, holding my hands up in mock surrender. "I've grown since then. Character development, Riley. It's a thing."

"Sure it is," she says. "So, what are these miraculous features you're so desperate for me to tear apart?"

"Glad you asked," I say, pulling out my tablet and swiping it to life. The screen lights up with the latest version of the app, looking sleeker than ever. "First off, we've improved the user interface—"

"Stop." She holds up a hand like a traffic cop, narrowing her eyes at the screen. "Define 'improved.'"

"Streamlined menus, easier navigation, better visuals—"

"Better for whom?" she cuts in, leaning forward now, her eyes sharp and unrelenting. "Your designers or your users? Because those aren't always the same thing, Danny."

"Users," I say firmly, though her skepticism undermines my confidence. "We've tested it internally, and the results have been—"

"Internally doesn't count," she interrupts again, waving a hand dismissively. "Testing with an echo chamber of people who built the thing isn't testing. It's self-congratulation."

"Fair point," I admit, nodding. "Which is why I'm here. You're not exactly known for sugarcoating things, Riley. If there's anyone who can poke holes in this, it's you."

"Flattery won't save you," she says, though the smile

suggests she's enjoying this more than she lets on. "What else?"

"Okay, okay," I say, scrolling down. "We've also added a rewards feature—"

"Why?"

"Excuse me?"

"Why does it need a rewards feature? What problem are you solving, or does it just look good in a pitch deck?"

"Well... it encourages stickiness," I say, which sounds weak even to my own ears.

"Translation: marketing told you to do it," she fires back, raising an eyebrow.

"That's... not entirely inaccurate," I mutter, making a mental note to revisit that particular decision later.

"Anything else?"

"Yes, actually," I say, straightening up and refusing to let her completely steamroll me. "We've added a feature that suggests local events based on user interests—"

"How are you sourcing the events?" she asks, already frowning.

"Through partnerships with local organizations and an API feed from Eventbrite," I explain, bracing for whatever critique she has loaded next.

"Partnerships, huh?" She leans back in her chair, tapping a finger against her arm. "And how are you ensuring those partnerships don't skew toward businesses that can afford to pay for placement? Because if smaller, community-driven initiatives get drowned out, you're just contributing to the problem instead of solving it."

"Good question," I say, whipping out my phone to jot it down. "I'll follow up with the team on that."

"Wow," she says, feigning shock. "You took that without arguing. Are you feeling okay? Need me to call someone?"

"Very funny," I shoot back, rolling my eyes. "Believe it or not, I actually care about getting this right."

"Mm-hmm," she hums, unconvinced but not as cutting as before.

"Look," I say, meeting her gaze directly. "I know I've got blind spots. That's why I came to you. Your feedback matters. Even when it's brutal."

"Especially when it's brutal," she corrects.

"Is this your version of neutral ground?" Riley asks as we slide into a booth at one of the town's two bars. Her tone is pure skepticism, with a twist of amusement. "Because it's pretty desperate."

"Not desperation," I counter, setting my laptop on the sticky table with a wince. "Ambition. It's the scent of dreams being brewed, one overpriced craft beer at a time."

"Dreams taste bitter, apparently." She eyes the imported ale in front of her like it's personally offended her.

"Careful," I say, grinning despite myself. "If you insult the beer too much, they might revoke your local card. Isn't this place a town institution or something?"

"Only because it hasn't been gentrified to death yet," she says

"Alright, let's get to it before the Wi-Fi gives out. Again."

"I'm ready," she says, leaning back with an expectant look that makes me feel like I'm about to present a middle school book report to the world's most unforgiving teacher. "Show me what you've got, tech bro."

"First of all," I say, ignoring the jab as I open the app, "I think we both know I'm more 'tech gentleman.'"

"That's generous," she mutters, but she leans forward to glance at the screen.

"Second of all," I continue, refusing to be derailed, "this version has some new features I think you'll appreciate. Cleaner UI, better navigation, and—"

"Spare me the sales pitch," she interrupts, holding out her hand. "Let me see it."

"By all means," I say, sliding the laptop toward her. "Tear it apart."

Her nails tap lightly against the trackpad as she starts poking through the app. The silence stretches, punctuated only by the occasional hum of acknowledgment or, worse, a faint scoff.

"Why does this button take me here?" she asks, frowning as she gestures to the screen. "Shouldn't it loop back to the main menu instead of opening a subpage?"

"Good catch," I admit, grabbing my notebook. "I'll fix it."

"Mm-hmm," she mutters, already clicking elsewhere. "And this filter option—you're prioritizing trending locations over smaller ones. That's counterproductive for local community engagement."

"Noted," I say, scribbling furiously.

"And this..." Her voice trails off as a pop-up animation of a cartoon mascot bounces onto the screen, complete with confetti and a cheery jingle. She freezes, staring at it like it just walked muddy boots through her cleanly mopped kitchen.

"Okay, hear me out," I say quickly, because I already know what's coming.

"Seriously?" She looks up at me. "A dancing fox? What is this, an app for toddlers?"

"We want to test gamification. Appeal to a broader demographic," I offer weakly, knowing how pathetic it sounds even as I say it.

"Broad demographic appeal," she says flatly, turning back to the screen. "You mean insulting anyone over the age of six?"

"Fine," I sigh, flipping the page in my notebook. "Goodbye, Foxy McFeedback."

"Foxy McFeedback?" she chokes out, half-laughing, half-appalled. "Please tell me you didn't actually name it that."

"Of course not," I say, affronted. "It's Mr. Feedbackington."

"Wow," she says. "You're really winning me over with this whole 'serious entrepreneur' vibe."

"Glad to entertain," I say dryly, watching as she clicks through another section with laser focus.

"At least you're taking notes," she says finally, glancing at my notebook.

"Always," I reply, meeting her gaze. "You make good points. Even if you deliver them like a sledgehammer to the face."

"Subtlety's overrated," she says, smirking.

"Well," I say, leaning back and closing my notebook, "anything else you'd like to brutally dismantle before we wrap this up?"

"Give me a minute," she says, scrolling again. "I'm sure I can find something."

Her elbow brushes mine as she leans closer to the screen, and I swear it's on purpose. Or maybe it's not. Either way, I'm hyper-aware of how little space exists between us in this cramped corner booth. The bar hums with low chatter and the clink of glasses being unloaded from the dishwasher, but all I can focus on is the faint scent of her citrusy shampoo and the fact that her knee is dangerously close to bumping mine under the table.

"So, final verdict? Is it a complete disaster, or just mostly a disaster?"

"You're getting there," she says, and for a second, I think I've misheard her. But no, she's looking directly at me now, her expression unreadable except for the slight furrow of her brow

—like she's annoyed by the words even as they leave her mouth.

"Getting there," I echo, testing the phrase like it's foreign currency. It doesn't sound like praise exactly, but coming from Riley, it feels suspiciously close.

"Do you mean the app, or..." I let it hang in the air, a smirk tugging at the corner of my mouth.

Riley pauses mid-reach for her bag, her eyes flicking to me with an expression that's equal parts exasperation and amusement—though she'd probably deny the latter if pressed.

"Don't push your luck, Danny."

"Ah, so vague praise *and* evasion," I say, tapping my pen theatrically against my notebook. "A bold combination. I'll take that as progress."

She slings the strap of her bag over her shoulder, the wildflowers poking out at odd angles like they're protesting their new home. "Take it however you want," she replies with a shrug so casual it could win awards. "Just don't start thinking we're friends or something."

"Wouldn't dream of it," I reply smoothly, though the grin I can't quite suppress probably gives me away.

There's something about the way she delivers these verbal jabs, each one sharp enough to nick but never deep enough to sting, that makes me feel oddly... buoyant. Like I've passed some sort of test I didn't know I was taking.

FOURTEEN

RILEY

The creak of my porch step pulls my eyes up from the tablet, and there he is—Danny Winter in all his disheveled glory, a takeaway bag dangling from one hand and that annoyingly earnest smile plastered across his face. His dark hair's doing this Hugh Grant windswept thing like he just stepped out of the set of a '90s romance flick. Meanwhile, I'm sitting on an old wooden chair in sweats, beginning to wish I had used a hairband instead of a biro to tie up my hair.

"Evening," he says, holding up the bag. "Figured you'd be inclined to provide more feedback on the app if I bribed you with food."

"Wow, subtle. But ten out of ten for honesty." I say, standing up and crossing my arms. "You're lucky I'm hungry."

"Great," he says with a wink, and approaches the other chair. "Mind if I—?"

"Too late to say no now, isn't it?" I gesture to the chair next to mine, then eye the bag suspiciously as he plops down. "What is it? And if it's sushi, we're gonna have words."

"Relax." He opens the bag and starts unloading cartons of noodles, the kind that comes drenched in sauce and smells like pure, unfiltered comfort. "Lo mein. Figured carbs might soften the blow."

"Of what, your existence?" I mutter, grabbing a carton and the pair of chopsticks he hands me. The smell alone almost makes me forgive him for... well, everything. Almost.

We settle into an uneasy rhythm, the sound of crickets filling the space between mouthfuls. He's got his own carton, twirling noodles around his chopsticks with surprising finesse.

"Alright," I say, breaking the silence as I wave a noodle-laden chopstick toward him. "Show me this magical feature you're so proud of. But fair warning: I'm still keeping score of how much this app sucks."

"Harsh," he says, but his grin doesn't waver. Instead, he sets his carton aside and leans forward, pulling his phone out of his pocket like it's a sacred artifact. "Okay, check this out. The tech team just pushed this feature live an hour ago. It's a community board, but hyper-localized. Think neighborhood announcements, lost pets, random acts of kindness—all tied to specific zip codes."

"Uh-huh," I say, scrolling through the new feature on his phone. "So basically Craigslist, but it doesn't make you feel like you need a tetanus shot after using it?"

"Exactly!" He points at me like I've just won the jackpot. "See? You get it. We wanted it to feel... safer. More personal."

"Yeah, yeah." I squint at the screen, flipping through screens and testing buttons. "It's not... terrible. The design's cleaner. Navigation doesn't make me want to throw myself off a bridge anymore. So, congrats, I guess."

"Was that... praise? From you?" His tone is mock-incredulous, but I catch the flicker of something else in his eyes—relief, maybe? It's fleeting, gone before I can decide if I imagined it.

"Don't get used to it," I say. "I still think you're trying too hard to make this app the second coming of sliced bread."

"Maybe," he admits, shrugging. "But hey, at least I showed up with noodles. That's gotta count for something, right?"

"Debatable," I reply. Damn him and his stupid, endearing attempts to charm his way out of criticism.

I glance back at the phone screen, my fingers idly scrolling. It really *is* better, and that fact irritates me more than I care to admit. Because the more improvements he makes, the harder it gets to keep dismissing him—and by extension, the app—as just another corporate gimmick. And heaven help me, the thought of admitting I might've underestimated him feels like swallowing glass.

"Wait a second, what on earth is this?" I ask, gesturing at the screen with my chopsticks. "A *virtual high-five?* What is this, 2010? Are we resurrecting Farmville now too?"

Danny, perched on the edge of my porch step like he owns the place, grins around a mouthful of noodles. "You're just jealous you didn't think of it first."

"Jealous?" I snort. "Of what? Your uncanny ability to make the corniest features sound groundbreaking? 'Tap here to send community vibes!' Oh please, spare me."

"Hey, those 'vibes' are getting stellar feedback in our European user testing," he shoots back, setting his carton down and leaning one arm casually on the railing. "Turns out people actually *like* feeling connected. Shocking, I know."

"Shocking," I say, shoving another bite of noodles into my mouth. Damn him. Why does he have to be so infuriatingly— What's the word? *Charming? No.* Annoyingly persistent. That's it.

"Admit it," he says after a beat, brushing a nonexistent speck of dust off his sleeve. "You secretly love it."

"Love *what?*" I narrow my eyes at him.

"That I'm right." His grin widens, full-on conceited now.

"About the app. About the noodles, obviously. And about the fact that you're having way more fun roasting me than you'd care to admit."

"Please. I'm doing a public service. Keeping your ego in check is basically charity work at this point."

"Alright, Ms. Philanthropy, let me show you something real quick."

His arm brushes against mine as he shifts, the warmth of his skin radiating through my flannel sleeve. It's barely a touch—light, fleeting—but it sends an electric jolt straight up my spine. My breath hitches before I can stop it, and for half a second, I consider pulling away.

But I don't.

"See this bit here?" His voice drops slightly, softer now, as he points to the screen. I nod, not trusting myself to speak. The faint scent of him mixes with the salt-tinged evening air, and suddenly, the porch feels a hell of a lot smaller.

"That button triggers a pop-up guide," he continues, oblivious—or maybe not—to the way my pulse has decided to audition for a drum line. "We added it based on feedback from—"

"From users who need their hands held to find a search bar?" I cut in.

"Exactly," he replies, turning his head toward me, his face now dangerously close. His smile softens, losing some of its cocky edge. "Hand-holding's underrated, don't you think?"

Oh, come *on*. I grit my teeth, willing myself to focus on literally anything else—the app, the noodles, the uneven crack in the porch floorboards—but instead, my gaze flicks to where our arms are still touching, his sleeve brushing mine with the slightest movement.

"Not when it involves patronizing design choices," I manage.

I glance up—big mistake. His eyes are already on me, deep blue and steady, and for a second, neither of us says anything.

The porch creaks softly beneath us, the only sound besides the dull hum of crickets. His gaze drops to my mouth, quick and subtle, but not nearly subtle enough.

"Blink twice if you're about to launch into another data point," I say, though my voice comes out quieter than I intend. My throat feels too tight. Why does my throat feel tight?

"Tempting," he murmurs, his lips curving just slightly. "But I was trying something new. It's called *not talking*. Revolutionary, isn't it?"

"Groundbreaking," I shoot back, but it's harder to keep the edge in my tone when my pulse is rioting in my ears. My fingers tighten around the tablet, the plastic suddenly slippery against my palm, and I realize with no small amount of horror that I haven't moved an inch. Neither has he.

"Relax, Riley," he says softly. "You're acting like I'm about to hack your brain or steal state secrets."

"Maybe you are," I reply. His cologne—clean, sharp, and confident—wraps around me like a net, and the way he's looking at me is really not helping.

"Wouldn't need to," he says, leaning just a fraction closer. "You wear everything you're thinking right here." He taps the side of his temple lightly, and I feel myself glaring before I can stop.

"Careful," I say. "That condescending streak of yours is showing."

"I prefer to call it... charisma with a dash of accountability."

The space between us feels thinner than thread now. I'm still staring at him—why am I still staring at him?—when his smile shifts, just barely, into something warmer. Something dangerous.

"Alright," he says after a beat. "You're looking like you're about two seconds away from combusting, so—" He pulls back, just slightly, and gestures toward the screen. "How about we get back to roasting bad UI decisions before you start accusing me of mind control?"

The laugh escapes me before I can stop it, sharp and sudden, and I hate how much relief it brings. He grins wider, clearly pleased with himself, and I shake my head, trying to summon annoyance but somehow landing squarely on amused instead.

"You're like a pop-up ad, you know that?" I say, leaning just far enough back to re-establish some semblance of personal space. Not too much, though. Because apparently, my self-preservation instincts are taking the night off. "Relentless, mildly irritating, and somehow impossible to ignore."

"I prefer to think of myself as... pleasantly persistent," he counters, his gaze steady on mine. "And, as I recall, persistence tends to get results."

"Results? That's what you're calling this?" I make a vague gesture between us, trying to encompass whatever this is—this thing that feels less like an argument and more like a live wire humming under my skin.

"Well, it's certainly not failure." His voice softens. "You'd have kicked me off this porch by now if it were."

"Don't tempt me."

"Riley," he murmurs, and somehow my name sounds different when he says it—like it means something. Like *I* mean something.

And then—because clearly, I've lost all sense of reason—I don't look away. I should. I *should*. But instead, I stay right where I am, frozen under the intensity of his gaze. The tension builds again, thick and electric, and before I can think to stop him—or myself—he leans in.

It starts so softly, so unexpectedly, I almost don't register it at first—the tentative brush of his lips against mine, barely there, testing the waters. It's not what I expected from him at all. It's hesitant. Careful. Like he's giving me every chance to pull away.

But I don't pull away.

Instead, something inside me snaps, or maybe fits. My hand moves before I realize it, fingers curling into the fabric of his shirt, anchoring him closer. And just like that, the kiss shifts—deepens—becoming something hungrier, messier. There's nothing careful about it now. His hand comes up to cup my face, his thumb brushing over the curve of my cheek, and the warmth of his touch sends a shiver down my spine.

My heart is pounding, loud and erratic, but it doesn't drown out the sound of his breathing—quickened, unsteady— mingling with mine. The world beyond the porch fades completely; it's just us, caught in this reckless, spiraling moment. I don't know who moves first, but suddenly there's no space left between us, just heat and friction and the undeniable press of his mouth against mine.

And for the first time in forever, I'm not thinking. Not analyzing. Not second-guessing. Just feeling.

My chest is heaving like I've just run a marathon, except I haven't moved an inch. Danny's face is still close—too close— his breath mingling with mine in the charged space between us. My fingers are locked in his shirt like they forgot how to let go, and his hand? Yeah, it's still on my cheek, warm and steady, like it belongs there.

This is fine. Totally normal. People do this all the time. Kiss their... *whatever Danny is*. Op-ed subject? Frenemy?

"Riley," he says quietly, his voice rough around the edges. His thumb twitches against my cheek—a barely-there movement, but it sends another jolt through me.

I should say something. Anything. A joke would work. Something snarky about boundaries or workplace conduct. Maybe a biting quip about how he's clearly been watching too many movies because this is not how software developers resolve UI disputes. But my throat refuses to cooperate. Instead, I just... stare at him, wide-eyed and mute, like some extra in a bad soap opera.

"Are you..." He swallows, his Adam's apple bobbing under his collar. "Are you okay?"

Mmmm. Fantastic question. Let me consult the committee of baffled emotions currently rioting in my brain. Lust says yes. Pride says absolutely not. Fear hasn't even voted yet—it's too busy screaming into a pillow.

"Yeah," I manage. I nod for good measure, though my head feels like it might actually disconnect from my neck if I keep moving it this fast.

"Okay," he says, his brow furrowing like he doesn't entirely believe me. Which, fair. I don't believe me either.

We're both still frozen, like two kids caught stealing cookies, except the cookies were... well, *that.* And the worst part? He's not gloating or smirking or doing any of the things I'd expect Danny Winter to do right now. He just looks... stunned. Vulnerable, even. Like he wasn't expecting it any more than I was.

"That was..." He exhales a shaky laugh. "Unexpected."

"Understatement of the year," I mutter before I can stop myself. My voice comes out sharper than I intend, but it's the only way I know to mask the fact that my heart is still doing somersaults.

His lips twitch—not quite a smile, but close. "Guess we have a talent for catching each other off guard."

"Talent is a strong word," I shoot back, finally loosening my grip on his shirt. My hand falls to my lap, where I clench it into a fist to stop it from shaking. My face feels hot enough to fry an egg, but I refuse to look away. If he's going to get all introspective on me, the least I can do is stay upright.

"Riley." His tone softens. It's gentle, careful, like he knows exactly how close I am to bolting.

"Don't," I say. "Don't make this a thing."

"Make what a thing?"

"Whatever *this* is," I gesture vaguely between us, hoping the motion distracts from the fact that I'm still trembling. "It's not a thing. It was—" I falter, swallowing hard. "It was nothing."

"Nothing," he repeats, his jaw tightening almost imperceptibly. For a second, I think he's going to argue, push back like he usually does when I throw out one of my definitive statements. But instead, he just nods, slow and deliberate, like he's filing the word away somewhere. "Right. Got it. I should probably—"

"Yeah," I cut in. "You should."

His brow furrows slightly. "I've got an early call with London tomorrow. Probably best I head out."

He gets up, but then pauses at the porch steps, glancing back at me, and for half a second, I swear he's going to say something monumental, something that will completely wreck whatever fragile equilibrium we have left.

But he doesn't. He just nods, almost imperceptibly, and then he's gone—his footsteps fading down the path, the sound swallowed by the quiet hum of the night.

I wait until the porch is empty before I let myself breathe, really breathe. My hands are shaking, my thoughts spiraling, and I can still feel the phantom imprint of his touch, his kiss, like my skin refuses to forget what just happened.

"Nothing," I remind myself under my breath, though the word tastes hollow now. "It was nothing."

But if it's nothing, why does it feel so much like everything?

I close the door behind me and lean against it. My fingers still clutch the edge of the doorknob like it's a lifeline, even though the only thing on the other side now is the night air and Danny walking away like he didn't just flip my entire sense of reality on its head.

"Okay," I mutter to myself. "That happened."

It doesn't help. The words hang in the air, flimsier than I'd like, because no amount of sarcasm is going to erase the heat still buzzing under my skin or the way my lips feel... used to his. Used to him. God, that's a dangerous thought.

I push off the door, shaking out my hands like that'll somehow get rid of this jittery electricity crawling up my spine. My feet move automatically—kitchen, glass of water, good old distraction—but my reflection in the microwave door catches me mid-step.

"Ugh," I groan, squinting at the distorted version of myself staring back. Messy hair, flushed cheeks, pupils so dilated I look half-feral. Perfect. Just the image of someone who *definitely* didn't just lose her mind over a kiss.

To hell with this. I march past the kitchen entirely, heading straight for the bathroom. Maybe if I splash some cold water on my face, I'll shock myself out of whatever ridiculous post-kiss haze this is. Except when I flick on the light and catch my reflection in the mirror, I freeze.

"Don't you dare," I tell the girl staring back at me. Her eyes are wide, searching, like she's looking for answers I'm not ready to give. "Don't even think about it."

She doesn't listen. Of course, she doesn't. Instead, she looks at me like she already knows the truth—that all my sarcastic quips and snide remarks tonight were just flimsy shields breaking apart one smirk and one stupidly tender kiss at a time.

"God, this is such a cliché," I mutter, gripping the edge of the sink. My knuckles go white from the pressure. "The girl who tells herself she doesn't care, only to—"

Nope. Not finishing that sentence. Because it's not true. It *can't* be true.

"Doesn't mean anything," I whisper to my reflection. The words come out shaky, like they're trying too hard to convince someone—me, him, the universe, I don't know. "It doesn't mean anything."

Except... it does. And deep down, I know it. I can see it, clear as day, in the way my eyes soften every time I picture him standing there on the porch. The way I worry at the thought of him leaving, of him not coming back.

"Dammit," I say, my voice cracking around the word like it's carrying the weight of everything I've been refusing to admit. Fear knots itself in the pit of my stomach, sharp and relentless. Wanting more—it's an abyss I've spent years avoiding, and now here it is, staring me in the face with Danny's name written all over it.

I straighten up, letting go of the sink and stepping back from the mirror like distance can somehow put space between me and the truth. But the reflection stays the same—raw, unguarded, undeniably me.

I'm willing the girl in the mirror to toughen up, to stop feeling so much. "It's just a kiss. That's all it was."

But as I turn off the light and walk away, all I can do is feel.

FIFTEEN

❤

DANNY

I yank at the knot of my tie for the third time, trying to convince myself it's not strangling me. But it very much is. The glass of the Willow Cove Inn's front window throws back my reflection—dark hair freshly tamed into submission, stubble trimmed to that perfect "I woke up like this" look (which took me twenty minutes), and a suit so sharp it could probably slice through the tension I'm already expecting tonight.

"You're fine," I mutter, leaning closer to adjust the pocket square. "Small-town charm, Danny. Be approachable. Smile. No tech jargon." My jaw tightens, and I force it loose again. These people don't care about market entry strategies or user engagement metrics. They want someone who looks like they belong in their little postcard of a town, not someone who just rolled out of a boardroom. Unfortunately, I scream "tech startup" from my Italian leather shoes to my overpriced watch.

The suit's too much. I know it. But when you've spent years building your image as the guy who knows what he's doing—even when you don't—you don't switch gears easily. Not to mention, I didn't pack much else, as I was only expecting to be here for two weeks. So here I am, dressed like I'm pitching to venture capitalists instead of a room full of people who make candles in between school pickups and want to sell them online.

"Okay," I exhale, squaring my shoulders. "Time to dazzle the folksy masses."

Pushing open the door, I'm hit by a wave of warmth that smells like roasted chicken and fresh-baked bread. The hum of conversation rises and falls, punctuated by bursts of laughter, clinking glasses, and the occasional scrape of silverware on ceramic plates. It's cozy chaos—an entirely different world from the sterile conference rooms I usually haunt.

The inn's dining room looks exactly how you'd imagine the heart of small-town America. String lights crisscross overhead, softening the edges of worn wooden beams. Mismatched chairs surround long tables, the kind you have to squeeze around sideways if you don't want to knock over someone's iced tea. A fire crackles in the stone hearth, fighting against the autumn chill seeping through the walls.

And the people—man, the people are *characters*. There's Mayor Thompson near the head of the main table, face flushed like he's already had one glass too many. He's laughing loudly at something a wiry guy in flannel said, his belly shaking in a way that makes his American flag pin jiggle.

At another table, Riley's boss, Elaine, sits ramrod straight, her wire-rimmed glasses perched low on her nose as she furiously scribbles notes on a pad. Probably already crafting tomorrow's editorial about the "slick colonial boy" invading their sacred traditions. *Perfect.*

Then there's the group of business owners scattered around the room—each one a walking cliché of small-town grit. One woman with forearms like tree trunks slaps the shoulder of the man next to her, nearly sending the poor guy's beer flying. Across the room, a retired couple is deep in discussion, looking like the human embodiment of pumpkin spice lattes and cozy scarves.

A Norman Rockwell painting come to life.

I step further inside, scanning the room for any potential allies—or at least someone who doesn't immediately look like they'd rather feed me to the wolves outside. All I get in return are curious glances, a few polite nods, and Elaine's steel-gray eyes narrowing like she's sizing me up for an obituary headline.

"Evening, Daniel!" A booming voice cuts through the din before I've even crossed the threshold into the main dining room. *Perfect. Exactly the kind of subtle, low-key start I was hoping for.*

I plaster on a grin so wide it feels like my face might crack. "Mayor Thompson," I say, extending a hand toward the mountain of a man heading my way. His handshake is as bone-crushing as his voice, and I can feel my knuckles protesting.

"Call me Ben," he says with a laugh that echoes across the room, drawing a few curious glances our way. "We don't stand on ceremony here in Willow Cove."

"Understood," I reply, pulling my hand back discreetly and flexing my fingers to make sure they still work. "And please, call me Danny."

"Well, Danny," he says, clapping a hand on my shoulder hard enough to dislodge my spine, "you've got your work cut out for you tonight. This crowd's not exactly... tech-savvy, if you catch my drift, but we're all very much looking forward to your talk."

"Tech-savvy" seems generous for a group that probably considers dial-up internet cutting-edge. But instead of saying that, I let out a polite chuckle and nod, scanning the room for a friendly face—or at least someone who isn't actively glaring at me like I've come to steal their cows.

"Good luck," Ben murmurs, his tone equal parts amused and pitying, before lumbering off toward the buffet table.

Fantastic. Nothing boosts confidence quite like being set up to fail by the town's jolliest executioner.

"Mr. Winter, is it?" A voice sharp enough to slice through steel interrupts my thoughts.

I turn to see Julie March, one of the town's preeminent bakers and proprietor of Scones & Stones, standing there, her glasses glinting ominously under the warm light of the chandelier.

"That's right," I say, keeping my smile firmly in place. "A pleasure to meet you, Ms. Marsh." I offer my hand, which she pointedly ignores.

"Let's hope you have more to offer than empty promises," she says. "The people of Willow Cove have a long tradition of—"

"Of valuing community over commercialization," I finish smoothly, cutting her off just before she can launch into what I suspect is her favorite rant. "And I couldn't agree more. My goal here is to enhance what makes this town special, not replace it."

Her eyes narrow, scrutinizing me like she's trying to decide whether or not I'm lying. Finally, she huffs and mutters something unintelligible before walking away. I'll take it as a win.

"Nice save," comes a low voice from behind me, dripping with amusement. I turn to see Riley leaning casually against the wall. Of course she's here. Because the universe clearly wants to make this evening as difficult as possible.

"Riley," I say, forcing my smile to stay in place despite the sudden urge to either groan audibly or walk straight out the door. "Didn't expect to see you tonight."

"Really? At a dinner about the Fall Festival? That thing I've been helping organize since high school?" She tilts her head, her expression pure mockery. "Why ever would I be here?"

"Sorry," I mutter, quickly shifting my focus back to the room. The last thing I need is to get sidetracked by whatever's going on between us.

"Don't worry," she adds, her tone light but her gaze sharp. "I hear you've been invited to give us all a little update on your app. I'll keep my heckling to a minimum. Wouldn't want to distract you while you're dazzling everyone with your cutesy London accent."

"Appreciated," I reply dryly, turning away before I say something I'll regret. Or worse, something honest.

An hour later, after a minefield of small talk and awkward dinner conversations, the plates are cleared, and the mayor stands to address the room. The chatter dies down as he raises his glass, a jovial grin spreading across his face.

"Now, before we overindulge on Peggy's famous snickerdoodles," he begins, earning a round of chuckles from the crowd, "I wanted to take a moment to talk about something near and dear to all of us—the Fall Festival."

There it is. My cue.

"Every year, this festival brings us together," Ben continues, his voice taking on a reverent tone. "It's a celebration of everything that makes Willow Cove special—our traditions, our creativity, our sense of community. And I know we're all excited to make this year's festival better than ever."

"Here goes nothing," I think, rising from my seat with what I hope looks like confidence rather than sheer terror. "If I may, Mayor Thompson?" I interject, my London accent cutting crisply through the room. All eyes swivel to me, and I resist the urge to tug at my tie.

"Go ahead, Danny," Ben says, gesturing for me to take the floor.

"Thank you," I begin, letting a practiced smile settle on my face. "First of all, I'd like to say how honored I am to be here tonight. It's clear that the Fall Festival holds a special place in this community, and rightly so. The energy, the passion—it's palpable."

"Palpable" earns me a soft scoff from somewhere to my left. I don't need to look to know it's Riley.

"But," I continue, ignoring her, "I believe there's an opportunity to ensure this festival reaches an even wider audience while preserving everything that makes it unique..."

I look around the room, at all the faces of tonight's guests, many of whom are artisans and craftspeople who I desperately need to impress enough for them to register with the app and start selling.

"Picture this," I say, pacing ever-so-slightly in front of my chair like a Silicon Valley prophet trying to sell salvation through Wi-Fi. The room is quiet—well, as quiet as it can get with the clink of dessert forks against plates and someone whispering, "Who does this guy think he is?" from the far end of the table. *Ignore it, Danny. Focus.*

"Imagine you're at the Fall Festival," I continue, letting my hands do some graceful choreography. "But instead of fumbling with paper schedules or asking Jim down the road when the pie-eating contest starts, you have everything you need right here." I pull my phone out for dramatic effect, holding it up like I've just solved world hunger.

"An app," I declare, pausing like they're supposed to gasp and applaud. Spoiler alert: they don't.

"Through the new live event feature in Makers' Mart, you'll have access to a sleek, digital schedule—color-coded by event type, mind you—" A few heads tilt in confusion, but I plow on, undeterred. "Plus, artist spotlights! Think bios, images, even behind-the-scenes videos. You want to know who's performing that acoustic set at sunset? Boom—tap your screen."

"Boom," Riley mutters under her breath from three seats away. It sounds like an insult disguised as an echo. I glance at her briefly, catching the faintest arch of her brow before I dive back in.

"Right," I say, clearing my throat. "And live feedback! Attendees can leave comments, share photos, even vote on their favorite food truck. This isn't about replacing your charming, small-town traditions. It's about enhancing them. Making them more accessible, more connected. A marriage between Willow Cove's authenticity"—I lower my voice for dramatic sincerity—"and modern convenience."

"Marriage, huh?" Riley interjects, louder now, her tone dripping with something dangerously close to mockery. "You sure you're not aiming for an arranged one, Danny?"

"Thanks, Riley," I say, plastering on a smile that feels more like a grimace. And now everyone's watching us like we're the halftime show they didn't pay for.

"Anyway," I push forward, glancing around the room to gauge the damage. "The point is, this app isn't here to take over. It's here to complement what makes this festival special."

"That's... interesting," pipes up Martha Caldwell, the retired teacher turned soap enthusiast, sitting directly across from me. Her gray curls bounce slightly as she speaks, and there's an unexpected twinkle in her eye. Finally, someone who doesn't look like they want to burn me at the stake. "I could see how that might help. I always struggle getting the word out about my booth—you know, other than taping flyers to the general store window."

"Exactly!" I seize the lifeline like a man drowning in skepticism. "With the app, you can merge your online and offline presence. Sell in person, or sell via the app. Visitors would know exactly where to find your booth, and you can even showcase your products and special event pricing ahead of time. Imagine uploading a quick video of how you make that lavender soap everyone loves."

"Well, that *would* be handy," Martha says, nodding slowly. "But only if it doesn't turn into one of those... What do you call 'em? Influencer things."

"Absolutely not," I assure her, raising both hands defensively. "No avocado toast sponsorships, I promise."

"Shame," Riley chimes in, her voice syrupy sweet and razor-sharp all at once. "You'd really nail the avocado toast crowd, Danny."

"Thank you for your... insight, Riley," I say through a clenched jaw, refusing to let her derail me. Again.

"Actually," Martha says, tapping a finger on the table thoughtfully, "if it helps me sell more soap without losing what makes the festival feel like home, I'd be open to trying it."

"That's the spirit!" I say, resisting the urge to fist-pump like an overexcited intern. Instead, I settle for a confident nod, scanning the room for more potential allies. Some faces remain skeptical, others contemplative. But Martha's cautious enthusiasm feels like a tiny victory—a foothold on an otherwise slippery slope.

"Of course," I add quickly, "this app will only work if it truly reflects what *you* want it to be. Your input, your vision— it's all integral to its success."

"Interesting pitch," Riley drawls, leaning back in her chair with arms crossed. "Just curious though—what happens if 'our vision' tells you this whole thing is a terrible idea?"

"Look, I know this might sound... unconventional," I say, standing straighter and gripping the edge of the table like it's the only thing keeping me tethered to earth. The words are already out of my mouth before I've fully thought them through, which isn't exactly comforting. But here we are. "But if this app is going to succeed—really succeed—it needs someone who understands both the technology *and* the community."

"Someone like you?" Riley cuts in.

"Not quite," I reply, shooting her a tight smile. "Actually, I was thinking... someone like *you*."

Her eyebrows shoot up, and for once, she's speechless. It's almost worth the impending fallout just to see that look on her face—a rare, unfiltered moment of surprise.

"Me?" she finally says.

"Yes, you." I nod, leaning into the idea. "You've got the technical background, the connections, and, let's be honest, the... *charm* to keep everyone engaged." That last part earns me a laugh from someone at the table—Martha, I think—but Riley doesn't join in. *Shocking.*

"Let me get this straight," she says, sitting forward, her eyes narrowing like laser sights. "You want me—someone who, by your own admission, has been pretty vocal about not trusting your little Silicon Valley pipe dream—to help you sell it?"

"Exactly!" I say brightly, as if I don't feel the noose tightening around my neck. "The Voice of the Customer. Who better than my most, uh, enthusiastic critic? If anyone can keep me—and the app—grounded, it's you."

"Riley," Mayor Thompson interjects, his deep voice cutting through the rising tension like a referee stepping onto the field. "Actually, I think Danny might be onto something."

"See?" I gesture toward the mayor with both hands, like I've just pulled off some kind of magic trick. "The mayor gets it."

"Don't push your luck," Thompson warns, though there's a glimmer of amusement in his eyes. He turns to Riley. "You're already one of the most influential voices in Willow Cove. People trust you. You understand all of this technical stuff.

And if Danny's app really does what he says it will, having you involved might reassure folks who are... hesitant."

"Which is putting it mildly," mutters one of the council members—a frail man whose name I've forgotten but whose perpetual scowl seems permanently etched into my brain. "But he's right. Riley, you've got sway in this town. Even the naysayers listen to you."

"Whether they like it or not," Martha adds with a wink.

"Okay, hold on," Riley says, holding up a hand like she's directing traffic. Her gaze swings back to me, sharp enough to draw blood. "Are you seriously asking me to put my name—and my reputation—on the line for your tech experiment?"

"Not *for me*," I clarify quickly, because that sounds far too self-serving, even for me. "For the community. For the festival. Think of it as... bridging the gap. You care about Willow Cove's traditions, right?"

"Obviously."

"Well, so do I. I mean, I'm still wrapping my head around what those traditions actually *are*," I admit, earning a few chuckles from the table, "but I'm not here to bulldoze them. I'm here to enhance them. And you're the perfect person to make sure that happens. You would be the community's eyes, ears, and first line of defense."

She stares at me for a long moment, her expression unreadable, and I resist the urge to fidget. Or bolt.

"Interesting proposition," she finally says, her tone neutral but her eyes still skeptical. "I'll think about it."

"That's all I ask," I say, exhaling a breath I hadn't realized I was holding. Small victories, Danny. Take 'em where you can get 'em.

"Well, I think it's a brilliant idea," Martha chimes in, smiling warmly at Riley. "You'd be perfect for the role, dear. And think of the possibilities! Why, just imagine how many more people I could reach with my lavender goat milk soap!"

"Or my honey," another voice pipes up from across the room.

"Exactly!" I say, latching onto the momentum. "This is about giving *everyone* in Willow Cove a chance to shine—not just during the festival, but year-round."

"Could work," the scowling councilman admits grudgingly. "If Riley's involved, that is."

"Alright," Mayor Thompson says, clapping his hands together. "Let's table the details for now, but I'd like to revisit this once Riley's had time to consider the offer. Fair?"

"Fair," Riley says, though the way she looks at me suggests that this conversation is far from over.

The room is finally clearing out, the hum of conversation tapering off as chairs scrape against wooden floors and the locals shuffle out into the night. I linger near the doorway, my grip tight around a half-empty glass of ice water that's long since gone warm. The air smells of roasted chicken, honey-glazed carrots, and—oddly—lavender goat milk soap. Somehow, it feels like an accomplishment that no one threw anything at me tonight.

"Well, that could've gone worse," I mutter under my breath, draining the rest of the water in one gulp. My tie, which started the evening perfectly aligned, now hangs loose around my neck, a casualty of too many forced smiles and overly firm handshakes. I feel like I've just walked out of a high-stakes boardroom where the PowerPoint slides were replaced by casseroles and skeptical stares.

But they listened. They didn't laugh me out of town—not entirely. A tentative win, even if I did just volunteer Riley for something without her explicit consent. *Bold move, Danny. Let's see how that plays out.*

I glance out the inn's smudged window, catching my reflection in the glass. My suit looks so out of place here, like wearing a tuxedo to a barbecue, but I can't bring myself to care. Tonight wasn't about fitting in; it was about proving I had something worthwhile to offer and that I was genuinely prepared to listen. And maybe—just maybe—I managed that. Even if it meant dragging Riley into the spotlight with me.

"Goodnight, Mr. Winter!" Martha calls from across the room, practically glowing as she waves a small bag of soaps in my direction. "Don't forget to take some home for your mother!"

"That's very kind," I reply with a smile.

As I step outside, the cool night air hits me like a reset button. The stars are scattered across the sky, bright and unapologetically clear, a stark contrast to the haze of city lights I'm used to. The streets are quiet, save for the occasional chirp of crickets and the faint laughter of the departing dinner crowd. It's... peaceful. Annoyingly so.

I shove my hands into my pockets, my polished shoes crunching against the gravel path leading back to my rental. The tension in my shoulders starts to ease, though my mind refuses to shut up. Instead, it replays snippets of the evening: the mayor's approving nod, the councilman's begrudging agreement, Martha's enthusiastic endorsement of Riley. And Riley herself—her sharp eyes narrowing as I said her name, the way her lips pressed together in what I'm guessing was an attempt not to throttle me in front of everyone.

For this to work, I need Riley on board. My thumbs hover over the phone keyboard as I try to string together words that don't sound like, "Hey, sorry for dropping that on you tonight."

"Hey, Riley," I type, immediately deleting it because no. Too casual. Too... weak. I try again:

"Riley, I wanted to let you know—" Delete. Still wrong.

"About tonight—" Ugh. Delete.

"Thanks for not murdering me in public" almost gets sent before I catch myself. God, why is this so hard? It's a text message, not a Shakespearean sonnet.

I stop walking, standing under the glow of a streetlamp as I stare at my phone. The stakes aren't just professional anymore —they're personal, dangerously so. Suggesting Riley for the committee wasn't just a strategic move; it was... something else. Something I don't have the bandwidth to unpack right now.

"Just send the damn message," I mutter, shaking my head. But the words stubbornly refuse to come. So instead, I shove the phone back into my pocket and keep walking, the sound of my determined footfalls muffled by the pavement as her house comes into view. Maybe I'll figure out what to say when I get there. Or maybe I'll just pace around like a lunatic until inspiration strikes.

Either way, I need to fix this. Preferably before Riley decides to kill me, after all.

I'm halfway up the driveway before I realize I've officially lost my mind.

The gravel crunches under my dress shoes—shoes that are wildly inappropriate for this whole small-town, rustic aesthetic Riley seems to embody in every possible way—and each step feels heavier than the last. My pulse is doing some kind of erratic tap-dance against my ribcage, and my palms are clammy enough to make me consider wiping them on my over-priced slacks.

That's a great look, isn't it? Sweaty corporate guy showing up unannounced at nearly nine o'clock at night, where I am very much not welcome. Brilliant plan, Danny.

But texting her didn't feel right. It felt... cheap. Imper-sonal. A cop-out. And while I could probably justify this as a professional courtesy—a face-to-face update on her newfound potential role in saving Willow Cove from its own stubbornness—I know better. This isn't just about the app, or the festival, or impressing the mayor. It's about *her*. And me. And whatever train wreck we've been skirting around since we first met.

The porch light glows softly, a wreath on the door that screams, "I'm approachable, but don't push your luck." There's even a pair of rain boots sitting neatly by the steps, because of course she has rain boots. Riley Hayes is the type of woman who probably plants vegetables in her spare time and makes sarcastic comments about people like me while doing it.

I stop at the base of the steps, staring at the door like it might slap me across the face if I get too close. What am I even going to say?

The wind picks up, cool against the back of my neck, and I shift on my feet, adjusting my tie out of pure nervous energy. For all my so-called charm and business acumen, I've got nothing. No pitch. No strategy. Just this gnawing, uncomfortable truth: I want to work with her on this. She is perfect for the role and doesn't hold back when it comes to feedback.

Or maybe this is just another excuse to see her. To watch her roll her eyes at me like I'm the most infuriating person on the planet, and feel that weird spark of satisfaction when I manage to crack her sarcastic armor. God help me, I think I *like* it when she's mad at me. *Is that normal? Weird? A kink?*

Before I can overthink myself into a full-blown spiral, I step up onto the porch, and my fist hovers in front of the door. One knock. That's all it takes. One knock, and then there's no turning back. I swallow hard, the lump in my throat refusing to budge. My hand trembles slightly, and I hate how exposed I feel standing here, like a teenager about to confess to breaking curfew.

"Just knock," I tell myself again, but my arm doesn't move.

Instead, I stand frozen on Riley Hayes' porch, debating whether this is the stupidest thing I've ever done or the bravest —or, somehow, both.

The light inside flickers, a shadow moving across the window, and my heart lurches. She's home. Of course, she's home. Because why wouldn't she be, ready to deliver the verbal smackdown I so clearly deserve?

"Here goes nothing," I whisper, finally summoning the courage to curl my fingers into a firm knock. The sound echoes loudly, sharp and final, and I brace myself for whatever storm is about to be unleashed when the door opens.

SIXTEEN

RILEY

When I open the door, Danny's standing there like he's auditioning for "Most Awkward Porch Moment of the Year." One hand is shoved in his pocket, the other holding— *What is that? A folder? Soap?* His tie is slightly askew, and the usual confident smirk is replaced with something closer to hesitant charm. *Great. He looks like a lost puppy.*

"Riley," he says, my name rolling off his tongue like it's both an apology and a challenge. "Hi."

"Hi," I reply, gripping the edge of the door. I don't step aside. Not yet. The last time I saw him—tonight's meeting excluded—his lips were on mine, and I've been trying very hard *not* to think about that. Spoiler alert: failing miserably. "If you're here to sell me something, I'm not interested. Unless it's coffee. Or a time machine."

"Neither." He flashes a lopsided grin that I refuse to find charming. "But if you want coffee, I can—"

"Stop." I cross my arms, leaning against the doorframe like

this is casual. Like my pulse isn't doing weird acrobatics. "What do you want, Danny?"

"Look, I know what you're thinking—"

"Do you?" I interrupt, because of course he doesn't.

"You're thinking this is some kind of PR stunt or another corporate power move. But it's not. This is genuinely about the town. About making sure the project works for everyone—not just me, or my company, or whatever headline you think I'm chasing."

"Wow," I say, voice dripping with sarcasm. "That's a touching speech. Did you rehearse it in front of a mirror, or...?"

"Okay, ouch," he mutters, scratching the back of his neck. "I deserve that. But seriously, Riley. You care about this town. You care about its people. That's exactly why we need you to be the Voice of the Customer."

"Why do you care so much about this?"

"Because it's important," he says.

"Important to who, Danny? You? Or the people you're supposedly doing this for?"

"Honestly? Both." He admits. "But I can't do it by myself; I need you."

"Need me," I repeat, my tone flat. "Is that supposed to be flattering?"

"Well, yeah." He shrugs, that crooked grin sneaking back onto his face. "I mean, you're stubborn, opinionated, and borderline terrifying when you're angry. Who wouldn't want you on their team?"

"Keep digging."

"Seriously," he says, his voice softer now. "You're smart, Riley. You see things other people miss. If anyone can keep this project grounded, and keep me honest, it's you."

I hate how his words linger, poking at the part of me that actually does care about this town. The part that wants to believe he might be sincere. But I also hate how he's looking at me—like he knows exactly what he's doing. Like he knows I'm already wavering.

"Let me guess," I say, masking my hesitation with a sardonic edge. "This is where I say yes, and you swoop in with a grateful smile, and we ride off into the sunset to save Willow Cove together?"

"Something like that," he says, grinning again. "Although I'm not much of a sunset guy. More of a sunrise person, honestly."

"Of course you are," I mutter, pinching the bridge of my nose. Because somehow, despite every instinct screaming at me to slam the door in his face, I'm still standing here. Listening. Considering. And that, more than anything, annoys me most of all.

"Fine," I say, the word leaving my mouth like an errant spark from a fire I thought I'd extinguished. "I'll be your Voice of the Customer."

Danny blinks at me, like he didn't actually expect me to give in this easily—or maybe just not this dramatically.

"Wow. Okay then. Brilliant," he says, the corner of his mouth twitching upward.

"Don't mistake this for enthusiasm," I shoot back, jabbing a finger in his direction. "I'm doing this for Willow Cove, not for you or your... sunrise optimism or whatever."

"Understood," he says, both hands raised in mock surrender. "Strictly for the greater good. Got it."

"Good night, Danny." I finally slam the door in his face, and boy, does it feel good.

The Fall Festival planning committee sits on chairs that squeak every time someone so much as breathes near them.

I'm surrounded by the kind of chaos that makes me question all of my life choices leading up to this moment.

"Welcome, welcome!" Mayor Thompson booms, his ruddy face practically glowing under the harsh fluorescent lights. He's already misplaced his glasses—they're perched on his head—and is squinting at the clipboard in his hand like it's written in a foreign language. "We've got a fantastic group here today, folks! Really top-notch!"

"Define 'fantastic,'" I mutter under my breath as I take an empty chair near the back, far enough away to avoid direct eye contact but close enough to fake interest if someone looks my way.

"Riley! So glad you could make it!" chimes Marlene Cartwright, the town's florist, who smells perpetually of rose water and always speaks in exclamation points. She's wearing a sunflower-print dress, her hair pinned back with a gardenia that looks suspiciously fresh for this time of year. "This is going to be *so* fun!"

"That's one word for it," I reply dryly, giving her a tight smile.

To Marlene's left sits Edna Fitzpatrick, the retired theater director who has inexplicably donned a feather boa for this occasion. She peers at me over her rhinestone-studded reading glasses, which are perched precariously at the end of her nose.

"This town deserves drama," she declares, not to anyone in particular. "And I intend to deliver."

"Great," I mutter, sinking lower in my seat. Between Marlene and Edna, I'm starting to feel like I've stumbled into a sitcom rather than a planning session for the town's biggest event of the year.

"Ah, Riley," comes another voice—this one smooth and measured, like butter melting on toast. Sam Hawkins, a baker, tips his flour-dusted hat (yes, an actual hat) in my direction.

"Glad you're here. Means we've got someone sensible in the mix."

"All right, everyone, settle down," Mayor Thompson calls, tapping his clipboard against the edge of the table for emphasis. The sound echoes through the room, cutting off Marlene mid-exclamation about artisanal wreaths. "Let's get started. We've got a lot of ground to cover, so let's stay focused, shall we?"

"Focused," Edna repeats, drawing out the word like it's a line from Shakespeare. "Yes, yes. But with flair."

"Kill me now," I whisper to myself.

"Careful," Danny murmurs, sliding into the seat beside me without warning. His shoulder brushes mine, and I shift slightly, pretending it doesn't set off a chain reaction of awareness I'd very much like to ignore. "You do this every year, remember?"

"Don't remind me," I say under my breath, glaring at him.

He grins like this is all some kind of game, like he's enjoying watching me writhe. And honestly? He probably is.

"Item one on the agenda," Mayor Thompson announces, adjusting his reading glasses with all the gravitas of a man declaring war instead of planning a community fundraiser. "We need to settle on the theme for this year's event."

"Bold choice, starting with the hard stuff," I mutter, scribbling a doodle in the margin of my notepad—an elaborate stick figure of a man getting whacked with a clipboard.

"How about something classic? Like 'A Night Under the Stars'?" This suggestion comes from Marlene, the florist, who has been meticulously rearranging her already-perfect stack of papers for the last five minutes.

"Groundbreaking," Danny murmurs, leaning slightly toward me. His shoulder brushes mine again, and I swear it's deliberate this time. My skin prickles where we've touched, like static electricity snapping to life. "You think Marlene came up with that all by herself?"

"Stop," I hiss under my breath, glaring at him sideways. He's too close, his tie slightly askew in a way that makes him look... human. "If you don't behave, I'm pinning this entire disaster on you."

"Disaster? Come on." He angles his head toward me, lips curving into that infuriating half-smile he seems to save just for me. "You mean *opportunity for growth*, right?"

"Opportunity for you to get punched," I reply.

"Focus, people!" the mayor calls out again, cutting through the room's growing hum of side conversations. He looks directly at Edna, whose theatrical sigh could rival a gale-force wind. The woman dramatically tosses her scarf over one shoulder and settles back in her chair, clearly unimpressed by the interruption.

"Don't make me regret sitting next to you," I whisper, sliding my notepad an inch closer to Danny and scrawling a quick note: *Do you actually work or just show up to meetings to torment me?*

He glances down at it, biting back a laugh, and grabs the pen from my hand before I can react. His handwriting is surprisingly neat as he writes back: *Tormenting you IS work. Full-time job, actually.*

"Are you two passing notes like middle schoolers?" Sam, the baker, hisses from across the table, eyeing us with mock disapproval. A faint smudge of flour lingers on the bridge of his nose.

I glare at him, willing him to mind his own business.

"Just brainstorming," Danny answers smoothly, flashing Sam his most charming grin. "Collaborative process, you know how it is."

As the discussion drags on—"Rustic Elegance" gets shot down faster than you can say "Pinterest"—Danny leans back in his chair, arms crossed, his knee brushing against mine. It's casual, accidental even. Except it happens again a minute later. And again. Each touch feels like a tiny spark igniting something I'd rather keep buried.

"Can you keep your legs to yourself?" I finally whisper, shooting him a pointed look.

"Not my fault there's no space," he says innocently, though his eyes gleam with mischief. "Small-town budget, small-town chairs."

"Excuses," I mutter, shifting away, only for him to lean closer under the guise of jotting something down.

"Don't look now," he murmurs, his tone suddenly conspiratorial, "but Edna's glaring at you like you insulted her cat."

"Probably because I exist," I reply dryly, stealing a glance at the retired theater director, who is indeed sending a death glare my way. She must sense my lack of enthusiasm for artisanal wreaths.

"Or maybe she thinks we're flirting," Danny adds, his voice dropping lower, teasing.

"Not in this lifetime," I reply.

"Whatever you say, Riley," he says lightly, tapping his pen against the table. But his gaze lingers on me a second too long.

"Next item," the mayor drones, oblivious to the silent battle happening at his table.

Danny finally looks away, his expression unreadable, and I exhale quietly, trying to shake off the weight of his attention.

SEVENTEEN

♥

DANNY

"Why does it have to be us?" Riley demands as we carry chairs from the meeting room, her expression set to *maximum disdain*. "Surely someone else is capable of collecting the chairs. The mayor has legs."

"Yes, but he also has gout," I reply dryly, gesturing toward the supply closet door. "And Edna looks like she might bite if anyone so much as breathes near her stage props. So, here we are." I put down my load and push the door open with an exaggerated flourish. "After you, Riley."

"Chivalry's not dead, just inconvenient," she mutters, carrying her stack of chairs inside.

The closet is cramped, even by small-town standards—a jumble of folding tables, half-empty paint cans, and a suspiciously large number of extension cords. Riley stops abruptly, and I nearly crash into her back.

"Personal space, Danny," she says over her shoulder.

"Apologies," I say, though I don't move back. Something about the way her ponytail brushes the nape of her neck keeps me rooted to the spot. "You make an excellent human barricade."

"That's what every girl dreams of being," she replies, shoving her stack of chairs into the corner. "A barricade. Super romantic."

"I took lessons." I quip.

Her lips press together, like she's debating whether to fire back or leave me dangling in my own awkward attempt at charm.

"Pass them here," she finally says, pointing at the chairs I'm carrying. Her tone is all business, but her fingers linger on mine for a split second as I hand them over. It's nothing, really. Barely a touch. And yet it feels like dropping live wires onto dry tinder.

"All yours," I say, but my voice catches slightly. She notices. Of course she notices. Riley doesn't miss *anything*.

"Careful," she says, a faint smirk tugging at her mouth. "Wouldn't want you pulling a muscle."

"Wouldn't dream of it," I reply, mirroring her smirk. But as we maneuver the chairs between us, the space between our bodies narrows, and suddenly I'm acutely aware of just how close we are. Her shoulder brushes mine, warm through the fabric of her shirt, and when she exhales, I feel it against my jaw.

"You're in my way," she says.

"Am I?" I ask softly, not moving. My gaze drops to her lips, and I can see the exact second she realizes it. Her breath hitches, and for once, Riley Hayes is speechless.

"Don't," she starts, but it's barely a whisper, and she doesn't step back. If anything, she leans closer, her hands tightening on the chair frame like it's the only thing tethering her to reality.

"Don't what?" I ask, my voice low enough to feel rather than hear. My heart is pounding like a drum, and every rational part of me is screaming to stop. To back away, crack a joke, do *something* to defuse this moment.

But I don't. Because even though I know this is a bad idea—maybe the worst one yet—I can't bring myself to step back. I see the faintest flicker of doubt in her eyes, too, like she's thinking the same thing but can't stop either.

But then she looks at me—really looks at me—and it's like gravity shifts. There's no air left in the room, no space between us, no time to think. Just her, and me, and the impossible pull drawing us together.

"Don't be smug about it later," she finally says, right before I kiss her.

It's not gentle. It's not calculated. It's messy and reckless and entirely too much, like we've both been waiting for this moment. Her lips are soft, but the way she kisses me back is anything but—fierce and demanding, like she's daring me to keep up. My hand finds her waist, pulling her closer, and her fingers tangle in my hair, undoing whatever semblance of composure I had left.

Somewhere behind us, a chair clatters to the floor, but neither of us stops. The world outside ceases to exist, swallowed whole by this one perfect, terrible, inevitable moment. And somewhere in the back of my mind, I know this will cost me. That we can't kiss like this and pretend nothing's changed. But right now, I don't care.

"Riley," I manage, breaking away just long enough to catch my breath. Her name tastes different now, like it belongs to me in a way it didn't before. Her forehead rests against mine, and her eyes are wide, pupils dark, like she's as stunned by this as I am.

"Shut up, Danny," she whispers, and then she's kissing me again, and I'm more than happy to oblige.

"Okay, so this is officially the worst idea I've ever had," I say, laughing as Riley fumbles with her keys at her front door. She's muttering something under her breath—probably about how this *isn't* my worst idea and that there are far worse examples—but she doesn't actually tell me to leave. That feels like progress.

"Shut up before I make you sleep in the hallway," she says, jiggling the key a little too forcefully until the lock finally gives way. The door swings open, and she steps through.

"Won't say a word, quiet as a mouse," I reply, stepping inside. Her place smells of... her, and it's exactly what I would've expected—cozy but slightly chaotic, with books stacked precariously on every available surface and a blanket draped over the back of the couch like it's been claimed by a very determined gremlin.

"Don't touch anything," she warns, kicking off her boots and tossing her bag onto an armchair. She's already pulling her hair out of its messy bun, shaking it loose like she's shedding the day.

"Wasn't planning on it." My jacket hits the floor with a soft thud, and I follow her lead, toeing off my shoes like I've been here a hundred times before.

"Uh-huh." She shoots me a suspicious look but doesn't argue. Instead, she crosses to the kitchen, grabbing two glasses and a bottle of wine from the fridge. "You drink?"

"Only when I'm trapped in close quarters with someone who kissed me like they were trying to prove a point," I say, leaning against the doorframe and watching as her lips twitch —just barely—in what might be the start of a smile.

"That wasn't a point," she says, pouring the wine and handing me a glass. "That was..."

"An experiment?" I prompt, taking a sip and raising an eyebrow at her.

"Don't push your luck."

"Wouldn't dream of it."

But I am pushing my luck, and we both know it. Because the space between us feels charged again, like it did back in that stupid supply closet when everything went sideways and upside down in the best possible way. And now we're here, alone, without the excuse of festival planning meetings or quirky townsfolk to keep things in check.

"Riley," I start, but she cuts me off, pushing me back against the wall with more force than necessary.

"Stop overthinking it," she says, her voice low and fierce. "Just... don't ruin it with words."

"Yes, ma'am," I manage, right before her lips find mine again, and this time it's less frantic, more deliberate—like she's daring me to figure her out one kiss at a time.

We don't make it to the couch. Or anywhere remotely civilized, for that matter. Somewhere between the hallway and the kitchen, my shirt ends up on the floor, and her flannel gets tangled around her elbows before she yanks it free and drops it unceremoniously onto the nearest surface.

"Your neighbors are definitely going to hate us," I mumble against her skin, earning an impatient huff as she pulls me closer.

"Then stop talking and make it worth their while."

"Your wish is my command," I say, before kissing her again.

My fingers trace the curve of her waist, the heat of her skin seeping into me. I can't help but notice how her bravado softens under my touch, accompanied by a quiet intake of breath. It's intoxicating, this power I hold over her, and it only fuels my desire to please her more.

She looks up at me, those eyes piercing through to my soul. Her hair tumbles down in loose waves, framing her flushed cheeks. I find myself lost in the sight of her, caught between wanting to devour her and memorize every detail.

"Like what you see, London?" she challenges, in between kisses.

"Oh, I do," I reply, letting my eyes wander from her face to the rest of her body. "Every inch of you."

A blush creeps up her neck, and she holds me tighter. The room seems to narrow around us, the outside world fading away until it's just us—two bodies navigating this unexpected connection. And yet, underneath it, there's this gnawing worry, quiet but insistent, that we're crossing some invisible line we won't be able to uncross.

"You're not so bad yourself, Danny-boy." She pulls me back into the moment, her voice barely above a whisper.

And then we're moving again, hands exploring, mouths meeting. Each touch sends a spark coursing through me, igniting a fire that threatens to consume me.

My fingers trace the curve of her hip, savoring the warmth of her skin beneath my touch. Riley's eyes flutter shut, her breath hitching again as I lean in to place soft kisses along her collarbone. As I continue to explore her body, I can't help but feel something more beneath it all. An intensity that goes beyond physical desire, something I'm not quite ready to name yet. But my actions speak louder than words, revealing the depth of emotion I'm unable—or unwilling—to voice.

I gently guide her down onto the couch, kneeling between her legs as I continue to worship every inch of her. Her hands thread through my hair, pulling me closer still, and I revel in the small gasps and moans that escape her lips.

The room's ambient light casts a golden hue, wrapping us in a cocoon of intimacy. As the moment stretches, I find my heart racing to match the urgency in her eyes.

Riley surprises me then, breaking the spell by leaning forward with a mischievous glint that suggests she's about to turn the tables. Her fingers move with an unexpected confidence, expertly unbuckling my belt as if she's done it a thousand times before. Each metallic click echoes in the space between us, matching the electric tension thrumming beneath our skin.

I watch her intently, captivated by both her audacity and her tender touch. There's something in the way she moves—a mixture of control and care that imbues each action with meaning. She tugs at my zipper, a gesture that feels less like undressing and more like unveiling.

Her eyes meet mine with a challenge that's as intoxicating as it is irresistible. This isn't about dominance or submission—it's a dance where we trade lead roles in seamless harmony. In those eyes, I see a reflection of my own desires mirrored back at me: the need to give as much as I am poised to take.

And then there's that smirk—a subtle tug at her lips that speaks volumes without uttering a single word. It says she's not afraid to steer us into unknown territories, that she's ready to explore every nuance of this connection we've stumbled upon. Her gaze holds not just desire, but an invitation wrapped in layers of trust.

The challenge in her eyes morphs into something more primal, and suddenly the air between us crackles with an anticipation that drowns out everything else.

"My turn," she murmurs, her voice a sultry whisper, rich with promise and need. It sends a delicious shiver up my spine, and I know I'm utterly powerless in the face of it.

With a deft grace that belies her earlier playfulness, Riley takes charge, her hands sliding across my chest with a deliberate slowness that speaks of both teasing and tenderness. It's as if each movement is choreographed to draw out this moment, stretching time until it feels like we've existed here forever, an eternity looping around our shared breath and heat.

Riley shifts again, her body fluidly moving like a dancer captivated by the music only she can hear. She explores with conviction and grace: each touch calculated yet organic, tapping into something deep within me that's never been touched before. We share this space where vulnerability masks itself as strength, where opening up feels less about risk and more about trust—fragile yet unyielding.

"Gotta keep you on your toes." She teases me with her hand, softly at first, before increasing the rhythm and tempo. Her smile holds myriad meanings; it's both an invitation into uncharted territories and a declaration of our shared understanding.

Her final move is a whisper against my ear—a gentle caress through sound alone—and then she guides me to the floor and straddles me, eyes warm despite their mischievous gleam. There's no doubt who's steering this moment now; neither captor nor captive, but equals exploring boundaries drawn anew.

As our surroundings recede into the periphery once more —the room reduced again to just us—I surrender completely to whatever connection we've unearthed together today: untamed yet breathtakingly familiar.

Her hips roll, deliberate and unhurried, a quiet assertion of power that sends a shiver through me. My hands find her waist instinctively, though it's her rhythm that dictates mine —every shift of her body pulling me further into the inevitable.

Her name escapes me in a low groan as the tension I've been holding unravels all at once, sharp and staggering, and I let myself fall—utterly undone beneath her.

When it's over, she leans down with a soft, knowing smile, brushing her lips across my jaw like punctuation. The world slowly seeps back in around us, but for a few precious seconds, all I can do is lie there, catching my breath, and marveling at how easily she's rewritten me.

Riley breaks the silence first, her laughter filling the air as she rolls onto her side, propping herself up on one elbow.

"Well, London," she says, a teasing note in her voice, "you sure know how to make a girl feel... appreciated."

I can't help but laugh, despite the awkwardness churning in my gut. Her humor is infectious, disarming. "I aim to please," I reply, smiling at her.

When it's over, I can feel her start to pull back almost immediately—not physically, but in that subtle way she retreats into her own head. Like she's already putting her walls back up. I lie there, staring at the ceiling. Riley is beside me, her breaths slowing to a steady rhythm. I can hear the soft hum of the refrigerator from the kitchen, the distant sound of traffic outside. My heart hammers, a mix of satisfaction and something else I can't quite place.

Her fingers trace idle patterns on my arm, sending shivers down my spine. I glance over at her, taking in her flushed cheeks, her disheveled hair spread out around her like a halo. She looks peaceful, content. Vulnerable. It's a side of her I haven't seen before, and it stirs something within me.

But as I look at her, really look at her, I feel a strange sensation creeping up on me. A realization that hits me like a punch to the gut. I might be in deeper than I ever intended to be. And I'm not sure if that's a good thing or not.

Later, when we're both lying on the rug in her living room—because apparently, beds are overrated—she stretches out beside me, her hair fanned across the carpet like some kind of auburn halo. I'm still shirtless, and trying to remember how words work.

"Well," I say after a beat, "that was... unexpected."

"Unexpected?" She turns her head to glare at me, though it's hard to take her seriously when her cheeks are still flushed and her lips are swollen from all the *not talking* we just did.

"Fine. Not unexpected," I admit. "But definitely not boring."

"Glad I could spice up your evening," she says, rolling onto her side and propping herself up on one elbow.

"Hey, I'm just saying, if this whole Voice of the Customer thing doesn't pan out, we could always start a—"

"Don't finish that sentence, Danny. There's a time to talk about work, and... this isn't it. You need to learn when to switch off," she says.

"Fair enough." I reach for her hand without really thinking, tracing lazy circles against her palm with my thumb. It's a small thing, but it feels bigger somehow—like I'm crossing some invisible line neither of us wants to acknowledge.

"Okay," Riley says, sitting up and wrapping herself in the throw from the couch. Her hair's a mess, her lips are red, and she looks like she just won a particularly brutal round of capture-the-flag. Against me. "We need to... figure out what this was."

"Ah, words every guy can't wait to hear after—" I gesture vaguely between us, my shirt still somewhere on her floor. "Whatever *this* was."

"Don't make me regret this more than I already do, Danny," she says as she tightens the blanket around her.

"So, what's on your mind? Rules for how often I'm allowed to bask in your glow?"

"Funny," she says. "No, this is about boundaries. You know? Those things people set so they don't accidentally ruin their lives?"

"Sounds bleak, but I'm listening." Even though every part of me is screaming to tell her I don't want boundaries, I bite my tongue. Because if I push too hard, I'll lose her entirely.

"Good. Because this"—she waves a hand between us now, mimicking my earlier motion—"can't turn into a... a *thing*." She says the last word like it leaves a bad taste in her mouth.

"Define 'thing,'" I say, because apparently, I've decided tonight is the night to test the limits of her patience.

"Don't make me spell it out." She sits forward, pinning me with that journalist glare of hers—the one that probably makes politicians sweat during interviews. "We work together now. Sort of. You're here, for what, a couple more weeks? And I don't want this"—another vague wave—"complicating anything. No expectations. No weirdness. Just... nothing outside of whatever this was. Got it?"

"Crystal clear," I say, even though it's not crystal *anything*. It's hazy, confusing, and absolutely not what I want to hear, but hey, I'll take what I can get. "So, purely professional from here on out. Like colleagues who occasionally—" I waggle my eyebrows.

"Don't finish that sentence," she warns, cutting me off before I can dig myself further into trouble.

"Right. No expectations," I repeat, holding up my hands as if to show my innocence. "Strictly business. Unless there's another community center supply closet involved, in which case—"

"Are you physically incapable of taking anything seriously?"

"Only when I'm trying to avoid thinking about how much I actually care," I admit, because apparently, I've also decided honesty is on tonight's menu. The words slip out before I can stop them, and her expression freezes for half a second—just long enough for me to notice.

"Well, don't," she says finally, shifting her gaze away. Her voice is quieter now. "Care, I mean. That's not part of the deal."

"Deal?" I tilt my head. "You make it sound like we're negotiating a hostile takeover."

"That's funny, coming from Mr. Corporate Speak." She rolls her eyes but doesn't look at me.

"Fine, Riley. Boundaries, it is. No crossing streams, no mixing business and... whatever this is. Zero expectations. Agreed?"

"Agreed," she echoes, her tone clipped and businesslike. But her fingers twitch against the throw, and I wonder if she's feeling that same pull—that stupid magnetic thing that keeps dragging us together no matter how much we pretend otherwise.

"Glad we sorted that out," I say, injecting as much casual indifference into my voice as I can manage. This thing between us already feels bigger than either of us will admit— and that terrifies me. "Anything else you'd like to add to the official rulebook? Maybe a clause about acceptable small talk topics or a maximum number of post-meeting glances?"

"Keep pushing, London, and I'll add a no-talking policy," she shoots back.

EIGHTEEN

RILEY

"One more thing," I say, slipping my jeans back on. My voice is perfectly steady—definitely not betraying the tiny, traitorous flutter in my chest. It's just a rule, that's all. If I say it out loud, I won't have to feel how much I already don't want him to leave. "No sleeping over."

Danny, who's halfway through buttoning his shirt, freezes. His head tilts, a single dark eyebrow arching upward.

"Is that so?" he says, his tone infuriatingly casual, but there's a spark of something—amusement, maybe?—in his eyes.

"Yes." I cross my arms for emphasis, even though it feels ridiculous when I'm still without socks, and crucially, my bra. "This isn't... You know, *that*. No cozy mornings or shared coffee mugs. You leave when it's done. That's the rule."

"Ah," he says, resuming his buttons with deliberate slowness, like he's savoring every second of drawing this out. "The old 'get out before dawn' clause. Classic. Very dignified."

"Don't mock me, Danny," I say, but my voice wavers between irritation and something closer to laughter. Damn him and his stupid smile. For a second, I almost say something different. Something stupid, like *stay*. But instead— "I'm serious. This isn't a relationship. It's a..." My brain scrambles for a word that doesn't sound pathetic or desperate. "Transaction."

"Right," he says, nodding solemnly now. "Strictly transactional. Like picking up a loaf of bread at the shop. Only, you know"—his gaze flicks over me, lingering just long enough to make my pulse spike—"more fun."

"Exactly," I manage.

"Got it," he says, smirking as he tucks in his shirt. "No slumber parties. No breakfast in bed. No awkward morning-after small talk about the weather."

"Or apps," I add quickly, narrowing my eyes at him for good measure.

"Wouldn't dream of it," he says. Then he extends a hand toward me, like we're closing some kind of bizarre business deal. "Shake on it?"

I hesitate, staring at his hand like it might bite me. But then I take it, because if there's one thing worse than Danny Winter being smug, it's Danny Winter thinking I'm scared of him. His grip is warm and firm, and for a second, neither of us moves. We just stand there, still holding hands, both a little too breathless, both grinning like idiots pretending this whole thing is just a joke we're in on together. And I hate how much I wish he'd push back. Call my bluff. But he doesn't.

"Deal," I say finally, pulling my hand away. "Now get out of here."

"Right, bye then," he says, grabbing his jacket from the back of the chair. He pauses by the door, glancing back at me with an expression I can't quite read. For a split second, I think he might say something else—something real—but then he just flashes me that insufferably charming grin and disappears into the night.

I exhale once the door clicks shut, leaning back against the couch as the silence settles around me. My heart's still racing, which is stupid because this was supposed to be simple. Rules are simple. Boundaries are simple. Adults make smart decisions all the time, right?

"Smart decision," I mutter under my breath, trying to convince myself as much as the empty room. Because that's all this is: two adults making a logical, mutually beneficial arrangement. Nothing messy, nothing complicated.

I stare at the door after it clicks shut. The silence feels heavier now, like the air's been sucked out of the room.

Before I can talk myself out of it, I stride over and yank the door open.

He's halfway down the walk, hands shoved in his pockets.

"Danny!" I call.

He stops and turns, and for once, he doesn't smirk. Just waits.

I swallow hard, then force a smile. "It wouldn't be very Willow Cove of me to send you out into the cold without at least offering a hot drink."

A beat. Then his mouth curves up, slow and warm. "Black, two sugars," he says, as he jogs back up the steps—and kisses me before I can think better of it.

NINETEEN

DANNY

The rich, nutty aroma of coffee fills Riley's kitchen as I stand barefoot on the cool tile floor, humming some half-remembered tune that's been stuck in my head since three a.m. The morning sunlight streams through her tiny window, catching the steam curling up from the French press like it's auditioning for a coffee commercial.

I'm still wearing yesterday's dress shirt, unbuttoned and hanging loose over my boxers because, apparently, I've lost all sense of personal dignity. But hey, at least I remembered to roll up the sleeves—small victories.

"You're aware this is against the rules, right?" Riley's voice slices through my morning reverie like a knife through warm butter.

"Good morning to you, too," I say without turning around, reaching for one of her mismatched mugs—this one has a cartoon cat saying something passive-aggressive about Mondays. A classic choice.

"Don't 'good morning' me, Danny," she counters, leaning against the doorway with her arms crossed. "You're *still* here."

She's wearing flannel pajama pants and an old band T-shirt, her hair doing its best impression of a bird's nest. It's criminal how good she looks disheveled.

"Technically, I didn't sleep over," I reply, pouring the coffee like I own the place. I glance at her counter and can't help noticing how her mugs are scattered randomly on different shelves, half of them chipped. "You know, you'd save about three minutes a morning if you organized this better. Streamline your whole workflow," I add with a grin.

"Don't 'optimize' my kitchen, London. It works just fine for me." She takes a long, deliberate sip of *my* coffee, her expression daring me to challenge her.

"First of all, rude," I say, folding my arms. "Second, you broke the no-sleepovers rule first. Remember last week? Movie night? You passed out on *my* couch."

"That doesn't count," she says quickly, waving me off. "There were extenuating circumstances."

"Sure, there were." I smirk. "Like the two margaritas and the extra-cheese pizza?"

"Exactly," she says. "Extenuating."

"Face it, Riley," I say, leaning casually against the counter. "We're terrible at rules."

"Speak for yourself," she says. "I'm just indulging your inability to stick to them. Someone has to keep you in check."

"Is that what this is?" I ask, gesturing between us. "You breaking your own rules just to make me feel better about breaking them first?"

"Obviously." She shrugs, setting the mug down with a clink. "I'm nothing if not selfless."

"Well, thank you for your sacrifice." I tilt my head, grinning. "*Saint Riley* has such a nice ring to it."

"Careful, Saint Riley might revoke your coffee privileges," she warns, reaching for the pot.

"Hey, hey!" I step in, grabbing the handle before she can. I pour another mug, sliding it across the counter toward her. "But for the record, I'm only sticking around because your coffee's better than mine."

"Mm-hmm." She picks up the second mug, her fingers brushing mine again. Then she steps back, her expression unreadable. "You're lucky I'm feeling generous today."

"Or you just like having me around," I say, testing the waters.

"Don't push it, London." She flashes a sharp smile over her shoulder as she walks out of the kitchen, leaving me standing there, holding my coffee and wondering when exactly I started liking the way she calls me that.

I lean against the counter, sipping coffee that tastes alarmingly better than it has any right to. Riley's kitchen still smells like her—coffee beans and something faintly floral that clings to her skin. The sunlight slants through the window, catching on the messy pile of her mail shoved off to one side of the countertop. Her life is here, tangible and chaotic, and for some reason, I feel like an intruder.

But not in a bad way.

Which is the problem.

This? This domestic, sunlit, *"let's have breakfast and pretend we're normal people" nonsense?* It feels too good. Like slipping into a pair of shoes you didn't know were missing from your closet. Except those shoes are labeled "Feelings," and trying them on means you're halfway toward buying the whole damn set: commitment, vulnerability, heartbreak—the works. No, thank you.

I drain my mug, setting it down with more force than necessary because apparently, I need to make a statement to myself. *Get a grip, Danny.* You're not here to play house.

You're here because... Why? Because she didn't kick me out last night? Because she lets me tease her without flinching? Because she laughs at my jokes, even when they're objectively terrible?

"Stop thinking," I mutter under my breath, scrubbing a hand down my face. "It's dangerous."

By the time we've both sat through the weekly marathon of a 'Voice of the Community' meeting—three hours of corporate jargon and PowerPoint slides so dull they could lull a rock to sleep—I'm ready to escape. Riley, naturally, looks almost smug about how unbothered she is by the ordeal. She's scrolling through her phone as we step outside, clearly hunting for something snarky to say about the state of my colleagues' collective stiffness.

"If they'd just implemented a proper stakeholder alignment model and tracked KPIs, half of this town hall circus could be solved overnight."

Riley stops and gives me a look. "God, listen to yourself. Do you ever switch that off?"

"What?" I say, feigning innocence.

"The way you talk about people like... moving parts in a system. Like we're just data points to be optimized."

I hold up my hands, half-apologetic. "I don't see people like that. I swear I don't. It's just—the app's on the line, and so is my career. If I can make it here, in Willow Cove of all places, then maybe it actually stands a chance. And maybe I do too."

She doesn't say anything, but the look softens just a little.

I nod toward the path ahead. "Come on. Let's take a walk before I say something else that makes you want to throttle me."

"Why not?" she says after a beat, tucking her phone away. "At least then I won't feel like I've wasted the entire day indoors listening to you mansplain the importance of clear communication in community engagement."

"First of all," I start, falling into step beside her as we head toward the water, "I don't mansplain. I professionally elaborate. Second, I only mentioned communication once. Maybe twice."

"Three times," she corrects, shooting me a sidelong glance. "And you used the phrase 'Unique Selling Point' four times. I counted."

"Okay, now you're just making things up." I bump her shoulder lightly as we walk, grinning when she rolls her eyes. The air smells like salt and seaweed, crisp and clean, and I can hear the faint cry of gulls overhead. For some reason, it all feels quieter out here, easier. Like the weight of whatever tension hangs between us gets carried off by the breeze.

"Admit it," I say after a moment, "you love these walks. You like hanging out with me."

"Sure," she says. "Nothing brightens my day like a little light corporate banter about Pantones and pixel resolution."

"See? I'm all about high-definition. You do like me."

"Keep telling yourself that, London," she says with the teasing edge she always uses when she's trying to keep me at arm's length. And maybe I should let her. Maybe I should stop leaning into moments like this, stop letting myself enjoy the way her laugh sounds.

But I don't.

We fall quiet for a while, the kind of easy silence that sneaks up on you, and I find myself watching the way the sunlight catches on the water. The waves lap gently against the shore, rhythmic and steady, and for half a second, I let myself imagine what it'd be like if it wasn't temporary. If Riley and I weren't two people who keep pretending this thing between us doesn't mean anything.

"Hey," she says suddenly, pulling me out of my thoughts. There's an edge to her voice, curious but cautious, and I glance over to see her watching me closely, her expression unreadable.

"Yeah?" I ask, keeping my tone light, deflective. Always deflective.

"Never mind," she says after a beat, shaking her head. "I'll save it for later. Let's just... walk."

The gravel crunches under our feet as we get closer to the waterfront, the smell of brine and seaweed hanging in the air. Riley's steps are confident, purposeful, like she's on a mission even when she's supposedly relaxing. Me? I'm just trying not to trip over my own damn thoughts.

"Spit it out, Danny," she says, her tone sharp but not unkind. Her hands are stuffed into her jacket pockets, and she doesn't look at me, which somehow makes it easier and harder at the same time. "You've been weirdly quiet for the last ten minutes. It's unsettling."

"Quiet can be charming, you know," I say. "Mysterious. Brooding. Like a Byronic hero."

"Mm-hmm. Or like someone who's about to vomit from nerves. Which one is it?"

"Well, now you're just wounding my fragile ego." I shove my hands into my own pockets, mimicking her stance, though hers looks natural and mine feels like a bad impression. "But fine. Since you're so insistent on prying..."

"Glad we're on the same page." She glances at me sideways.

I exhale sharply, kicking at a pebble on the path. It skitters forward and bounces off the edge of the walkway, disappearing into the water below. "So, fun fact—turns out I'm really good at giving advice to others, but when it comes to me, I'm absolutely rubbish at relationships. Who knew?"

"Shocking revelation," Riley says. "Go on."

"Right, well, picture this: young, ambitious Danny Winter, fresh out of uni, full of ideas and charm—" I glance over, waiting for her inevitable interjection.

"Still waiting for the shocking part," she cuts in.

"Patience, Saint Riley," I say, holding up a finger. "Anyway, there was this girl. Amelia. We met at some bar—I don't even remember which one now. She was brilliant, you know? Witty, clever, the whole package. And for a while, everything was... great." The word feels too big and too small all at once. "Until it wasn't."

"Let me guess," Riley says, her voice softer now, like she's treading carefully. "Work got in the way."

"Work always gets in the way," I mutter, more to myself than her. Then I shrug, pushing the weight of it off with practiced ease. "But no, that wasn't the kicker. The real problem was me being, well... me. Always *on*, always hustling, always thinking five steps ahead. Turns out that's not super conducive to, you know, *feelings*."

"Feelings are overrated," she says, but there's something—a hint of understanding—that keeps me going.

"See, that's what I thought, too. Until Amelia told me I was emotionally constipated."

"Did she actually use those words?" Riley asks, biting back a laugh.

"Verbatim," I say. "She said I was 'charming but ultimately exhausting,' which, honestly, might be the most poetic breakup line I've ever received."

"Wow," Riley says, shaking her head. "Sounds like a keeper."

"Right?" I laugh. "Anyway, lesson learned: maybe I'm just not cut out for the whole relationship thing. Too much baggage, too little patience. Or maybe I'm just... not enough."

The words hang in the air between us, heavier than I intended, and I immediately regret letting them slip out. But Riley doesn't pounce on them like I expect her to. Instead, she stops walking, turning to face me fully.

"That's crap," she says bluntly, crossing her arms. "You're not 'not enough.' You're just human. And humans screw up. A lot."

"Very inspirational," I say, deflecting again, because that's what I do.

"Shut up and listen," she says. "You think you're the only one who's messed up? Please. I burned out so hard in Seattle, I practically left scorch marks."

"Burned out?" I ask, surprised by the admission. Riley doesn't exactly scream 'fragile' to me.

"Yeah," she says, her gaze drifting out toward the water. "Turns out working eighty-hour weeks and fighting with your boss about ethics every other day isn't sustainable. Who knew?"

"Shocking revelation," I echo, earning a faint smile from her.

"Anyway," she continues, "I quit. Kissed the salary and the stock options goodbye. Packed up my life and moved back here, thinking I'd figure it out, eventually. Spoiler alert: still figuring it out."

"Well, at least you didn't run off to Bali to find yourself or something equally cliché," I say, and she snorts.

"Not my style," she replies. "But hey, if you ever need someone to remind you that perfection is overrated, I'm your girl."

The bench creaks under our weight as we sit down, side by side, a little closer than necessary. The wood is warm from the sun, and I can feel the heat seeping through my shirt. There's a breeze coming off the water, carrying traces of salt and seaweed, and somewhere nearby, a kid is shrieking with laughter—probably at some poor parent's expense.

"Nice spot," I say, stretching my legs out in front of me. My polished loafers look almost absurd against the uneven gravel path beneath us. "Very... picturesque. Almost makes you forget about the crippling small-town vibes."

"Careful," Riley says, leaning back on her elbows. "You're starting to sound dangerously close to relaxed. Wouldn't want anyone in Willow Cove thinking you're softening up."

"Perish the thought," I say.

"Bet you didn't have spots like this growing up," she says, her tone light but probing, as always. "What was it? Some posh London mansion with manicured flowerbeds and those weirdly aggressive swans?"

"Close," I say with a smirk. "Hampstead Heath, if you must know. And yes, the swans were terrifying. Practically sociopathic. Not exactly the kind of wildlife encounter that warms the heart."

"Figures," she says, shaking her head. "Meanwhile, I was running barefoot through the woods here, climbing trees and scraping my knees on every available surface. My mom used to call me her 'feral child.'"

"That explains so much."

"Shut up," she says, shoving my shoulder lightly. "It was great, actually. No screens, no schedules... just endless afternoons pretending to be an explorer or a pirate or whatever else my overactive imagination cooked up. What about you? Were you a... What's the British equivalent of a Boy Scout? A Beefeater in training?"

"Ha-ha." I roll my eyes but can't help laughing. "No, I wasn't a Scout. More of a bookworm, really. Spent most of my time indoors, building elaborate Lego cities or getting lost in fantasy novels where elves and dragons did all the adventuring for me."

"Seriously?" She raises an eyebrow, clearly amused. "Danny Winter, future corporate overlord, was a Lego nerd?"

"Don't knock it," I say. "I had a very sophisticated system. Color-coded bricks, strict zoning laws—urban planning at its finest."

"Of course you did," she says, her laugh bubbling up like soda fizz. "Let me guess: even your imaginary cities had spreadsheets."

"Naturally," I reply, feigning offense. "How else would you track dragon-related property damage?"

"God, you're such a dork," she says.

"Better than being feral," I shoot back, though the word feels oddly affectionate now. Like a compliment.

"Feral. Wow, compliments like that make me feel so special," she laughs, tilting her face up toward the sun. For a moment, neither of us speaks, just listening to the rhythmic lap of the water against the shore and the distant hum of a boat engine. It's... nice. Too nice, probably.

"Funny, isn't it?" I say finally, breaking the quiet. "How two people can grow up so differently and still end up here, on the same park bench, debating Legos versus tree climbing?"

"Yeah," she says, her voice softer now. "Guess life's funny like that."

"Or cruel," I say, mostly to needle her.

"Definitely funny," she counters. "Because now I get to picture you in your childhood bedroom, surrounded by neatly stacked Lego towers, probably wearing a sweater vest or something equally tragic."

"Not a sweater vest," I say. "A bow tie. Obviously."

"You're staring," Riley says, not even looking at me. Her voice is smug, like she knows she's caught me red-handed.

"At what?" I counter, leaning back on the bench and crossing my arms in what I hope reads as casual indifference. "The seagulls? Sure. Very majestic creatures."

She snorts, turning her head so I catch the faintest smirk tugging at her lips. Damn her and that smirk. "Right, because you've always struck me as a big avian enthusiast. Admit it, London. You were staring."

"Maybe I was trying to figure out if you're capable of being quiet for more than thirty seconds," I say.

"Nice dodge," she murmurs, still smirking as she picks at a loose thread on her messenger bag.

I glance away, focusing on the water instead. The sunlight ripples across its surface, bright and endless, and for a second, I almost say it. Not *it* it—I'm not completely reckless—but something dangerously close. Something about how easy it feels, sitting here with her, trading barbs and pretending neither of us is keeping score. How much I want to keep doing exactly this... indefinitely.

But then she shifts beside me, her arm brushing mine, and the thought evaporates faster than a puddle on hot asphalt. Because that's not what this is. It's not supposed to be, anyway. Rules or no rules, we both know where this ends, and it's not on some romantic park bench with violins swelling in the background.

"Stop overthinking," she says suddenly, her eyes locking onto mine like a heat-seeking missile. "You get this weird furrow in your brow when you do. It's distracting."

"Thanks for the unsolicited feedback," I say dryly, nudging her shoulder with mine. It's meant to come off as playful—a light jab to shift the mood—but the contact lingers a half-second too long, and I swear I feel her lean into it. Or maybe I imagine that part. Hard to say.

"Anytime," she replies, bumping me back with more force than necessary. It sends me rocking slightly on the bench, and she grins like she's won some unspoken battle. "I live to make your life harder."

"Mission accomplished," I mutter, shaking my head.

We sit there for another beat, the silence stretching between us, taut but not unpleasant. I could say something now—something real, something honest—but instead, I let my shoulder drift against hers again, the barest brush of skin. She doesn't pull away, and neither do I.

"Alright," Riley says, standing up from the bench and brushing invisible dust off her jeans like she's preparing for a fight. "Let's just get this out of the way."

I blink up at her, squinting against the afternoon sunlight haloing her head like she's some kind of angel. A sarcastic, no-nonsense, rule-enforcing angel.

"Get what out of the way? My inevitable apology for how charming I am?"

She snorts. "No. The fact that we're terrible at rules. Like, objectively bad. Embarrassingly bad."

"Speak for yourself," I say, dragging myself to my feet. She steps back to give me space, but not much. Close enough that I catch the faintest hint of her shampoo—something citrusy and sharp, like her—and it makes my brain go fuzzy for half a second. "I've been excellent at following rules. You're the one who keeps breaking them."

"Excuse me?" Her hands go to her hips, head tilting in disbelief. "Who was it that stayed over last night, huh? Because it definitely wasn't me hanging out in *your* kitchen making coffee this morning."

"Technically," I counter, already grinning because I know this will rile her up, "the rule was *no sleeping over*. No one said anything about leaving immediately after waking up. Loophole."

"Loophole," she repeats flatly, narrowing her eyes. "That's your defense? You're worse than a politician."

"Wow, low blow," I say. "If you're going to insult me, at least compare me to someone cool. Like a rebellious rockstar or a really clever con artist."

"Fine," she says. "You're like one of those smug lawyers in courtroom dramas who always gets the guilty client off on a technicality. Congratulations, Danny, you're TV villain material."

"Thank you," I reply with a mock bow. "I'll take it as a compliment."

"Of course you will."

We start walking again, weaving through the thin crowd along the waterfront. The breeze off the water carries the faint tang of salt, and the sun hangs low enough now that its reflection shimmers like molten gold across the waves. It's annoyingly romantic, the kind of setting that feels tailor made for deep confessions or declarations of undying love. Naturally, I try to ruin it by talking.

"Okay," I say, stuffing my hands into my pockets because if I don't, I might be tempted to reach for hers. "How about this? A new rule."

"Seriously?" She glances at me. "Didn't we just establish that rules are not our thing?"

"Exactly," I say, turning to walk backward so I can face her. Her expression hovers somewhere between skeptical and amused, which is honestly where I like it best. "This is the ultimate rule. The rule to end all rules."

"Go on," she says cautiously, crossing her arms like she's bracing for impact.

"No more new rules," I declare, spreading my arms wide like I've just delivered a groundbreaking philosophical revelation. "There. Problem solved."

She stops walking, blinking at me like I've just grown a

second head. And then she laughs—a quick, sharp burst of sound. "That's the dumbest thing I've ever heard."

"Is it, though?" I ask, stepping closer, close enough that I can see the faint freckles scattered across the bridge of her nose. "Think about it. If there are no rules, there's nothing to break. We win by default."

"Or," she counters, fixing me with a look that's both challenging and fond, "we crash and burn spectacularly because we have zero boundaries."

"Could be fun," I say lightly, though my pulse kicks up when her gaze stays locked on mine a beat too long. "High risk, high reward, right?"

"Come on," she finally says, breaking the tension as she starts walking again. "We'll call it a truce—for now. But if you come up with another 'rule,' I'm filing a formal complaint."

The town comes into view as we follow the curve of the path, its familiar streets bathed in the warm glow of the setting sun.

"Hey," I say eventually. "You realize this whole 'no more rules' thing means we're officially winging it, right? No safety net."

"Good," she replies, though her smile feels a little sharper now. "Maybe. Or maybe it's just reckless."

But she's smiling, so I let it go.

TWENTY

RILEY

My fingers hover over the keyboard like they're waiting for divine inspiration to strike, but all I get is a blank screen and the ghost of Danny's stupid smirk flashing behind my eyes. It's infuriating how vividly I can summon him—the way he smiles right before he says something incredibly cocky, or how his laugh rumbles low when he catches me off guard. Like last night.

I groan and drop my head onto the desk with a dull *thud*.

Focus, please.

"Trouble in paradise, Riley?"

Elaine's voice bursts through my spiraling thoughts like a confetti cannon, and I jerk upright so fast my chair squeaks in protest. She's already halfway across the newsroom, marching toward me, her red boots tapping out a rhythm that screams, *you're late.*

"Please tell me you're here to fire me," I say.

"Not a chance," she chirps. "At least, not until you file your article."

I bite my lip, officially I'm not late yet, but I know I'm cutting it fine.

"Where's my feature on the man who wants to catapult Willow Cove into the future?" she asks, practically glowing. "You spend enough time together, the app's got the town talking. Surely the article should write itself? It's got everything: innovation, community impact..."

On paper at least, this is all true. But I've seen the other side of Danny Winter. The part that still treats community like it's a market segment to be optimized.

Elaine continues, "a charming underdog success story—"

"Charming?" I cut in. "*Really?*"

"Absolutely!" she shoots back without missing a beat. "Plus, it's local, it's human interest gold. I was expecting a love letter to the app's success—"

"Love letter?" I choke out, sitting bolt upright. "Elaine, no offense, but have you met me?"

"All the more reason it's perfect," she says, completely unfazed. "Your voice, Riley. Your insight. Your... unique perspective on Mr. Winter."

"That's one way to put it."

"Either way," she says, tapping her watch with a perfectly manicured nail. "This could be huge—for you, for the paper, for—"

"Yeah, yeah," I cut her off, waving a hand in surrender. "For truth, justice, and the American way. I get it."

"Good." She stands, brushing imaginary dust off her skirt. "This is a chance to make our readers proud of their town, a chance to make them smile."

"Okay, but what if I'm fundamentally opposed to making people smile?" I counter, plastering on my most innocent expression. "Like, philosophically?"

"Then fake it," she replies, all too cheerfully. "You're a professional, aren't you?"

"Debatable," I mutter under my breath, but Elaine hears me anyway. She tilts her head, giving me that look—the one that makes it clear it's an order, not a request.

"Look, Riley," she says, her tone softening. "I get that you're... apprehensive. But this isn't just another article. This is a chance for you to show the world what you can do. To really connect with people. And let's be honest"—she leans in slightly, lowering her voice—"it's not like you don't already have a connection to Mr. Winter."

My throat tightens. "What's that supposed to mean?"

"Only that you've spent more time with him than anyone else in this office," she says innocently, but there's an edge to her smile that makes my palms sweat. "You've got insight no one else has. Use it."

"Insight," I repeat, my voice cracking just a little. "Sure. Let's call it that."

"Exactly," Elaine says, completely missing—or ignoring—the panic bubbling just beneath my surface. "So, dig deep, and write something that'll knock my Jimmy Choos off by four pm. Got it?"

"Crystal clear," I manage to choke out through gritted teeth as she saunters away, leaving behind the faint smell of expensive perfume and the crushing weight of expectation.

As soon as she's out of earshot, I slump back in my chair, staring at the closed folder on my desk like it might spontaneously combust. A love letter to Danny's app. Right. Totally doable. Except for the tiny, insignificant fact that my brain short-circuits every time I think about him. About us. About the way he looks at me when we're alone, like I'm the only person in the room—

"Stop it," I hiss under my breath, shaking my head violently. No. Absolutely not. There is no *us*. There's just me, trying not to implode, and him, probably somewhere right now, being infuriatingly charming and British and—ugh.

The office door swings shut behind me with a hollow thud, and the mid-morning air smacks me in the face like a cold, unwelcome reality check. My boots scuff against the concrete trudge down the sidewalk, shoulders hunched under the weight of my messenger bag and, oh yeah, the crushing realization that my career might implode by morning.

"Love letter to Danny's app," I mutter under my breath, my voice dripping with sarcasm. "Sure, Elaine. Why not? Maybe I'll add some glitter hearts and a soundtrack while I'm at it."

The streets blur around me—cars honking, pedestrians weaving past with their umbrellas and hurried steps—but it all feels distant, muffled, like I'm wading through fog.

I groan, loud enough that a guy walking his dog gives me a wide berth. Fine. Let them think I'm unhinged. It's not like they're wrong.

"Professionalism first," I mutter, biting down hard on my lower lip until I taste something metallic and a darker thought worms its way in: *What if all that smooth talk about 'shared purpose' is just... packaging?*

By the time I reach my house, I've worked myself into such a spiral of indignation and panic that I nearly trip over the threshold. The door creaks open, and there she is—Ava, queen of unsolicited truths, perched cross-legged on my couch like she owns the place.

"Coffee's on the table," she says without looking up from her phone. Her oversized sweater swallows her frame, one fuzzy sock dangling lazily off her foot. She glances at me, raises an eyebrow. "You look like you got hit by a bus. A feelings bus."

"Don't start," I say, tossing my bag onto the chair with

more force than necessary. The leather slumps pathetically, clearly reflecting my mood. "I'm on a deadline."

"Uh-huh." Ava sets her phone aside and leans forward, both elbows on her knees. "What'd Elaine do this time? Assign you another puff piece about how we do Halloween better than anyone else?"

"Close." I grab the mug she's gesturing to and take a scalding sip, ignoring the way it burns my tongue. "She wants a new angle on my Makers' Mart article."

"What sort of angle?"

"A love letter."

"To who?" Ava smirks, already sensing where this is going. "Wait, let me guess—Danny. Mr. Tall, Dark, and British, right?"

"To his *app*," I clarify, leveling her with a glare. "Not him. Definitely not him."

"Uh-huh," she says again, dragging out the syllables like she doesn't believe me for a second. "And how exactly are you planning to write this 'objective' article without turning into a puddle of awkward, repressed emotions?"

"That's not—" I set the mug down harder than I intend to, coffee sloshing dangerously close to the rim. "There are no emotions. Not repressed. Not awkward. None. Zero."

"Right," Ava says, leaning back and folding her arms. "Because you're totally unaffected. That's why your face looks like you just swallowed a lemon every time someone mentions his name."

"Okay, you know what? I don't have to take this from you." I point an accusatory finger at her, but she just grins like the cat who ate the canary.

"Relax, Riley," she says, waving me off. "I'm just saying— this could be good for you. Get all those *feelings* out of your system, channel them into the article. Catharsis or whatever.

Just write about him, and write about the app. What's the problem?"

"It's dishonest," I snap, pacing the length of my living room. "He still treats the town like it's a market opportunity, not a community. Like we're just... metrics he can show off on a slide deck. And now I'm supposed to write about how brilliant that is? No way."

"He is hot though," Ava cuts in, smirking. She takes a long, obnoxiously loud sip of coffee, clearly enjoying this way too much.

"Infuriating," I correct, glaring at her. "The whole thing's a conflict of interest. How am I supposed to write some glowing feature about this guy when—" I stop short, clamping my mouth shut before I can say something incriminating.

"Mm-hmm." Ava raises an eyebrow, daring me to continue. When I don't, she shrugs. "Seems like you're making a bigger deal out of this than it needs to be. Just write the article, Riley. You're a pro. Stick to the facts, slap on some heartfelt nonsense about community ambition or whatever, and call it a day."

"That's not the point!" I throw my hands up. "The point is... I can't just 'stick to the facts.'" My voice cracks slightly, which Ava notices immediately, because of course she does. I plop down on the couch and bury my face in my hands. "The facts aren't the problem. The problem is... me."

"Wow, groundbreaking insight." Ava leans forward, resting her chin on her palm. "So, what's the real issue here? Is it that you're scared you'll fluff this up because you've got hearts-eyes for Mr. Smooth? Or"—she pauses dramatically—"are you worried he's going to read it and figure out how hard you're crushing on him?"

"Crushing?" My head snaps up. "No one's crushing on anyone! This isn't high school, Ava. I'm a professional journalist—"

"With a soft spot for dashing Brits who use words like 'brilliant' and 'splendid,'" she interrupts, grinning like the Cheshire cat.

"Stop!" I groan, crossing my arms like a petulant teenager. "This isn't about feelings. It's about integrity. About boundaries. About not turning into one of those cliché movie heroines who sabotage her career over some guy with nice hair and a stupid accent."

"Ah yes, boundaries," Ava says, raising her mug like she's toasting me. "You're doing a stellar job with those, by the way. Really setting an example for the rest of us."

"God, why do I even talk to you? Why are you even in my house?" I mutter, pinching the bridge of my nose. But deep down, I know exactly why. Because, for all her teasing and sarcasm, Ava has this annoying habit of cutting through my bullshit like a hot knife through butter.

"Because I'm right," she says smugly, as if reading my mind. "And because you need someone to tell you what you're too chicken to admit to yourself: You care about this guy, Riley. Like, *care* care. And that's why this whole assignment is freaking you out so much."

"That's ridiculous," I say automatically, but the words feel hollow. Ava doesn't miss a beat.

"Is it though?" She tilts her head, studying me like I'm one of her true-crime documentaries. "Look, I get it. You're scared. If you mess this up, it's not just your reputation on the line—it's his too. And yeah, maybe that's because you're emotionally invested. But that doesn't have to be a bad thing."

"Emotionally invested," I repeat, rolling my eyes so hard it's a miracle they don't fall out of my head. "Thanks, Dr. Phil."

"Hey, don't knock it," she says with a shrug. "Emotions make people human. Maybe instead of fighting them, you could actually use them to, I don't know, write something honest for once."

"Honest," I echo quietly, the word landing heavier than I expect. I look away, staring at the half-empty coffee cup on the table. *Honest.* The idea terrifies me almost as much as it intrigues me.

"Yeah, honest." Ava leans back, folding her arms behind her head. "But hey, no pressure. If you'd rather play it safe and churn out another cookie-cutter piece, go for it. Just don't come crying to me when Danny reads it and thinks you're a soulless robot."

"Ugh, you're impossible," I say, but damn it, she might actually have a point.

I open my notebook, flipping past pages of meticulous shorthand. Danny's voice practically jumps off the paper as I read back through my notes. "The Makers' Mart App is about connecting people, not just through technology but through shared purpose." His words are perfectly polished, like they were hand-delivered by his PR department.

But then there's that other quote, scribbled hastily in the margin because he'd said it almost as an afterthought: "*Honestly, I didn't think anyone here would care about what I'm building.*" That one hits differently.

I chew on my lip, staring at the jagged scrawl, remembering how his voice had softened when he said it. Not the clipped, confident tone he uses when pitching to his bosses or potential vendors, but something rawer. Hesitant, even. Vulnerable. Damn him.

That's the problem, isn't it? I don't know which one is real — the guy who fidgets with his tie when no one's looking, or the one who calls people 'user cohorts' and means it.

"Purely journalistic perspective," I remind myself, sitting up straighter. "Focus on the app. The community impact. This isn't about him."

But every note feels personal. Every observation loops back to him. The way he fidgeted with his tie during our first meeting, like it was choking him. The slight smirk when I scoffed at one of his over-rehearsed soundbites. The unguarded laugh when I called him out for using corporate buzzwords like "synergy" without irony. I shake my head like that'll somehow clear the memories away, but they stick like gum on the bottom of my shoe.

I try again: *The Makers' Mart app has revolutionized the local artisan economy, proving that innovation can thrive in small-town America.*

I stare at it. Delete. Too stiff. Too sterile.

"Danny Winter, the charismatic yet infuriating Brit behind the Willow Cove Makers' Mart app, has managed to do the impossible: make me care about artisanal sourdough."

"Ugh, no." Delete. That's... way too personal. And snarky. And probably not great for staying objective. Not to mention, if Danny ever read that, I'd have to move to Siberia out of sheer humiliation.

"In a town where tradition often overshadows innovation, one man's vision is bridging the gap between old-world crafts-manship and modern technology."

I squint at the screen. It's better... kind of. But it still feels flat, lifeless. Like it's missing something vital. Something... honest.

I rub my temples, resisting the urge to chuck the laptop across the room. Why is this so hard? I've written hundreds of articles—covering everything from city council meetings to cupcake wars—and I've never struggled like this. But none of those stories involved *him*. None of them made me feel like my heart was doing cartwheels while simultaneously being squeezed in a vise.

"God, Ava was right," I groan, slumping back against the couch cushions. "This is either going to be my best work or a complete train wreck."

At three p.m., it's done. I scroll back to the top of the article, taking a sip of lukewarm coffee as I start reading. The opening is strong—sharp, concise, and just the right amount of sentimental without veering into cheesy territory. It paints a picture of Willow Cove's resilience, of how the town has rallied around progress without losing its soul. Progress that, annoyingly, has Danny Winter's fingerprints all over it.

And then there's the part about him. Or, more accurately, the part where I try *not* to make it about him, while still acknowledging his role in everything. I read the paragraph again, my stomach twisting tighter with every sentence:

"At the heart of Willow Cove's transformation is not just technology, but people—resilient, stubborn, hopeful people— who refuse to let their town fade into obscurity. And, yes, it takes visionaries too, even if they come with an English accent and a penchant for unsolicited advice."

God. Why did I add that last bit? It's not even subtle. Ava would die laughing if she saw it.

I bite my lip hard enough to sting, and force myself to keep reading. The rest of the piece flows well—better than well, actually. It's good. Great, even. But as I reach the final lines, it hits me: for all its polish, for all the ways it captures the town's story... there's way too much of me in here. My perspective. My feelings. My stupid, tangled-up mess of admiration and frustration and whatever else Danny manages to pull out of me without even trying.

"Ugh," I groan, slumping back in my chair. The leather creaks in protest, and I glare at the blinking cursor again.

"Just hit send already," I say aloud, as if that'll somehow make it easier. My mouse hovers over the button, my hand frozen like it's been possessed by some malevolent spirit, determined to keep me from making a decision.

What if Elaine hates it? What if the town hates it? What if Danny reads it and—oh God—*despises* how I see him? Heat rushes to my cheeks at the thought, and I shake my head like I can physically dislodge it.

I take a deep breath, close my eyes, and count to three. Then five. Then ten, because apparently, I'm emotionally incapable of letting go. My finger twitches over the mouse pad, and for half a second, I consider scrapping the whole thing. Starting over. Pretending I never tried writing something this personal in the first place.

But then Ava's voice echoes in my head, smug and annoying and unfortunately right: "*Just write what's real.*"

"Fine," I mutter, mostly to her imaginary presence. "But if this blows up in my face, I'm blaming you."

Before I can talk myself out of it, I click the send button. One quick motion, and it's done. No take-backs. No revisions. Just... final.

I sit there for a moment, staring at the confirmation message on the screen. All I can do is wait and hope I didn't just set myself up for disaster.

"Well," I say, leaning back in my chair with a humorless laugh. "Guess we'll find out."

The rest of the day passes in a blur. I can't really settle in the house, and there are only so many times you can vacuum a floor. I put on my coat and pocket my house keys, and go for a walk.

The air outside is cool but not biting, a slight breeze carrying the scent of saltwater and freshly baked bread from the market square. I shove my hands deep into my jacket pockets as I weave through the Saturday Market crowd, letting the noise and chaos drown out the relentless buzz of my thoughts.

"Candy apples! Sweet as a kiss!" a vendor calls out, waving a basket in the air like it's some kind of trophy. I manage a half-smile before ducking past him, dodging a kid chasing a runaway balloon. The square feels different today—buzzing, alive, like someone flipped a switch I didn't know existed.

Danny's fingerprints are all over this place. Not literally, thank God—I'd have to burn the square down if I found his smarmy grin plastered on the bakery window—but figuratively? Oh yeah. The new solar-powered streetlights approved and installed by Mayor Thompson, the 'free Wi-Fi' signs hanging above vendor stalls, even the little card payment devices now sitting alongside the tip jars at every booth. It's all very *him*—polished, efficient, exactly what Willow Cove never knew it needed—and now can't stop showing off.

"Try our mixed berry honey," an elderly woman says, shoving a tiny spoonful toward me before I can politely decline. I take it anyway because, apparently, saying no to grandmas is against the law here. The honey melts on my tongue, floral and sweet, and for just a second, I forget about the heavy weight of the article sitting in my sent folder.

"Good, isn't it?" she beams, and I nod awkwardly, mumbling something about coming back later before slipping away. My boots scuff against the cobblestones as I make my way toward the waterfront, the growing hum of waves drawing me like a magnet.

When I reach the bench near the edge of the harbor, I sink onto the worn wood, huffing out a breath. The sun dips lower over the horizon, painting the water in streaks of gold and orange so picturesque they'd look fake in a photo. The kind of sunset that practically screams. "Everything will be fine," while you sit there wondering if the universe actually knows how to keep its promises.

I lean forward, resting my elbows on my knees, and stare at the rippling surface of the water. It's both calming and infuriating—how something so chaotic can still seem so steady. The same could probably be said about this town. About Danny. About... well, everything lately.

"Resilience," I mutter under my breath, repeating the word like it'll give me answers. That's what I tried to focus on in the article, right? The resilience of this community. How they've adapted, grown, and thrived even, with all the change. But the truth is, I don't know if I believe half of what I wrote. Sure, the town looks shiny and new on the outside, but what about everything underneath? What about the people who feel left behind?

What about me?

I shake my head, trying to dislodge the thought, but it's sticky, clinging to the corners of my mind. Writing that article peeled off layers of armor I didn't even realize I wore. Now I'm sitting here, raw, wishing I'd kept a few pieces intact. Wondering if I've just handed Danny—and the world—a piece of myself that I might never get back.

A seagull swoops down, snatching up something shiny from the shoreline, and I watch it disappear into the distance. Lucky bird. No deadlines, no editors with hidden agendas, no smug tech moguls making you question your entire existence. Just freedom and instinct, simple and uncomplicated.

"Must be nice," I say softly, to no one in particular.

The breeze picks up, tugging at the strands of hair escaping my ponytail, and I pull my jacket tighter around me.

There's no going back now, no undoing what's been done. All I can do is wait—wait for the fallout, the praise, the silence, whatever comes next. And hope, maybe foolishly, that I've managed to tell the story this place deserves.

Everything's different. The market square didn't hum like it does now—alive with energy, new vendors setting up shop where "Stall Available" signs used to hang like tombstones. It's not just the town's transformation that wraps itself around me, though. It's something deeper, something uncomfortably tangled up in *him*. Danny Winter, with his tailored suits and his cocksure smirk, strutting into Willow Cove like he'd been sent to rescue us all. And—ugh—the worst part is, maybe he kind of did.

I hate admitting it, even silently to myself, but I see it now. The revitalized storefronts, the arts and crafts workshops pulling teenagers off the streets and into something brighter, the subtle buzz of hope weaving its way through conversations at the coffee shop. His fingerprints are everywhere.

And mine? Mine feel... faint. Smudged. Like they're fading away, no matter how tightly I try to cling to the pieces of this place that used to define me. Used to ground me. Used to make me feel irreplaceable. That sharp pang of jealousy twists again, and I press my palms together like I'm trying to squeeze it out.

My fingers toy with the edge of my jacket sleeve, pulling at loose threads. I hate this feeling—the weight of too many thoughts piling up, none of them willing to settle neatly into place. It's like trying to organize a closet when the hangers keep breaking: pointless and mildly destructive.

Danny Winter. Just the thought of his name makes my jaw tighten. Not because he's done anything particularly offensive —this time—but because he exists in this weird liminal space in my head where I can't decide if I want to strangle him or...

well, something else entirely. Something softer, more vulnerable, and infinitely more terrifying.

The tide is coming in, slow but inevitable, dragging with it bits of seaweed and driftwood and whatever else got caught adrift. Fitting, really. That's me—a tangled mess bobbing along, unsure if I'm being pulled toward something or away from it.

The truth is, I'm scared. Scared of what his presence means. Scared of what his absence would feel like. Scared that my heart skips around him like a faulty Wi-Fi signal—and that maybe, I like him more than I'll admit.

And now I have to share a stage with him to convince the last of the Cove's artisanal naysayers to sign up to his app. Joy.

TWENTY-ONE

DANNY

Riley Hayes is waiting on the steps of the town hall with a stack of printouts balanced on one hip and an annotated run sheet in her other hand. Her hair's pulled back into a no-nonsense ponytail, but there's a faint smudge of ink on her cheek—just enough to remind me she's human beneath all that hyper-competence.

"Well, well," she calls out as I approach, her tone laced with mockery. "If it isn't Danny Winter, savior of small towns."

"Riley," I reply, forcing what I hope passes for a grin onto my face. "Always a pleasure."

"Is it?" She arches an eyebrow, holding up one of the printouts like it's Exhibit A in a murder trial. "Because judging by these slides, you seem more committed to Helvetica than actual substance."

"Ah, yes. Critique by font choice. Classic move." I pluck the paper from her hand and flip through it, pretending not to notice the red circles and scrawled notes littering the margins. "I'll have you know, Helvetica is timeless. Iconic, even."

"Sure, if you're designing a subway map." She crosses her arms, clearly enjoying herself. "But for a community-focused app presentation? Maybe aim for something less... sterile."

"I'll take it on board." I toss the offending page back onto her pile and step past her toward the double doors. "Anything else you'd like to nitpick moments before we start? My tie? My haircut? The existential futility of it all?"

"Actually," she says, falling into step beside me, "your tie's fine. For once. But don't think that means I'm going easy on you in there."

"Wouldn't dream of it," I reply, though my pulse kicks up a notch. Riley's the kind of person who keeps you on your toes—whether you like it or not. And right now, I need all the edge I can get.

By the time the Makers' Mart US re-launch event kicks off, the town hall is buzzing. Local artisans file in one by one, their chatter filling the space as they claim seats in mismatched rows of folding chairs. The backdrop is simple—a banner strung across the stage reading: *Willow Cove: Where Tradition Meets Tomorrow*. Riley insisted on the tagline. I didn't argue.

"Alright, here we go," she murmurs beside me, clutching a clipboard with one hand and smoothing her flannel shirt with the other. Her version of dressing up. "Deep breaths, London."

"Thanks, Coach," I reply, tugging at my tie. It suddenly feels too tight, like it knows I'm about to stand in front of a room full of skeptics who would probably still rather hurl tomatoes than download my app.

"Relax," she says, her tone softer now. Reassuring, even. "You've got this."

Before I can respond—before I can decide whether her words are comforting or terrifying—Riley steps forward, taking center stage with a natural confidence that makes the room go quiet almost instantly.

"Good evening, everyone," she begins, her voice steady and clear. "Thank you all for being here tonight. For those of you who don't know me, I'm Riley Hayes, and like most of you, I've called Willow Cove home for as long as I can remember. Tonight, we're here to talk about something new—something that could change the way our community connects and grows."

She pauses, scanning the room with a warm yet commanding presence that I can only dream of emulating. As she speaks, I feel an unexpected swell of pride—not just in the project, but in her. In the way she owns the moment, bridging the gap between tradition and innovation with nothing more than words and sheer force of will.

"I'm very excited to announce the official launch of Makers' Mart here in the United States of America. Let's get started, shall we?" she finishes, stepping aside and gesturing for me to take the stage.

"Break a leg," she whispers as I pass her, and though her tone is teasing, there's an undercurrent of sincerity that steadies me.

"Don't tempt me," I mutter back, but my lips twitch into a small grin as I turn to face the crowd.

"So, we've been working very hard to incorporate all of your feedback and give you the tools you need to sell locally, nationally, and beyond," I start, clicking the remote to bring up the first slide of my meticulously crafted presentation. The projector hums softly as the screen illuminates with the app's sleek new interface. My voice is steady—thank God—but I'm a bag of nerves underneath.

"Willow Cove Connect," I announce, gesturing toward the

logo that Riley insisted we redesign because, and I quote, "It looks like something you mocked up in an afternoon, blindfolded." Fair point, she wasn't wrong. "This isn't just an app. It's a digital bridge, designed to link the traditions you value with the tools you need to thrive in today's world."

A polite murmur ripples through the room. No one's stormed out yet. That's what I call winning.

"Now, I know what some of you might be thinking," I continue, pacing slightly. "Why do I need another app? My phone already does too much, and besides, I've managed just fine without one of these... *widgets*." I throw in the last word deliberately, mimicking the way a gruff older man in the back corner had said it when I'd had the pop-up stand here four weeks ago. A faint chuckle rolls through the crowd, and I latch onto it like a lifeline.

"Good point," I say, nodding. "But this isn't about replacing what you do. It's about enhancing it. Let me show you how."

I click again, pulling up the newly updated homepage. The colors are warm, inviting—Riley's suggestion, naturally. The categories are tailored to the town: local crafts, small business promotions, upcoming events at the community center. Each one is a result of weeks spent listening to their feedback, incorporating their quirks, their needs, their *essence*.

"Take the community calendar," I say, zooming in on the feature. "Instead of relying on the bulletin board outside the diner—which is fantastic, by the way, if you enjoy deciphering faded Post-it Notes—you can now check every event in town from the palm of your hand. Farmers' markets, art classes, Ava's art workshops..." I trail off deliberately, glancing toward Ava herself, who beams proudly from the front row.

"Better yet," I add, "you can RSVP, pay fees, or even share the event with friends—all in one place."

"Fancy," someone mutters, not unkindly, and a few heads nod. Encouragingly. I can manage encouraging.

"Moving on," I say, shifting to the next feature: the Artisan Showcase. "This section is specifically for local vendors. Think of it as your own online storefront. You can upload photos, set prices, take orders—"

"Let's hope it doesn't crash like it did a few months back," a middle-aged man interjects, arms crossed over his flannel shirt. His tone is more amused than accusatory, but it still stings. My spine stiffens reflexively.

"Funny you should mention that," I reply, forcing a smile. "We've rebuilt the system from the ground up, ensuring stability and ease of use. Our beta testers have given us great feedback—"

"Speaking of beta testers," Riley cuts in smoothly, stepping forward from her spot near the side of the room. "May I?"

"By all means," I say, stepping aside with exaggerated politeness. "The floor is yours."

"Thanks," she says, turning to face the crowd. "So, about that Artisan Showcase Danny mentioned..." She pauses, glancing around the room before zeroing in on Ava. "Ava, mind if I share your story?"

"Go right ahead," Ava chirps, her excitement bubbling over.

"Perfect." Riley pulls out her phone and taps the screen. "Here's where things get interesting. A couple of weeks ago, Ava decided to list a new set of postcards on the app. Within hours"—she glances at Ava for confirmation—"you had your first order from a customer in Bridgeport, didn't you?"

"That's right!" Ava says, practically glowing. "And then three more the next day!"

"Exactly," Riley continues, her voice gaining momentum. "Not only did Ava sell out of her stock within a week, but her new customers also signed up for her studio classes. That's the kind of impact we're talking about here—real, tangible benefits for real people in Willow Cove."

The room shifts. Conversations ripple quietly between neighbors, heads nodding with more conviction now. Even the skeptical honey vendor looks mildly impressed, which feels like a minor miracle.

"Thank you, Riley," I say, injecting as much sincerity into my tone as possible. She hands the metaphorical mic back with a subtle smirk.

"Anytime," she replies, the word dripping with sardonic charm. And for the first time tonight, I think we might actually pull this off.

"Does it integrate with existing inventory systems?" Priya Sharma's voice cuts through the murmurs in the room, cool and clipped like she's cross-examining a witness. Her pen hovers over her notebook, poised for judgment. She was one of the early adopters who had embraced the app as a way to promote her handmade silver jewelry. Plagued by payment issues from day one, she soon abandoned her online storefront and was one of the case studies Riley had used in her initial article, lambasting Makers' Mart.

"Yes," I say, forcing my tone to stay even while I click to the next slide on the projector. "Through open APIs, we've designed it to sync seamlessly with any off-the-shelf inventory software you are already using. Minimal setup required."

I glance at Nora, the skeptical soy wax candle-maker who's leaning back in her chair, arms crossed, giving me the kind of look that says she's still deciding whether I'm full of it.

"How minimal?" Her question lands with a challenge, her New England drawl stretching out the vowels to make it sound like he's not entirely buying it.

"Minimal as in 'a couple of clicks and you're good to go.'" I let a faint smile tug at the corner of my mouth, hoping to disarm her. "Even for someone who—hypothetically speaking, of course—might still be using dial-up internet."

There's a low chuckle from the audience. Riley, off to the side with her annotated run sheet, smirks into her cup of coffee but doesn't look up. Of course not. She wouldn't want me to think she's impressed.

"Okay." Nora shifts forward now, uncrossing her arms. "And what about customization? Can vendors adjust their storefronts to reflect seasonal products or promotions?"

"Absolutely. That's one of the key features we've added after feedback from... Well, folks like you." I decide not to mention that "folks like you" translates to Riley dragging me around Willow Cove and forcing me to talk to every single artisan in town. "You can change banners, highlight specific products—it's all customizable from the dashboard."

"That could be useful," Priya murmurs, scribbling something down. Progress. Her skepticism is cracking, though she's trying hard not to show it.

"Could be?" Riley pipes up suddenly, raising an eyebrow as she leans against the wall. "You mean *is* useful. Don't be shy, Priya—you're allowed to admit when something's smartly designed."

"Riley," I mutter under my breath, shooting her a warning glance. But Priya actually smiles, which catches me off guard.

"Fair point," Priya concedes, meeting Riley's gaze briefly before turning back to me. "It does seem like you've thought this through more than I expected. It's practical."

"High praise," I say, clicking to the final slide. "I'll take it."

"One last question," Nora says, lifting a hand. "What measures are in place to protect vendor data? You're asking people to trust their livelihoods to this app. How do they know it's secure?"

"Good question." I nod, appreciating the shift in her tone —less combative, more curious. "We've implemented end-to-end encryption for all transactions and personal information. Security updates roll out automatically, so there's no risk of outdated software creating vulnerabilities."

Nora exchanges a glance with Priya, and for the first time tonight, they both look... satisfied. Or close to it. I resist the urge to exhale too loudly.

"Well," Priya says. "It's clear you've put a lot of work into this. It's impressive."

"Thank you." The words come out steadier than I feel. She said, *"impressive."* Not a phrase people typically use to describe me—or my work—in a sincere tone.

"Alright, folks," Riley announces, stepping forward with a clap of her hands, instantly reclaiming the room. "Let's give Danny a round of applause for surviving our interrogation and actually making tech sound... dare I say it... useful."

The laughter and light clapping that follow feel like a release valve being turned. My shoulders drop half an inch, and I allow myself a small moment to bask in the relief. Priya and Nora are nodding along with the other vendors now, who are chatting animatedly amongst themselves. Even Ava looks ready to nominate me for sainthood.

"Nicely done," Riley murmurs as she passes me, low enough that only I hear it. "Didn't even trip over your own ego once."

"Surprising even myself," I reply, keeping my tone dry.

She grins, but it's gone in a flash, replaced by her usual air of brisk competence as she ushers everyone toward refreshments laid out in the back.

As the crowd disperses, Priya approaches, Nora trailing just behind her. "I'll admit, I came here expecting a sales pitch that didn't understand our community," she says. "But you've clearly listened. This app has potential—not just for Willow Cove, but for places like it everywhere."

"Coming from you, that means a lot. I'm sorry we let you

down badly before. I assure you that was never our intention. I hope you'll give us another go," I reply honestly.

Nora nods in agreement, offering a quick handshake. Their approval feels like a stamp of legitimacy I didn't realize I needed until now.

"Not bad," Riley says, sidling up beside me again, her arms folded as she surveys the scene. "They didn't laugh you out of the room. In fact, they might actually respect you now."

"Don't ruin this for me," I shoot back, but there's no heat in it. Just a quiet gratitude I don't quite know how to express yet.

Riley moves off to join Ava and Priya at the refreshment table, leaving me standing amid the slowly dispersing crowd. I take a quiet moment, letting the buzz of conversation and the faint smell of coffee and paper settle around me. My shoulders finally drop, muscles loosening for the first time all week.

That's when my phone buzzes.

I glance down out of habit, thumb already swiping the screen before my brain catches up. An email notification glows against the lock screen, the subject line catching my eye like a flash of neon in the dark.

I freeze.

It's from Callum. My breath sticks halfway in my throat as I tap it open.

The words blur for a second before they snap into focus— short, formal, and devastating in their precision.

My stomach twists.

This isn't just an email. It's... life-changing. Career-defining. The kind of thing you wait your whole professional life for.

And it's the worst possible timing.

I glance up, instinctively finding Riley across the room. She's laughing at something Ava just said, her ponytail swinging as she shakes her head. Completely oblivious.

My thumb hovers over the screen.

It shouldn't feel like a choice. But it already does.

I slip the phone back into my pocket, forcing a neutral expression as Riley glances over at me from the other side of the room.

For the first time tonight, I don't feel triumphant.

I feel like the ground just shifted under my feet.

And I have no idea which way to fall.

TWENTY-TWO

❤

RILEY

By the time we stumble out of the town hall, it's well past midnight. The buzz of a hundred handshakes, awkward elbow bumps, and forcibly upbeat small talk still thrums in my eardrums, but the rest of Willow Cove is already in a sugar coma. The air is heavy and sweet, thick with the ghosts of donut holes past and the civic pride of a population who want to believe they matter.

Danny is three paces ahead of me, which would be impressive if I weren't actively trying to keep up. He's got his hands shoved deep in his pockets, shoulders hunched like he's auditioning for the role of "Human Parenthesis." He's been in a strange mood since he finished his presentation.

I catch up and nudge him gently with my elbow. "Hey," I say, mustering my best imitation of casual. "Did you catch the mayor's tie situation? I'm pretty sure it was on upside-down. At one point, I swear it started blinking."

He doesn't look at me. "Mmm," he says, noncommittal, eyes trained on the sidewalk.

"Glad you're so invested in the local flavor," I say, hoping he'll bite. He doesn't.

We walk in silence for half a block, the only sounds are the rhythmic squeak of my boots and the lonely whir of a distant street cleaner. The lampposts stretch our shadows out across the concrete, huge and spindly and always a few steps ahead.

"Did you try the cider?" I offer desperately. "Ava said it was spiked, but I think she just doesn't know what fermentation is."

"Didn't have any," he replies, monotone. He's not even pretending to play along.

This is the third time in as many blocks that I've tried to engage him, and the third time he's responded like I'm a telemarketer with his number on speed dial.

"Okay, I'm going to say something, and I need you to promise not to make it weird," I say, stopping in the middle of the sidewalk. He stops too, finally, but doesn't face me.

"Sure," he says, which is basically a contractual agreement in Danny-speak.

I clear my throat. "Tonight went pretty well. People were actually... happy." The word tastes foreign, like I'm trying it out for the first time. "I mean, no one threw a custard pie at you, and the mayor's speech only contained two factual errors. That's gotta be a record."

"Yeah," Danny says, voice flat. "It was fine."

I blink. "Fine?"

He glances at me, just for a second, then back at the ground. His jaw is tight, the muscle in his cheek working overtime.

"What is going on with you?" I demand. "You've been in a mood since we left the town hall."

He sighs and pulls his phone from his pocket, checking the screen like he's expecting a rescue text from NASA. "Nothing," he says, locking the phone and shoving it back in. "Just tired."

"Uh-huh." I cross my arms and keep walking, deliberately slowing my pace so he can't outdistance me again. "Because you're usually such a ray of sunshine."

He lets that hang in the air. We walk in tandem, our steps out of sync. Every time I look over, he's watching his feet or the horizon, anywhere but at me.

The silence thickens, grows claws.

When we hit my block, I try again. "You know, I'm starting to think you only stick around for the free carbs."

He manages a ghost of a smile, but it dies before reaching his eyes. "Maybe I just like the company," he says, but there's no conviction behind it.

I want to push—hell, I want to shake him until whatever's eating him falls out of his mouth and onto the sidewalk—but I don't. Not yet.

Instead, I slow to a stop and look up at him, searching for a crack in the armor. "You want to tell me what's actually going on, or should I just guess?"

He hesitates, and in that hesitation, I see a thousand unsaid things crowding behind his teeth. But then he shakes his head, lips pressed together in a hard line.

"Later," he says. "Not tonight."

And I let it go, because the alternative is risking the whole brittle mess shattering right in front of me.

We stand there, neither of us sure what comes next. The street is empty except for the occasional cat and the echo of our own breathing.

After a beat, I try one last joke: "If you don't cheer up soon, I'm assigning you to help with next year's parade float. I'm thinking papier-mâché narwhal."

He huffs a short, almost-laugh. "Yeah. I'll get right on that."

He's already looking at his phone again.

We reach my building in a fugue of silence. The porch light—installed by the world's most sadistic landlord—casts our shadows in stark relief, like two criminals caught at the scene of an emotional hit-and-run. The air has that hollow, after-dark chill that makes you question every life choice, starting with the one that landed you here in the first place.

Danny stops at the bottom of the steps, not even bothering to follow me up. For a second, I consider just letting him stand there, marinating in his own weirdness, but if there's one thing I'm good at, it's not letting sleeping dogs lie.

I pivot. Arms crossed, voice sharp as a box cutter: "You're not even here right now. What's going on?"

He blinks, looks away, and then—classic—runs a hand through his hair, screwing up what was left of the careful styling. "It's nothing," he says, but even he knows that dog won't hunt. "Just a work thing. Not important."

I laugh. It's not a nice sound. "Liar."

He winces like the word physically stings. "Riley—"

"No," I say, stomping down the steps until we're toe to toe, well within range for maximum withering glare. "You don't get to shut down now after a few weeks of being all in, just because something spooked you. That's not how this works."

He hesitates—tiny shift in his jaw, the barest narrowing of his eyes. "I don't want to do this right now."

"Too bad," I snap. "Because we're doing it."

For a second, he says nothing. Then, like someone deflating a balloon very slowly, he exhales and mutters, "I got an email."

I blink. "And?"

"And it's from the exec team." He's studying his shoes like

they're about to offer up the answer to world peace. "They want me to take a senior position. Perth, Australia."

For a second, I'm sure I've misheard him. "You're kidding."

He shakes his head, still not looking at me. "It's a promotion. A real one. And... they need an answer by next week."

It hits me like a punch to the diaphragm, except instead of doubling over, I laugh. Hard. Too hard. "Well, that's great, right? Dream come true. You can get out of this backwater and live somewhere with actual nightlife and, I don't know, kangaroos."

He flinches. "It's not like that."

"No? Then what's it like?" I say, voice brittle. "Because you sure didn't mention you were job-hunting. Or that this"—I gesture between us, like maybe he'll finally see it—"was just a warm bed on your way to the next big thing."

His hands are in his pockets again, thumbs worrying at the seam. "I wasn't looking. They reached out."

"Well, aren't you just the hottest commodity?" I fire back. "Everyone wants a piece of the Danny Winter Experience."

"Stop," he says. If anything, he's folding in on himself, like he's trying to disappear from his own news.

"Were you going to tell me at all?" I ask, the words practically spitting themselves out. "Or were you just planning to disappear into the night with an email after the fact, with some bullshit about 'pursuing exciting global opportunities?'"

"I didn't want to make a thing out of it until I decided," he says, voice barely more than a whisper. "I didn't want to mess this up."

"Oh, sure," I say, unable to stop myself. "God forbid you mess up your precious streak of Not Giving A Shit."

He says nothing. The silence is so complete I can hear a moth kamikaze the porch light.

I press on because I can't help myself. "You know, you could have just said it. 'Hey, Riley, this was fun, but I'm not sticking around.' Would have saved us both some time and—" my voice hitches on the word "—energy."

His shoulders droop, the posture of someone who's been told he's terminal, only it's just my words killing him.

"I'm sorry," he says, and I hate how small it sounds.

I want to scream. Or laugh. Or take it back. Instead, I fumble with my keys, hands suddenly clumsy. One slips through my fingers and lands on the stoop with a sound that's way too loud for the hour. I'm hyper-aware of him standing behind me, silent and so still he might as well be part of the scenery.

I bend to grab the keys, and as I straighten up, I half-turn to face him. For a moment—just a fraction of a second—I almost say it. *"Come inside."* Like nothing happened. Like everything that just spilled out onto the street could be swept under the rug if we tried hard enough.

But I see the look on his face: tired, sad, and somewhere behind the practiced neutrality, scared. Scared of what comes next. Scared that this is the end.

My throat locks up. I clamp down hard, force the words back.

I turn to the door, keys in hand. "It's probably not a good idea for you to come in," I say. My voice is as brittle as the frozen grass in January. "Not tonight."

He doesn't argue. He doesn't even sigh, just nods once. "Right. Not tonight."

I watch him walk away, his footsteps slow and deliberate, like he's measuring out the distance between us inch by inch. I want to call after him, want to say something that will undo the last five minutes, the last five weeks, maybe the whole damn timeline.

But I don't.

Instead, I lean against the doorframe, white-knuckling the paint until it creaks. I watch his silhouette fade into the shadows at the end of the block, and when he finally rounds the corner, I wait another ten seconds, just in case he comes back.

He doesn't.

The key clicks in the lock, loud and final. Inside, the house is dark and cold, every sound magnified. My shoes make little squeaks on the tile, and the air tastes like the leftovers of an argument I can't stop replaying.

I close the door behind me softly, but the click is loud enough to echo all the way to the end of the empty hall.

TWENTY-THREE

DANNY

I wedge my hands deep into my pockets and start walking, because that's what you do when you've just torched the one good thing you had going in a town that isn't yours.

The street is empty, dead silent except for the off-kilter stutter of a distant crosswalk sign and the bone-dry crunch of salt on the sidewalk under my boots. Above, streetlamps do their best impression of a noir film, throwing spindly shadows that tangle and twitch with every step. I count the pools of light like mile markers, daring myself to go just a bit further before looking back.

I manage ten more strides.

Behind me, Riley's house sits dark and indifferent. One window glows blue from the flicker of a television. She's probably already decided never to speak to me again, or maybe she's analyzing the evening's emotional carnage in one of those battered spiral-bound notebooks she keeps stacked on every available surface. I almost laugh, but my face is too numb for it to come out right.

My breath comes out in little clouds—smoke signals, if anyone cared enough to decode them. I keep walking.

The fight replays in my head, every syllable of Riley's voice sharpened and multiplied by the echo chamber between my ears.

You could have just said it. 'Hey, Riley, this was fun, but I'm not sticking around.' Would have saved us both some time and—energy.

There's something about the way she said "energy," like the word itself tasted of ash. Or maybe that's just me, marinating in my own brand of self-flagellation. Either way, she wasn't wrong. I am good at leaving. I've made an entire lifestyle out of preemptive exits, cutting ties before the rot can set in. It's cleaner that way, or at least it used to be.

Another block. The air gets colder, or maybe I do as I fight the urge to check my phone for a message that will never come.

"Don't let Willow Cove hold you back."

She'd said it so offhandedly, as if I might be capable of being held by anything. But I'd seen her jaw set, the flicker of something—regret, anger, heartbreak—in her eyes just before the mask came back down. Maybe she did care. Maybe that made it worse.

A trash bin, rusted to hell and back, stands sentry at the corner. I pitch a pebble at it, just to hear the clang. The sound is hollow and sharp and instantly swallowed by the night.

I round the corner, pace picking up as if I can outrun the part of my brain dedicated to overthinking. It's a doomed effort. Every step just turns up more detritus: her laugh, the way she'd tuck her hair behind her ear when she thought I wasn't watching, the unguarded look on her face during those rare moments when she actually let herself believe in us.

God, I'm a sap.

I mutter it out loud, voice scraping the inside of my throat: "Absolute sap, mate. Well done."

There's no one to hear it but the raccoon raiding the trash can, who glances up, unimpressed, and resumes his rummaging.

The world keeps moving, as if daring me to keep up. So I do, even though each stride feels like I'm walking further away from the only person who ever called me on my shit and made me like it.

By the time I reach the co-sharing office that's been my home-away-from-home for the last five or six weeks, my face aches from the cold, and my lungs burn like I've run a marathon instead of a few blocks. I hesitate at the front door, uncertain whether to go in or just keep walking until I hit the water and let the Atlantic sort it out.

A shiver racks my whole body, not entirely from the wind.

I look back once, just to check if I'm being watched. I'm not. There's nobody. Not even a passing car.

I go inside.

The warmth of the vestibule is immediate but superficial, like a compliment from someone who hates you.

For a second, I picture Riley's face at the door, the set of her jaw, the way her voice went tight just before she told me to leave.

My hands are shaking as I fish the keys out of my pocket. I can't blame the cold anymore.

The office is exactly as I left it—messy, lonely, smelling faintly of printer ink and wet concrete. I lock the door behind me, lean against it, and slide to the floor.

For a while, I just sit there, letting the silence take over. Letting it feel like punishment or penance or maybe just what I deserve.

Eventually, I get up. The night is only half over, and I've still got hours to kill before dawn.

But there's no running from it. Not anymore.

Outside, the wind picks up, whistling through the ancient window frames. I listen to it, counting the seconds between each gust. I don't remember how to be alone, but I'm about to get a refresher course.

If I'm lucky, she'll never find out how much it stings.

First order of business: whiskey. I fish the bottle from the bottom drawer—a gift from Ed Baldwin after he received his first commission via the app—and pour a generous three fingers into a coffee cup. The sound of the liquid hitting ceramic, for a fleeting moment, is almost meditative. I settle into my chair, which registers its disapproval with a groan.

The laptop screen flickers to life, the harsh blue glow illuminating a constellation of sticky notes and printouts orbiting the keyboard. Front and center, top of my inbox, is the digital equivalent of a loaded gun: "PERTH POSITION - CONFIRMATION REQUIRED." The subject line practically shouts, as if sheer volume could force my hand.

I click it open. The body of the email is a masterclass in corporate seduction, every sentence a siren song of upward mobility and international "opportunity." There are words like "synergy" and "global impact" and "generous relocation package." There's a number, too—a big one, enough to buy a car that's actually half decent, and a flat with an actual view, if I cared about those things.

My finger hovers over the Reply button.

I take a sip instead, letting the whiskey burn a path down to my stomach. The heat barely makes a dent.

The mini-fridge, which houses the communal milk and some yogurts I bought on a whim during my first week, rattles to life behind me, providing a low, mechanical soundtrack. I stare at the screen until the text blurs. I could do this. I should do this. It's what I've always done: leap at the first sign of escape, then justify the running after the fact. Wash, rinse, repeat until the past is just a trail of vapor.

But every time I try to click, my brain short-circuits and dumps me back at Riley's front stoop, her voice flat and final: *"It's probably not a good idea for you to come in."*

I try to focus. I read the offer again, line by line, like maybe this time I'll find the clause that will make me care more about money than about the way she used to squeeze my hand under the table at Voice of the Customer meetings, or the way she'd mock my accent but then use it to get free coffee at the bakery, or the way her hair would smell like burned sugar after a day at the paper.

I close the laptop. The room snaps into shadow, details melting into the edges. I lean back, glass balanced on my thigh, and stare at the water stains on the ceiling tiles.

The plan was always to leave. Get the US ticking over, take the credit, head back to London before the roots set in. But now, the idea of leaving feels less like liberation and more like self-immolation. Like I'd be amputating the only piece of myself that's worth anything.

My mind wanders back to the last time I was offered an out—my first job in Manchester, fresh after graduation, a blank slate where no one knew my middle name, let alone my flaws. I'd jumped at it, convinced myself I was allergic to commitment, that I thrived on motion. It worked, for a while. But by the end of the year, I was hollowed out, orbiting from job to job, city to city, always a step ahead of the emptiness.

I'm so tired of running.

Another sip of whiskey, this one more desperate than the last. My phone buzzes on the desk, screen lighting up with a WhatsApp notification. For a split second, hope flares in my gut—maybe it's her, maybe she's forgiven me, maybe she wants to talk.

It's Lara. The text is a single question mark.

I ignore it, which is probably the most honest thing I've done in months.

The minutes drag on, the office growing colder as the heat cycles off. I glance at the boxes of branded merch lined up against the wall: water bottles, mouse pads, pens. The sight of it all makes me irrationally angry, so I kick them over, their contents spilling onto the floor.

I lean against the window, forehead pressed to the glass, and watch the world outside. It's empty. Nobody coming or going. Just a pale reflection of myself, stuck in place.

Living out of a suitcase was never meant to be a lifestyle. It was a stopgap. A habit. A hedge against committing to a place that might not want you back.

The apartment is colder than the office, which is saying something. There's no central heat, just a rattling radiator and a stack of wool blankets that smell faintly of wet dog and cedar. My overnight bag still sits at the foot of the bed, open, like a dog waiting to be fed. I never unpacked. Not really. Shirts folded, socks balled, toiletries zipped into the same compartments I've used for years of conferences and quarterly meetings.

I move around the cramped bedroom without purpose, half-heartedly sorting a drawer that barely needs sorting. Most of the clothes inside still have their factory creases.

I reach for a fresh t-shirt and pause, hand hovering over a lump of navy fabric. It's the 'I ♥ Willow Cove' hoodie Riley bullied me into buying at my first Saturday market. I can still hear her, half-mocking, half-genuine: "You can't keep wearing button-downs to everything, London. People will think you're allergic to fun."

She'd said it with a smirk—and that look. The one that meant she cared, in spite of herself. She made me try it on right there in front of a table stacked with artisanal pickles and beeswax candles. When I protested, she threatened to post photos of me in the changing tent. I caved. She paid in cash, dropped the receipt in my hand, and said, "Consider it your passport to fitting in."

The memory lands with a thud. I pull the hoodie out, thumb brushing the Willow Cove logo embroidered across the chest. For a second, I hold it close—like a keepsake, or a question I still don't know how to answer.

I sit on the edge of the bed, hoodie bunched in my fists, and stare at the wall.

The radiator gurgles, like it's trying to warm a space it doesn't believe in. Outside, wind whistles through the sash windows. A car alarm hiccups and dies. The rest of the town is still, suspended in one of those coastal nights that dares you to hope for permanence.

This was always going to be a temporary posting. A one-bedroom rental over a bakery. A borrowed town, borrowed time. No shelves. No wall hangings. No declarations of home.

And yet... the hoodie. The Saturday markets. The way Riley said my name when she wasn't angry. The version of me I almost started becoming.

I don't know if that version deserves to stay—but I know he doesn't want to leave.

I set the hoodie beside me, not in the drawer, not on my shoulders. Just in the empty space between.

Then I sit there. Fully dressed. Staring at the slow spin of the ceiling fan and wondering how long I can stay in limbo before I either move in... or move on.

TWENTY-FOUR

RILEY

My phone glows in my hand, dimming and brightening in a rhythm as desperate as my thumb, which has been hovering on refresh for the better part of an hour. The living room is shrapnel from last night's emotional implosion: crumpled tissue casualties and the lingering stench of self-pity.

For the fourth—or maybe fortieth—time, I open the last message from Danny. Nothing special.

Let me know if you want to talk.

Like he's the reasonable one, the adult, and I'm the rabid animal best left to chew through her own arm.

The worst part? He's right.

My stomach churns as the memory unspools, sharper now than it was in the heat of it. *Well, don't let Willow Cove hold you back, London. Go save the world somewhere else. Or don't. Whatever. Nobody's stopping you.*

The look on his face when I said it—tight-lipped, polite, hurt underneath—has been on repeat in my brain ever since.

Ava breezes in from the kitchen, barefoot and carrying a mug emblazoned with the words *I Make Poor Life Choices*. The steam rising from the top does nothing for the temperature in the room, but it has a certain ritualistic comfort.

She surveys the scene—me in the fetal position, phone welded to my hand, hair an active crime scene—and sets the mug on the coffee table with surgical precision. "You look like you just got ghosted by Mr. Darcy," she announces, perching on the edge of the sofa with the practiced sympathy of a therapist.

"Isn't Darcy supposed to be the prize?" I ask, not looking up. "You know, aloof, emotionally constipated, rich. And then you fix him, and he becomes a solid boyfriend. Or whatever."

Ava shrugs. "Maybe, but you look like you caught him at the part where he's still a raging asshole."

I grunt, which in this context passes for laughter. "Great. Can't wait for the happy ending where I learn to accept his failings and inherit a mansion in Derbyshire."

"Could be worse," she says, stretching her legs across my lap. "You could be stuck in a fixer-upper with a cat who pees on your laptop every time you're late with dinner."

"That only happened twice," I grumble, shifting my phone to avoid her toes. "And he was on a hunger strike."

She leans in, voice dropping just above a whisper. "Okay, I'll bite: did you actually say what you wanted to say? Or did you just... do that thing where you try to win the argument and forget why you're in it in the first place?"

I force myself to look at her. "It's not like it matters. He's already halfway out the door. I just gave him a little push."

Ava raises an eyebrow, a move she's honed to lethal effect. "That wasn't the question, Riley."

I wrap both arms around a throw pillow and anchor my

chin to its fuzzy surface. "I said what I needed to say. Which was... not much, okay? Mostly anger. Maybe a few sarcastic barbs. I basically told him to enjoy Perth and get the hell out of my town. Which, in hindsight, is not exactly the love letter I meant to write."

"Classic." She sighs, reaching for the tea and blowing on it like she's waiting for the heat to do the emotional heavy lifting. "You didn't tell him, did you?"

"Tell him what?" I snap, then immediately regret it. The answer is obvious, neon-lit.

She just stares, giving me the rope.

I tug it around my own neck: "That I... That I don't want him to leave." The words taste like pennies.

Ava doesn't gloat—she's better than that. Instead, she pats my knee with the patience of a parent and the tact of a wiseass. "You know, you can be terrifyingly smart and also the world's biggest moron. It's almost impressive."

I snort, hollow. "What difference would it make? It's a massive promotion. He's going to Perth. End of story."

"Bullshit." She sets the mug down, leans in so close I can count the freckles on her nose. "Don't let him leave thinking you don't care. Even if he still goes. Especially if he still goes."

I want to argue, to defend the barricade I've built out of pride and old wounds. Instead, I retreat into my own brain, cycling through every fight, every almost-confession, every time I opened my mouth and let sarcasm out instead of truth.

My finger starts tapping the rim of the mug, a nervous Morse code for "I wish I were someone braver."

Ava doesn't look away, and she doesn't let me. "You deserve to say it," she says quietly. "He deserves to hear it. Whatever happens after that... is not the point."

I blink back something wet. "I hate you for being right."

"You're not the first," she says with a smirk, "and you will not be the last."

For a long, slow minute, I sit in the glow of my phone, letting Ava's words sizzle against my skin. My stomach flips, my pulse screams retreat, but Ava just waits me out like she knows I'll move. And I do.

She moves her legs, and I stand. My legs feel like driftwood, hollow and unsteady, but the resolve in my gut is a different beast entirely.

"You're right," I say, my voice stronger than I feel. "I have to tell him."

I take the stairs up to my room two at a time, nearly slip on the top step, and catch myself with a curse that would make a sailor blush. No time to wallow—not when I've just declared a dramatic change of heart in front of my best friend and there's a ticking clock on my pride.

I wrench open the door to the wardrobe and pull out my ancient navy peacoat—a garment better suited to dramatic departures than actual warmth. My keys are buried under a stack of unopened mail, right where I left them after yesterday's minor meltdown. The fumble for them is loud and uncoordinated, every jangling noise announcing just how little control I have over my own hands.

Ava appears in the doorway, arms folded, silhouette backlit by the hall light. She's swapped her I Make Poor Life Choices mug for a glass of wine, which she swirls like an Olympic judge waiting to see if I'll stick the landing.

"You're not even going to pretend to brush your hair?" she asks, smirk firmly in place.

"Gotta strike while the humiliation is fresh," I shoot back, shoving my arms into the sleeves and wincing as the seam catches on my elbow. "Besides, I think the disheveled look really captures the moment."

She nods, like I've just confirmed a scientific hypothesis. "If you show up looking too put together, he'll know you rehearsed this. Go raw. Like an oyster."

"Never say that again," I beg, but the joke lands, loosening some of the tension between my shoulder blades.

She leans against the doorframe, glass dangling from two fingers. "Seriously, Riley—don't bail on this with some metaphor about mold or a bad one-liner about how he 'deserves better.' Don't armor up. Just say what's actually in your head and your heart."

"I'm not an idiot," I say, but even I can hear the wobble in my voice. "I get it."

She tips her head, a slow grin spreading. "I know you do. Now go before you combust."

The hallway is narrow, and as I march down it, every creak of the old floorboards feels like a countdown. At the front door, my hand lingers on the knob, palm slick with sweat. Outside, the porch is blue-black with night, the yellow streetlight carving out a lonely spotlight on the stoop. The shadows fall long, stretching down my driveway and out toward the sleeping town.

I glance back once. Ava's still there at the far end of the hallway, wineglass in hand, eyes soft but posture pure steel.

"Even if he leaves," I whisper, mostly to myself, "he has to know."

The words hang in the foyer, thick and uncomfortably earnest. I wait for the inner critic to jump out and mock me, instead, there's just silence. And the sound of my own lungs drawing breath. I square my shoulders, channeling every ounce of what passes for courage in this family.

Ava raises her glass and salutes me, the smirk gone now, replaced by something oddly maternal. "Bring me back a good story."

The latch clicks. The world is cold, the night air slicing

through my coat and waking every nerve ending. I step onto the porch, down the stairs, and into the quiet stretch of Willow Cove that runs between here and Danny's rented office.

No plan. No script. Just a head full of chaos and the dangerous hope that this isn't the dumbest thing I've ever done.

Willow Cove at night is a different beast: the tourists are gone, the shops are closed, and the only witnesses to my march of shame are a handful of bored seagulls and the blinking orange eyes of a street-cleaning truck making its slow, existential journey down Main Street. My boots ring out on the sidewalk with a confidence I definitely don't feel, every stride a desperate bid to outrun the tidal wave of second-guessing gathering at the back of my skull. The wind off the harbor is sharp, threading through my coat and slicing through whatever bravado I managed to cobble together at home. I pull the lapels tight and walk faster. My mind races faster than my legs, tripping over every possible way this could go nuclear.

Option A: Knock on the door. Say, "We need to talk," and immediately vomit all over his shoes.

Option B: Ring the bell, pretend I just happened to be in the neighborhood at eleven-thirty p.m., and accidentally recite my apology in the voice of a Victorian ghost.

Option C: Collapse on the stoop and hope he's a mind reader.

None of these inspires confidence. But momentum hates being wasted.

The town square is littered with folding tables, spools of extension cord, and cheap plastic bunting that probably violates at least two environmental ordinances. Festival workers move like ghosts, hauling crates and duct-taping signs for tomorrow's *Lobsterpalooza* or whatever quaint nightmare we're calling it this month. It's a reminder that the world keeps spinning even when you've torched your personal life. The sight makes my throat tighten.

I almost stop, just for a second. There's a stupidly tempting urge to blend in with the work crew, pick up a box, and disappear into the comfort of manual labor until sunrise. But the glow of the office windows up ahead pulls me on. The first-story suite is the only one still lit, its fluorescents burning like a beacon. He's still there.

A fresh wave of doubts hit. What if he's on a call with London? What if he's already packing? What if he's with someone else and I'm about to walk into the world's worst episode of *The Office?* I nearly turn back, but the memory of Ava's voice—*No metaphors. No armor*—drives me the last block.

TWENTY-FIVE

DANNY

I'm sitting at my desk, scrolling through the same two emails for the fourth time. One is the Perth conference call confirmation, now canceled and glowing angrily in red. The other is a draft, addressed to no one, with the subject line: Sorry.

All I can think about is last night.

Her voice, sharp and bright as shattering glass.

Her face, more hurt than angry.

The coffee on my desk is cold now, leaving a sticky brown ring that matches the scatter of mockups and draft designs littered around me. I pick one up, crumple it, then flatten it again, staring at nothing.

This job was supposed to be easy—a quick win, a few weeks of work, and on to the next shiny opportunity. Instead, it's become a holding pattern. A quiet little town I can't seem to leave, and a woman I can't seem to get out of my head.

I hear myself say it out loud before I even think:

"What's the point of staying if she won't even respond to my text?"

The words sit there in the air like a dare.

The Perth thing was never really about Perth. Not even about the title. It was about escape velocity—how fast you need to go to break free. And maybe, just maybe... I don't have it in me anymore.

My thumb hovers over the glowing screen of my phone, scrolling past emails, Slack notifications, and a message from Lara reminding me to *"stop being a workaholic for five seconds."*

Yeah, thanks for that insight, Lara.

I glance up from my phone, gaze landing briefly on the half-empty coffee cup sitting on the windowsill, its contents cold and bitter, forgotten hours ago. That feels appropriate. I came here to launch an app, fix some bugs, get buy-in from the local community, and leave. Not to get tangled up in a town where everyone knows your name—or worse, have actual feelings about it.

A notification pings across the top of the screen: *"Willow Cove Gazette: New Editorial by Riley Hayes—"*

Oh, for the love of—

I click on it before I can stop myself. The headline glares at me like it knows exactly what it's doing. I hesitate, thumb poised above the screen again. Rational Danny would ignore it. Rational Danny would not care about what some hot, flannel-wearing journalist thinks.

But Rational Danny must be taking a coffee break, because Emotional Trainwreck Danny is now scrolling down to read it.

The text loads slowly, or maybe that's just me. My brain's already running a mile a minute, trying to guess what Riley Hayes has unleashed this time. A hit piece? A thinly veiled diatribe on why my app is the modern equivalent of unleashing locusts upon Willow Cove?

But as the first paragraph comes into focus, I stop breathing.

"Change often arrives uninvited, wrapped in sleek branding and glossy promises. It's easy to distrust it—easier still when it feels like a threat to the things we hold dear. But sometimes, change surprises you. Sometimes, it learns. And if we're brave enough to meet it halfway, it can remind us of who we are, and who we want to be."

What the hell? This... isn't what I expected. No sarcasm. No razor-sharp critique designed to fillet my ego in public. Instead, it feels like being handed an olive branch by someone who usually pelts you with rocks.

I read on, each line hitting me harder than the last. She doesn't name me, but I feel exposed anyway. She talks about the app's transformation—not just the technical tweaks, though she gives a nod to those, but the way it's started connecting people in ways no one predicted. The way local businesses are thriving because of it. The way neighbors are talking again, sharing tips, stories, even recipes, through something that once felt cold and impersonal.

"Trust isn't built overnight," her words continue, *"and it isn't built without effort. But when it starts to grow, when it's nurtured—when it's earned—it can turn even skeptics into believers."*

My throat tightens. Is she talking about herself? About the town? About me? Probably all three, because apparently, Riley's gift for words includes the ability to punch me directly in the gut while making it sound poetic.

And then there's the closing line, the one that stops me cold: *"The question now isn't whether we should embrace change, but how we can rise to meet it—and what kind of future we want to build together."*

Together.

It's one word, but it echoes like thunder in my head. Riley Hayes, queen of skepticism, practically allergic to collaboration, just said "together" in reference to this app—and by extension, me. If that's not a miracle, I don't know what is.

I lean back in my chair, staring at the glowing screen as her words imprint themselves onto my brain. My heart's doing that annoying thing where it races like I just ran up a flight of stairs, except I've been sitting still this whole time. Damn her. Damn her for seeing something in this project, in me, that even I couldn't articulate.

I push back from the desk, the wheels of my chair squeaking against the wood floor as if they, too, are protesting this sudden onset of emotional vulnerability. I stare at the screen again, Riley's words still glowing in that infuriatingly perfect serif font.

"Together."

The word has rooted itself in my brain, looping over and over like an annoying pop song you pretend to hate but secretly hum along to in the shower. I rub the back of my neck, feeling the tension radiating up into my skull. Pride bubbles up first—damn right this app is making a difference. Damn right she noticed it.

She gets it. She gets *me*.

And that's the part that scares me, because I've spent years perfecting this polished, untouchable exterior only for Riley Hayes to waltz into my life with her combat boots and pointed questions and absolutely shred it with a few hundred well-placed words. It's like she reached inside my head, pulled out all the messy bits I try to hide, and laid them bare for everyone —including me—to see. Vulnerability isn't exactly my strong suit, and yet here I am, feeling like someone just peeled back my armor and left me standing in the middle of the town square in nothing but my boxers.

"Bloody hell," I mutter under my breath, scrubbing a hand down my face.

My mind drifts, unbidden, to one of our conversations. The one where I'd tried—badly, I'll admit—to explain why this app mattered to me, why it wasn't just another notch on my career ladder. Riley had stood there, arms crossed, eyebrows raised, looking at me like I was trying to sell her a timeshare. And maybe I deserved that skepticism. I hadn't exactly been forthcoming about my motivations. Hell, I hadn't even been sure of them myself at the time.

"Why do you care so much about this?" she'd asked, her voice sharp enough to cut through steel.

"Because it's important," I'd said, which was possibly the least convincing answer I could have given.

Her eyes had narrowed, and for a second, I thought she was going to walk away. Instead, she'd leaned in, close enough that I could smell the faint hint of coffee on her breath, and said, "Important to who, Danny? You? Or the people you're supposedly doing this for?"

It hadn't been a question. It had been a challenge. And instead of rising to meet it, I'd floundered, retreating behind my usual wall of sarcasm and deflection. Now, sitting here with her editorial in front of me, I feel the full weight of that moment—and the regret that comes with it.

I should have told her the truth. That I cared because, for the first time in years, something felt real. That building this app, seeing how it brought people together, made me feel like I was part of something bigger than myself. That she made me want to be better, even when she was driving me up the bloody wall.

"Together," I mutter again, the word tasting bittersweet on my tongue.

It's not just her belief in the app that's shaking me—it's the possibility that she might believe in *me*, too. And God help me, I want that more than I want to go back to the UK, or to accept the Perth deal, more than I want the shiny career accolades I've been chasing since I was twenty-two. I want *her* belief. Her approval. Her fire.

But instead of saying any of that, I'd let her walk away thinking I was just another standard-issue tech exec with a slick pitch and a fragile ego. I'd let my fear of being seen—truly seen—get in the way. Typical Danny Winter move, really. Always so busy trying to control the narrative that I miss the opportunity to actually connect.

"Well done, mate," I say to myself, my tone dripping with sarcasm. "Top marks for emotional intelligence. Really nailed it."

There's a knock at the door.

Not a bright, cheery rap—just one single, deliberate thump that cuts through the quiet.

I freeze, pen still in my hand, and listen. Could be anyone.

But I know better.

I look at the door, then across to my laptop, then back at the door.

For half a second, I consider hiding. But no—avoiding things is what got me here in the first place.

I put the pen down, stand up, and wait.

The handle turns. The door creaks open.

And there she is.

She's soaked.

Her coat clings to her shoulders, dark with rain, and strands of her hair stick to her cheek in damp curls. A bead of water slides from her temple to her jaw, and for a second, all I can think is: *I should grab her a towel. I should... something.*

But I don't move.

We just stare at each other, the kind of stare that feels like it could burn a hole through steel. I'm the first to blink—always am.

"Saw the light on from the street," she says finally, her voice low and hoarse, like she's been shouting or crying or both.

"Couldn't sleep," I answer, and instantly regret it. It sounds unhinged. Or worse—pathetic.

She shuts the door behind her with a quiet click and steps forward, just far enough into the light that I can see how much this is costing her. She stands on the rug like it's a tightrope, her fists curled at her sides.

"I came here…" She hesitates, swallows hard. "No metaphors. No jokes. No bullshit."

I hold my breath.

"I don't want you to go," she says.

There it is. The thing I hadn't even dared to imagine.

I try to play it cool, but my hands are trembling. I jam them into my pockets and force a smile that feels like it's carved into me.

"I thought you made that pretty clear last night," I say, trying for levity, but my voice cracks halfway through.

She gives me a look—half a scowl, half something else entirely. "Yeah, well," she mutters, hugging herself now, "I was an ass. You tried to be honest with me, and I… threw it back in your face. So." Another shrug, small and jagged. "I don't want you to leave thinking I don't care."

I can't quite meet her eyes. It's like looking into the sun.

"So," I say, softer this time, "you're here for closure?"

She actually laughs—sharp and shaky. "You're impossible," she says, swiping at her cheek. "No, you idiot. I'm here because I can't let you leave. I don't *want* you to leave. Not to Perth. Not to anywhere."

She exhales like she's been holding it for a week. "I want you to stay. Here."

She drops her arms and just stands there, open and exposed, daring me to break her heart anyway.

I want to tell her everything. That she's the reason I haven't already boarded a plane. That she's been in my head since the day we met, whether I wanted her there or not. But the words stick.

So instead, I just say, "I declined the role."

That stops her cold.

Her eyebrows draw together. "What?"

I finally look at her, really look at her. "The job in Perth. I let them know this morning. Told them I was staying."

For the first time tonight, the weight in the air lifts just a little.

"Why?" she whispers.

I let out a breath I've been holding for months. "Because… this place, this job, this *thing* between us… It's the first thing in years that feels like it's worth sticking around for."

Her jaw tightens. Her eyes shine. "You're such a jackass," she says, but it comes out softly, almost like a prayer.

I can't help it, I grin. Crooked. Honest. "Yeah. But I'm your jackass. If you'll have me."

She laughs then, sharp and wet around the edges. "You're really staying?"

I nod. "I'm really staying."

She shakes her head, but she's smiling now. "You know what happens next, right?"

I raise an eyebrow. "Do tell."

She takes one step forward, until the damp chill of her coat seeps into my shirt. She looks up at me, smirking faintly through the tears.

I reach for her hand. It's cold and clammy but strong, her fingers curling around mine like she's never letting go.

We stand there for a long time, quiet except for the rain on the windows and the soft tick of the wall clock.

At some point, I realize I'm still holding her hand.

Her fingers are chilled from the walk, but they've stopped trembling. So have mine.

The silence between us is thick, but it doesn't feel heavy anymore—it feels like a bridge. Like maybe we've finally stopped standing on opposite sides of the river and started building something in the middle.

I flex my fingers slightly, just to see if she'll let go. She doesn't. In fact, her grip tightens. A laugh—quiet, shaky, but real—slips out of me before I can stop it.

She tilts her head up, eyebrows raised in suspicion. "What?"

I shake my head. "Nothing. Just..." I hesitate. "You."

Her eyes narrow, but there's a softness there now. "You're ridiculous."

"Not denying it."

She huffs a laugh through her nose and leans against the edge of the desk, arms folding more loosely now. I let her hand slip away, but only because I can tell she needs it free to cross her arms and pretend she's still skeptical.

"You know," I say, leaning back on my heels, "I used to think change was just... momentum. Keep moving, keep climbing, don't stop. Don't get stuck."

She gives me a look. "That sounds exhausting."

I smirk faintly. "It was. Still is, some days." My shoulders drop as I add, quieter: "Turns out... it's not about moving at all. It's about knowing when to stop. When to stay."

Her head tilts, that familiar journalist's skepticism lighting her face. "You're not about to quote *Eat, Pray, Love*, are you?"

I grin, just a little. "No promises."

Her lips curve, but she doesn't press.

I step closer, one slow step at a time, until we're standing so close the faint scent of rain in her hair is all I can smell. "I thought..." I swallow, trying to untangle it all. "If I kept moving, I wouldn't have to... want anything. Or anyone. But apparently I'm spectacularly shit at not wanting you."

Her gaze drops to the floor, then slides back up to meet mine. She bites the inside of her cheek, then admits, "I was scared too. Not that you'd leave. But that I'd..."

She trails off, her voice catching.

"That you'd start hoping I wouldn't," I finish for her.

She closes her eyes for half a beat, then nods.

"Hey," I murmur, letting my fingers brush hers again. "If we're going to be scared, we might as well do it honestly."

She lets out a sound halfway between a laugh and a scoff. "God, you're insufferable when you're right."

I chuckle, low and warm. "Doesn't happen often. You should savor it."

We stand there for another long moment, the air between us finally peaceful, finally settled. I reach for her other hand, and this time she lets me take it without hesitation.

"Guess we're stuck with each other, then," she says, her tone dry but her mouth twitching like she's holding back a smile.

"Could be worse," I reply.

Her smile finally breaks through, and it's like the sun rising after weeks of rain.

I grab a towel from the little kitchenette and drape it over her shoulders. She dabs at her hair, then tosses it onto the chair and exhales shakily.

"I should go home," she says, but she doesn't move.

"Yeah," I say, but I don't let go of her hand. "You probably should."

We don't move.

After a long moment, she lets out a soft snort. "This is pathetic. I'm going to have to bleach my memory of this."

I grin. "If it helps, I've already repressed half of it."

She shakes her head but doesn't pull away. "You know we're going to be a disaster, right?"

"Absolutely," I say. "But at least it'll be our disaster."

That earns me another laugh that's full of something I haven't heard from her in weeks: hope. Eventually, she steps closer, resting her forehead against my chest. My arms come up around her almost without thinking.

TWENTY-SIX

DANNY

TWO MONTHS LATER

The Fall festival is chaos. Absolute, unfiltered chaos. Children streak past like caffeinated squirrels, clutching sticky cones of cotton candy that seem to defy the laws of physics by being both a solid and a liquid at once. A band somewhere off to our left is valiantly butchering what I think was once a folk ballad, while the air reeks of fried dough and caramel apples. It's the kind of scene that should set my teeth on edge. Yet here I am, strolling right through the madness, hand firmly clasped in Riley's like some small-town convert.

"Try not to make that face," Riley says, her voice cutting through the din with ease. "You look like you're plotting how to shut this whole thing down and turn it into a luxury condo complex."

"Now there's an idea," I reply. "Willow Cove Residences: where quaint charm meets overpriced square footage. Has a ring to it, doesn't it?"

She smirks, giving my hand a quick squeeze. "You'd be run out of town before you could even hang up the first 'Coming Soon' sign."

"Tempting, though," I mutter, as we dodge a toddler wielding a bubble wand like a medieval mace. The kid aims for Riley, misses spectacularly, and ends up drenching his own shoes. She laughs—a low, genuine sound that cuts straight through the jangling music and noise around us.

"Careful there," she teases, catching my expression. "I think you almost smiled. That might ruin your whole big-city mystique."

Before I can retort, something—or someone—slams into my side with the force of a battering ram. I stagger slightly, just managing to stop myself from toppling into a nearby popcorn stand.

"Sorry, bud!" comes a muffled voice.

I glance down and find myself face-to-face—or face-to-claw—with a giant papier-mâché lobster. Its bulbous eyes wobble precariously as its owner adjusts the oversized headpiece, revealing a teenage boy drenched in sweat and regret. His apology, thick with a New England accent, is almost drowned out by Riley's sudden bark of laughter.

"Of course," I say flatly, brushing imaginary dust from my shirt. "Because what's a fall festival without being assaulted by seafood?"

"Not just any seafood," Riley corrects, still grinning like this is the funniest thing she's seen all year. "That's Larry the Lobster, Willow Cove's official mascot."

"Official mascot?" I arch an eyebrow at her, then turn back to the boy. "Really? You signed up to parade around in... that? Voluntarily?"

"Community service hours," he says with a shrug, his voice muffled again as he adjusts the claw apparatus. "Better than picking up trash, ya know?"

"Debatable," I murmur, though I can feel a laugh bubbling dangerously close to the surface. This place. This ridiculous, bizarre little town. What has it done to me?

"Hey, Larry," Riley calls, her grin now downright mischievous. *Oh no.* "Make sure you get Danny here a photo op later. He's dying to memorialize this moment."

"Will do, ma'am!" Larry salutes clumsily, one enormous claw flopping sideways. With that, he lumbers off into the crowd, leaving me standing there, staring after him in stunned disbelief.

"Don't worry," Riley says breezily, tugging me back into motion. "You'll learn to love it."

"Love being mauled by oversized shellfish?" I ask dryly.

"Love the chaos," she counters, glancing up at me. There's something softer in her gaze now, beneath the sarcasm. "It grows on you."

"Like mold," I mutter, but I don't let go of her hand.

"Ah, Danny!" Ava calls out as we approach her stall, her voice warm and welcoming like the first sip of coffee on a brutally early morning. She's mid-paintbrush stroke over a wooden sign that reads "Locally Sourced Joy" in looping script, but she sets it down to beam at me. "You're practically a local now."

"Practically," I echo, glancing at Riley with a raised eyebrow. "Is there an initiation ceremony I should be worried about? Will Larry the Lobster come back for me in the night?"

"Don't tempt fate," Riley says under her breath.

"Not officially," Ava replies, ignoring both of us as she waves her hand toward her display of art prints and canvases. "But buying one of these is step one. Go ahead, Danny—pick your poison."

I scan the abstract paintings and illustrations, each one

labeled with names as absurdly self-important as they are specific: *Saltwater Serenity, Autumn Harvest Reverie, Midnight Pines*. It's like walking into a personality test I didn't sign up for.

Riley leans against the edge of the booth, arms crossed, watching me with her patented amused expression—the one that says she's already decided everything about me before I've said a word.

"Well, this one screams 'personal growth,'" I say, finally plucking up a predominantly mint green and powder blue interpretation of the Cove's waterfront labeled *Perfectly Imperfect*. I hold it up between us like a trophy. "I've been working on myself this whole time and didn't even know it."

"That, or you have no idea what you're actually buying," Riley quips, reaching over to take the canvas from my hand. She looks at the piece and over to Ava. "It's beautiful. Good choice."

"Fitting, then," I say as she hands it back.

"Perfect choice, Danny," Ava says brightly, bagging the canvas before I can change my mind. "You'll fit right in around here in no time."

"Comforting," I murmur, sliding a bill across the counter.

Riley snorts beside me, but when our eyes meet, the teasing softens for just a moment. I don't know what it is about her tonight, but every glance feels like a dare I'm not entirely sure I want to lose.

We wander further into the maze of stalls, the hum of chatter melding with the faint strumming of a guitar. Ahead, a small crowd has gathered near the makeshift stage where a folk band has begun their set. The lead singer—a man with more beard than face—leans into the microphone, crooning something slow and mournful.

"Is it just me, or does his voice sound like a dying cat trying to seduce another dying cat?" I whisper to Riley, leaning down so only she can hear.

"Shh!" she hisses, though her shoulders shake with barely contained laughter. "You can't say stuff like that here. These people take their folk music *seriously*."

"Do they?" I ask, feigning wide-eyed innocence. "Because I think I just heard him rhyme 'heart' with... 'fart.'"

"Stop it," she says, elbowing me in the ribs. "I've already told you we keep the pitchforks sharpened specifically to run naysayers like you out of town."

"Fair enough," I say, grinning despite myself. Her laugh—low and unguarded—is worth every bruise her sharp elbows have gifted me tonight. As the song drags mercilessly onward, I nudge her again. "Admit it. You're impressed by how bad this is."

"Impressed isn't the word I'd use," she fires back without missing a beat.

The applause rises as the song ends, and the band launches into another bout of nasal wailing. Riley shakes her head.

"They grow on you, too, you know," she says, her tone lighter now. "Like mold."

"Good to know I'm not the only one who's evolving here," I reply, letting my shoulder brush hers as we turn away from the stage. Her chuckle follows me, warm and close, and I wonder—not for the first time—just how much trouble I'm getting myself into tonight.

"Danny! Finally tracked you down!"

The voice cuts through the festival's din like a foghorn, and I barely have time to brace myself before my newly hired US team descends upon us in a flurry of enthusiasm and questionable fashion choices. Leading the charge is Tyler, my senior software engineer, whose Hawaiian shirt—complete with flamingos wearing sunglasses—makes me want to reconsider every hiring decision I've ever made.

"Tyler," I say, pasting on a smile that I hope doesn't look too much like a grimace. "I see you've embraced the local... aesthetic."

"Damn right I have," he replies, clapping me on the shoulder hard enough to make me stagger. "Small-town festivals are where it's at. Free samples everywhere. You can't beat this vibe."

"Free samples?" Riley interjects, eyebrows raised as she takes in his attire with a smirk. "I think you mean free rein for crimes against fashion."

"Ah, you must be Riley," Tyler says, undeterred by her jab. He offers her a hand with an easy grin. "Danny's told us all about you."

"Has he now?" Riley shoots me a sidelong glance that's equal parts curiosity and challenge. Her handshake is firm, her tone sharper than the cider donuts we passed earlier. "All good things, I'm sure."

"Mostly," Tyler quips, earning himself a glare from me.

"Right," I cut in, clearing my throat. "Riley, meet Tyler and the rest of my US team. Everyone, this is Riley Hayes. She's—"

"His better half," Tyler interrupts, grinning like he's just delivered the punchline of the century. A ripple of laughter spreads through the group, and I can feel Riley stiffen beside me, though her expression remains neutral.

"She's *not*," I correct quickly, my face heating. "She's a journalist. And a—"

"Power couple alert!" another team member pipes up, raising an imaginary alarm with his hands.

"Okay, that's enough out of all of you," I say. They're

enjoying themselves far too much at my expense, and judging by the grin on Riley's face, so is she.

"Nice to meet you all," Riley says finally, her tone light but her gaze sharp as it flicks between them. A quiet satisfaction settles over her features, and I realize with a jolt that she's not annoyed at the teasing—she's pleased. Pleased at being acknowledged, at being included.

"Come on," I mutter, steering her away from the group before they can start planning our imaginary wedding. "Let's get out of here before they start picking out china patterns."

"Aw, but I was starting to enjoy myself," she teases, letting me guide her toward the quieter edge of the festival. The crowd thins as we near the harbor, the light of the setting sun casting long shadows across the wooden docks. Seagulls wheel overhead, their cries mingling with the distant hum of the festival.

"Your team seems... lively," Riley says after a moment, her tone carefully neutral.

"That's one word for it," I reply, shoving my hands into my pockets.

"Spit it out, London," she says finally, stopping to lean against the railing overlooking the water. Her profile is outlined in gold, her hair catching the last rays of sunlight like it's been set aflame. "You've got that look—the one where you're either about to pitch a business idea or confess to a murder."

"Neither, thankfully," I say, though my laugh comes out more strained than I'd like. I join her at the railing, the wood cool beneath my palms. For a moment, I watch the rippling water, trying to gather my thoughts.

"Look," I begin, exhaling slowly. "I don't know how this is all going to pan out. But now..." I trail off, the words tangling in my throat.

"Now what?" she prompts, her voice quieter now, less sharp.

"Now I'm standing on a dock, watching the sunset with someone who makes me question everything I thought I wanted," I admit, the words tumbling out before I can stop them. I glance at her, half expecting to see skepticism or amusement in her eyes, instead, there's something softer there.

"That's a lot of pressure to put on one person," she says.

"Trust me, it's not intentional," I say, managing a weak laugh. "I'm just saying... I don't have all the answers. But I know I want to figure it out with you."

Her smile falters, and for a moment, I think I've said too much. But then she looks back at the water, her expression unreadable. The silence stretches, heavy but not uncomfortable, until finally, she speaks.

"Well," she says, her tone lighter now, almost playful. "At least you didn't confess to murder."

"Yet," I reply, unable to resist a grin.

"Fair warning," she says, glancing at me out of the corner of her eye. "If you turn out to be a serial killer, I'm writing the exposé of the decade."

"Deal," I say, and this time, when she smiles, it feels like the first crack of light after a storm.

She takes a step closer, her arms dropping to her sides. "I'm scared too."

"Of what? My idiocy?" I try to grin, but it feels off-kilter.

"Of this," she admits, gesturing vaguely between us. "You. Me. The fact that every time I look at you, it feels like... I don't know, like I'm standing on the edge of something huge. And if I take one more step, there's no going back."

"That's oddly specific," I say, though my throat tightens at her words. "Were you always this poetic, or is it a new development?"

"Shut up." She rolls her eyes, but there's no heat behind it. "I'm being serious, Danny."

"Okay, okay," I say quickly, holding up my hands in surrender. "No more jokes. Promise." A beat passes. "Well, maybe one or two. But only the good ones."

"God, you're impossible." She shakes her head, but she's smiling now. "The point is... I feel it too. Whatever this is. And it scares the hell out of me. But it also..." She exhales sharply, like she's trying to push out the last bit of doubt. "It also makes me excited to see where it goes."

"Really?" The word comes out before I can stop it, laced with equal parts hope and disbelief.

"Really," she says firmly. Then, because she can't seem to help herself, she adds, "But don't let it go to your head, London Boy."

"Too late," I say, grinning despite myself. "My ego's inflating as we speak. I'll probably need to buy a bigger house to fit it in."

"Great," she says. "Because nothing screams 'personal growth' like an over-inflated ego."

"Speaking of which," I say, leaning casually against the railing, "have I mentioned how much I've grown since moving to this charming little town? Why, just last year, I was living in a flat with more wine stains than furniture. And now"—I spread my arms theatrically—"here I am, embracing artisanal candles, Ava's abstract art, and seafood festivals like some sort of New Englander."

"Wow," she says, mock-impressed. "Such depth. Such transformation. You should write a memoir: *From Cockney Chaos to Coastal Chic.*"

"Not bad." I nod thoughtfully. "Although, I was thinking more along the lines of: *How to Survive New England Without Losing Your Accent—or Your Mind.*"

"Catchy," she says, laughing softly.

The crowd swells around us, a living, breathing thing made out of cotton candy and funnel cakes. Kids with sticky fingers dart between legs like hyperactive squirrels, and someone's Great Dane in a patriotic bandana lumbers past, drooling on everything in its path. The air hums with the kind of energy that only comes from small-town festivals, where everyone knows everyone else and gossip is traded as freely as lemonade refills.

"Is it always like this?" I ask, sidestepping a rogue beach ball that ricochets off a vendor's tent and nearly takes out an elderly woman.

"Like what?" Riley says, her tone as dry as the dust underfoot.

"Chaotic. Wholesome. A bit... sticky," I say, gesturing vaguely at a toddler who appears to be glued to both a balloon and a melting ice cream cone.

"Welcome to Willow Cove," she replies with a smirk. "Where chaos and wholesomeness go hand-in-hand. Kind of like us."

"Ah, yes, because nothing screams 'wholesome' like our relationship dynamic," I quip. "A journalist with trust issues and a corporate sellout—truly, a love story for the ages."

"Don't forget the part where you're emotionally stunted," she shoots back, biting into a caramel apple she's somehow acquired without my noticing.

I grin despite myself.

The chatter around us grows louder, the anticipation building as the sun dips lower, painting the sky in streaks of pink and orange. Somewhere behind us, a group of teenagers bursts into laughter, and the scent of fried dough wafts through the air, mixing with the saltiness of the harbor breeze.

"Looks like everyone's gearing up for the big finale," Riley says, nodding toward the waterfront where people are staking out prime viewing spots. Blankets are spread, chairs are unfolded, and coolers are cracked open. There's a palpable buzz in the air, the kind that makes you wonder if maybe magic exists in places like this—if only for one night.

"Let me guess," I say, eyeing her sideways. "You've seen this fireworks display a million times, and you're about to tell me it's overrated and predictable."

"Pretty much," she admits, shrugging. "But hey, it's tradition. And unlike some people"—she arches a brow at me—"I don't think there's anything wrong with a little predictability now and then."

"Predictability is just code for boring," I counter, leaning casually against a nearby lamppost. "Which, by the way, is not something you can accuse *me* of."

"Trust me, Danny," she says, her lips twitching in amusement. "'Boring' isn't even in your vocabulary. But let's not pretend you didn't Google 'small-town festival etiquette' before showing up here tonight."

"That's slander," I say. "And I'll have you know I'm adapting quite well to small-town life. Exhibit A: I bought a soy candle earlier. Exhibit B"—I gesture dramatically to the festive scene around us—"I'm voluntarily participating in this... celebration of lobster-themed kitsch."

"Next thing we know, you'll be wearing flannel shirts and drinking craft beer," she teases, her eyes glinting in the fading light.

"Steady on. Let's not get carried away," I reply.

A loudspeaker crackles to life, announcing the imminent start of the fireworks. The crowd shifts, all bodies and voices and shared excitement, and we're swept along toward the edge of the harbor. The water glistens darkly below, reflecting the first pinpricks of stars overhead.

"Here we go," Riley murmurs beside me, her voice quieter now, almost contemplative.

"Brace yourself for mediocrity," I reply, but the sarcasm feels half-hearted, like my heart's not really in it anymore. Because for the first time in a long time, I'm struck by how... full this moment feels. How alive it all is—the laughter, the warmth, her presence at my side.

And then the first firework explodes above us, a burst of blue and white that lights up the sky and ripples across the water. The crowd lets out a collective "ooh" and "ahh" as more quickly follow—reds and whites and greens, each one brighter and louder than the last.

"Not bad," I admit, tilting my head back to watch the display.

"See? Tradition's not so terrible," Riley says, nudging me lightly with her elbow.

"Maybe not," I concede, glancing at her. The colors reflect in her eyes, and for a second, I forget about the noise, the crowd, everything except her. She catches me looking and raises an eyebrow.

"What?" she asks, her tone guarded but her expression soft.

"Nothing," I say, unable to fight the smile tugging at my mouth. "Just... glad you're here."

"Me too," she admits after a beat, smiling back at me.

Another firework goes off, showering the sky in silver sparks, but I barely notice. Because in this moment, with her hand brushing mine and that smile lingering between us, I realize something terrifying and wonderful: I've stopped looking for an exit strategy.

The crowd cheers as another firework cracks open above us, a cascade of golden light scattering across the night sky. The reflection shimmers on the harbor's still water, and for once, I don't feel the urge to check my phone or calculate how many emails are piling up in my inbox. I'm here, fully and inexplicably *here*. And it's... not terrible.

"You're staring again," Riley says, her voice cutting through the crackle of the next explosion overhead. Her tone is dry, but there's a warmth in it too—subtle, but it's there if you know where to look. And I do. God help me, I do.

"Can you blame me?" I shoot back. "It's hard not to when you've got glittery explosions doing their best impression of a Jackson Pollock painting right behind you."

"Nice dodge," she quips, though her lips twitch like she's fighting a smile. "You're deflecting."

"Am I?" I ask, leaning slightly closer. I let my fingers slide between hers, locking us together. Her grip tightens instinctively, and something inside me settles—a quiet click, like the world shifting infinitesimally into place.

Another firework bursts above, dazzling the sky with streaks of green and red.

"Alright, fine," I admit after a moment, keeping my eyes on the fireworks because looking directly at Riley feels too much like surrender. "Maybe... Willow Cove isn't the worst place I've ever been."

"High praise," she says.

"Fine," I add with exaggerated drama, squeezing her hand for emphasis. "Maybe this place isn't so bad. And maybe... you were right. About all of it."

"Wow," she says, mock-gasping. "Did Danny Winter just admit someone else was right about something? Somebody mark the calendar."

"Enjoy it while it lasts," I reply, smirking. But beneath the banter, there's a sincerity I can't quite mask. Because the truth is, she *was* right. About Willow Cove. About slowing down. About me.

And maybe I needed this quirky little town more than it ever needed me.

The final fireworks explode—a thunderous burst of silver and gold that bathes the crowd in light, their faces tilted skyward, aglow with collective wonder. I look over at Riley one last time, catching her watching the display with the faintest hint of awe, softening her sharp edges.

"Hey," I murmur, pulling her attention back to me.

She raises an eyebrow, waiting.

"Thanks," I say simply. It's not enough to cover everything I mean, but from the way her expression shifts—guard dropping just a fraction—I think she understands.

"Don't mention it," she replies, her voice quieter now, almost lost in the crowd's cheers.

We stand here, hand in hand, as the last of the fireworks fade, leaving trails of smoke curling into the night sky. The harbor glows faintly with their remnants, and the air hums with a kind of peace I didn't realize I'd been chasing. Or maybe it's not the air at all—maybe it's her.

Not bad for a guy who used to think home was just a marketing tagline, I think with a wry grin, squeezing Riley's hand as the crowd begins to disperse around us.

Hand in hand, we stay rooted where we are, the lights of Willow Cove reflecting off the water and the echoes of laughter fading gently into the distance. For the first time in a long time, I don't care about tomorrow, or the next deal, or the next big move.

Right now, this is enough.

SUBSCRIBE TO ALIA'S MAILING LIST
&
RECEIVE YOUR FREE NOVELLA

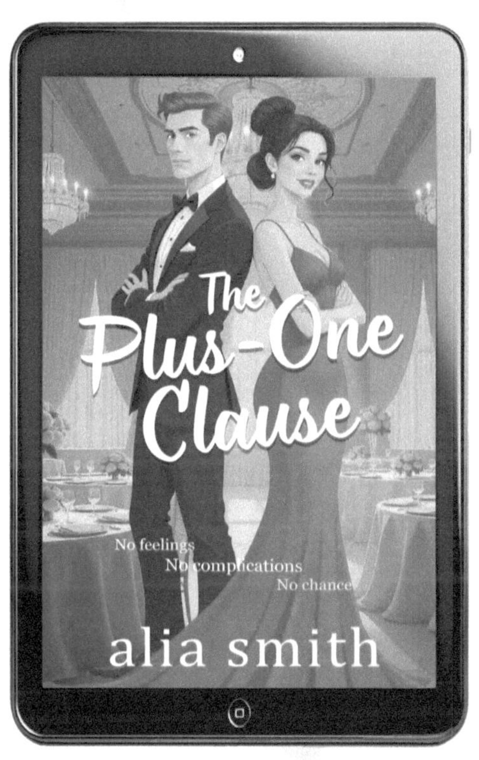

www.aliasmithbooks.com

AUTHOR'S NOTE

Hi,

Thanks so much for reading *Mind the App*!

It was a lot of fun to write. I truly hope it was an entertaining read.

If you enjoyed it I would be incredibly grateful if you'd be so kind as to leave a review.

Reviews really help authors for a number of reasons, not least, providing feedback on what readers like and improving visibility of the book on online retail sites.

Thanks in advance and I look forward to reading your thoughts.

Alia xx

ABOUT THE AUTHOR

Alia Smith writes heart-warming romantic comedies filled with wit, charm, and just the right amount of chaos.

When she's not crafting love stories, she can usually be found curled up with a book, getting emotionally invested in reality TV, or attempting to keep Galaxy—her cat and chief muse—from sitting on her keyboard.

She lives in a cosy Oxfordshire home, where she firmly believes that every great romance starts with a good cup of tea.

www.aliasmithbooks.com

instagram.com/aliasmithbooks

amazon.com/author/aliasmith

BINGE THE SERIES